CARNABY

CARNABY

CATE SAMPSON

SIMON AND SCHUSTER

First published in Great Britain in 2013 by Simon and Schuster UK Ltd
A CBS COMPANY

1 3 5 7 9 10 8 6 4 2

Simon & Schuster UK Ltd
1st Floor, 222 Gray's Inn Road
London
WC1X 8HB

Simon & Schuster Australia, Sydney

Simon & Schuster India, New Delhi

A CIP catalogue record for this book is available from the British Library.

PB ISBN: 978-1-4711-1581-3
EBook ISBN: 978-1-4711-1582-0

Printed and bound by CPI Group (UK) Ltd, Croydon, CR0 4YY

www.simonandschuster.co.uk
www.simonandschuster.com.au

For Alistair, Rachel and Kirsty.

ONE

Every day after school I lug my bike up one hundred and sixty-eight steps to our flat, and every day my bike turns into a mad thing. I try to take control by grabbing the handlebars and lifting them in the air so the back wheel bounces up the steps behind me. But the front wheel goes mental because it can't see the ground and the pedals jab at my calves giving me bruises and tearing holes in the holes in my tights. It's November and it's pissing it down, so I'm soaked and frozen from the ride home and the bike is wet too, all cold slippery metal. Two times I lose my balance and have to grab onto the wire mesh they've put around the stairwell to stop people falling down and smashing themselves into bits on the concrete at the bottom.

To take my mind off my psycho bike, each time I reach a landing I glance up at the walls to take in the graffiti. Usually it's words, but sometimes, when they've got something really special to say, they draw a picture. On Level 5 someone's painted a dick. His, I assume.

He's pissing out his territory. I know that. I'm thirteen, but that doesn't mean I'm stupid. Still, you've got to ask yourself what kind of dickhead wants this territory where there are discarded syringes in the stairwell, and the lifts don't work, let me think . . . oh yes, nothing works, and anyone who's got any functioning brain cells left long ago. Which makes me stupid, after all.

Just before I get to Level 7, I hear footsteps running down the concrete steps towards me. The footsteps are soft, like a pitter-patter. I'm holding my breath. I get a better grip on my bike, hugging it tight against me. No one's nicking my bike off me.

Then the feet appear, and they're attached to Omar, so I can start to breathe again. Omar's in Year 11 at school, and he thinks he's David Blaine or Derren Brown or something. He's always pulling things out of people's ears or reading people's minds. He's got long thin hands, and his fingers are always flexing like they're practising to make things disappear. It's not going to put him on TV, but one of his tricks is changing out of school uniform in, like, a millisecond. Seriously, I've never seen him in school uniform anywhere but school. Today he's wearing jeans and a leather jacket.

'Hey, Carnaby,' he says.

I feel stupid in my school kilt with my hair plastered to my face and rain dripping off the end of my nose that I can't wipe off because I've got to keep hold of my bike.

'Hey,' I say.

We kind of pause as we pass each other on the stairs. When we see each other in the corridor at school he always teases me. I think he can read my mind well enough to know I'm afraid he'll play a trick on me. Once, in the school canteen, he pretended to pull an orange out of Zoe's bum, and she was so embarrassed she nearly died. Then he hypnotised Martin, although he got suspended for two days for that. I'd hate it if he did that to me. I don't want to encourage him, so I don't speak to him.

'Carnaby, I'm having a vision of the future,' he says.

I scowl at him. So much for not encouraging him.

He puts his long thin fingers to his forehead and screws his face up like he's concentrating hard.

'I see . . .' he pauses, frowns, 'I see a man . . . in your flat.'

'I'm not lis—'

'Wait!' He lifts his long palm towards me to stop me speaking. He opens his eyes wide. 'It's Borys!'

I roll my eyes. Borys is my sister's Polish boyfriend, and it's not unusual to see him in our flat. Anyone can see him there, he's there all the time. Not today, maybe, not after the row he had with Mum last night. But the future is a long time. He'll definitely be back.

Omar grins at me and I try not to smile back. Everyone always forgives Omar.

I turn away from him and I start lugging my bike up the steps.

I hear his voice behind me.

'Hey, Carnaby?'

I turn my head, giving him a look which I hope makes it clear that I don't think anything of him.

'What?'

'Nothing,' he says. And then he grins again.

I give him the finger and he laughs.

A few steps later and I hear his voice again, from a couple of flights below.

'Hey, Carnaby?' he calls out again.

But I'm not going to say 'what?' and have him say 'nothing' again. He seems to think that's hilarious. So I ignore him.

3

'Hey, Carnaby,' his voice rises up from the stairwell again, 'do you want a hand?'

I'm tempted. For a millisecond. Then I tell myself not to be stupid. If I say yes, he'll probably pull a plastic hand out of his jacket or something. So I don't reply. I just keep going.

When I get to the landing at Level 8, I see someone at my door, which is near the far end, eight flats along, and I stop before I step out onto the walkway. He's squatting down, facing away from me. Now I know where Omar's vision came from. It's Borys. Omar must have seen him on his way down.

Although he's got his back to me I can tell it's Borys because his shoulders slope down and his ears are pink and his hair's so short I can see the skin of his skull, and the back of his neck and his arms are all covered in tattoos. He's got a snake winding round his arm. It climbs up his left arm and slithers all the way across his shoulders and down his other arm. It took hours and he says it really hurt when they did it but it was worth it. From where I am I can see he's got his bag open in front of him and he's moving stuff around as though he's trying to fit something inside it. I don't know if he's just come out of our flat or if he's been getting no answer at the door and is giving up now. I don't call out to him because I don't want to talk to him. Not now, not after last night. I wait there until he stands up and walks off in a hurry and then he's gone, breaking into a jog and heading down the steps at the other end. That's when I wheel the bike out of the stairwell and onto the open walkway.

You can say what you like about Shepherd's Way, and none of it would be good, not any more, but when I walk along these walkways I feel like I'm walking across the sky. Up above me – not counting the bottom of the walkway that's directly over my head – the sky is dark with a fat inky cloud. Down below me is the round flat roof of the Egleton Shopping Centre, and then streets of terraced houses. Because of the rain, the rooftops are glinty, like metal, but it still looks cosy where people have lights on inside their houses. I can see a strip of the river. The water is dark and oily. On a sunny day, when the sky is blue and London's shining, the rich people would pay a fortune for a view like this. They'd kill to be able to see a bit of water. But they wouldn't touch Shepherd's Way. No way. They wouldn't even come as far as Level 8 because they'd stop at the first step and decide they didn't want to get their lovely shoes dirty. It's like Cinderella backwards. Put your foot on the step and someone waves a magic wand and everything vanishes – all your money and your lovely castle, all your crowns and dresses.

Number 87 is home. I rest the bike against the wall while I dig out the keys. I've got a zip-up pocket in my hoody, and that's where I keep anything I don't want to lose. That's basically my keys and any cash that comes my way. Right now the only thing in my pocket is my keys. The padlock on the security grille is locked, which means no one's in. I'm guessing Borys came by but no one was in to answer the door. I unlock the padlock and then stick my key in the door. Once the door's open, I wheel the bike in. I try to shove it right up against the wall so it doesn't take up any space, but there's no way round it. I mean literally there's no way round it. Mum yells at me to move it any time she needs to get out the house, which isn't as often as you might think.

I stick my head around the door to the lounge. Mum is in actually, which is a surprise. She's having a nap on the couch with her back to me.

'Is there anything for dinner?' I ask. But Mum doesn't answer. She's out of it. I'm guessing she never heard Borys at the door, which is just as well under the circumstances.

Nobody's good company when they're asleep. So I head into the kitchen. I open the fridge door, then cover my nose and breathe through my mouth because it smells of stale food, although how it smells of any kind of food is one of the wonders of the world because there's hardly ever any in there. I unplug the fridge to save money – it's just electricity wasted if there's nothing in there. I know it's the unplugging that makes it smell worse, but I can't help that.

Anyway, I still always open the fridge because you've got to hope for the best. If Mum works a shift at the shop, which she does one or two times a month, she might bring something back with her, and I think I'm in luck because there's a bottle of lemonade. Except that's empty too, so I take it out and bin it. Then I switch the radio on and glance at Mum, but she doesn't move, so I turn it up. I don't mind cleaning up, but it would be nice to have someone to chat to while I'm doing it.

I go through the lounge again to get to the room I share with Jude and Em, taking the radio with me. It looks like a bomb's gone off: there are clothes all over the floor, Em's milk bottles rolling around, their teats all fluffy and sticky, and dirty nappies rolled into tight little balls, fat and smelling stinky-sweet. I take off my uniform and change into my jeans, and then I start picking stuff up, chucking nappies into a plastic bag. All the time I'm singing along to the radio so I don't have to think about what I'm doing. I dance around a bit, too, because there's no one looking, and because it keeps me warm.

When the flat's half decent I go back to the kitchen. I find my pair of rubber gloves, pull them on, scrub out Em's bottles and rinse them with boiling water from the kettle. Then I run some water into the sink and add a squirt of washing-up liquid, and I swish my school shirt and my tights and knickers around quickly, then hang them to dry by the window, except it's been raining so the air's wet which means it'll all still be damp when I put it back on in the morning. Still, the shirt doesn't need ironing if I hang it up, which is good because we haven't got an iron.

All of a sudden my tummy starts to ache, and then it starts groaning at me really loudly. On school days I always think if I eat enough school dinner I'll be able to go without when I get home, but sometimes it doesn't work.

Dinner at school was lasagne: lumps of gristly meat and cubes of hard carrot layered between pasta which tasted like you imagine a tyre might taste if it was smeared in gravy. I know beggars can't be choosers but I couldn't bring myself to eat a second portion. Although if you put it in front of me now, with my belly aching and nothing in the fridge, I'd scoff it down no problem.

If I get really hungry, like so hungry I can't bear it any longer, I go round to Sheena's mum's café under the railway arch, and she gives me a plate of sausage and beans. But it's only when I'm so hungry that being hungry is worse than being embarrassed. I was there two times last week. So right now I'm too embarrassed to go and beg for food from Sheena's mum again.

I should go and buy a loaf of bread and make toast, maybe fry an egg, but I need something right this minute. I can't wait. If I get bread I'll eat it straight from the packet, which isn't a good look. Chips are better because you can stuff them in your mouth as quick as you want right there in the street and no one thinks anything of it.

I put my head round the lounge door again. The music from the radio sounds too loud now I'm this hungry. My brain's concentrating so hard on finding food that the music is screeching in my head.

'I'm going to get chips,' I say. 'Can I have some cash?'

I wait in the doorway.

Mum doesn't move a muscle. It's like she can't hear me. Like she hasn't heard the radio blaring, and me bashing around in the kitchen doing the washing-up. I think she's faking it because she doesn't want to admit to me that she hasn't got any cash.

I go over to the couch and look down at her. I can't see her face at all because her long hair has fallen across it. She's all curled up like a baby, so I can't even see her breathing. If she does have any cash it will be in her pocket, but she'll go mad if she wakes up and finds my hand stuffed in there.

'You're hungry too, aren't you, Mum?' I suggest loudly. 'I bet you'd really fancy some chips.'

My tummy's beginning to eat itself and I'm feeling all shaky. All my brain can think about is how hungry I am.

'Chips and a wing?'

Chips and a wing is £1.99 at the Sunshine Café in the Egleton or £2.79 if you add a drink. Chips and a piece of chicken is £2.20 and a drink is £3.

'I can get you a piece of chicken,' I suggest to Mum. 'It's only an extra 21p, it's well worth it.'

Still she doesn't budge.

Then I tell her if she's got enough cash we can get two wings and a piece of chicken and chips all for £2.79. That way we can share it. We don't have to add a drink – we can just have the food.

I'm trying to tempt her, but it's just making me hungrier.

'Mum!' I lean over and speak right into her ear. 'Wake up, you're starving!'

When she still doesn't move, I reach out and I poke her shoulder.

Her shoulder moves a bit under my finger, but she doesn't wake up.

Gently, so she doesn't yell at me, I shake her.

TWO

It's June 20th. Which means it's seven months since Mum was found dead on the couch. In two weeks, Borys goes on trial for killing her. In three weeks I'll turn fourteen . . .

At school they've found me a shrink. Her name is Mrs Franklin, and I see her two times a week in a really small room called The Student Counselling Office. I'm The Student. I've never had an office named after me before. As far as I know, none of the other kids have to see Mrs Franklin, although in my opinion there are lots of them who could do with her help more than me. Clare, for instance, who always gives in her homework early. Don't tell me *that's* not a mental health issue.

'Did you know they used to keep bog roll in here?' I say to Mrs Franklin. 'What do you think they did with it when you moved in? Did they just chuck it all out?'

'Sarah,' she says, 'I need to bring you back to the point. We need to make sure you're prepared psychologically. The trial's what, two weeks away?'

'I can't think they'd make the school go without bog roll just so I can have counselling, can you? I mean I'm flattered, obviously, but . . .'

Mrs Franklin smiles, but not like she really wants to.

10

'No, Sarah, I haven't noticed a shortage of bog . . . of lavatory paper.'

'I mean, which would *you* rather have? Bog roll or counselling?'

'Sarah . . .' She shakes her head. 'You can't pretend the trial's not happening . . .'

Mrs Franklin always dresses well. She's got on a draped top with a leopard-skin print on it, and a black skirt to her knees, and patent black open-toed sandals. Her skin is brown and smooth and her hair has a sheen to it, like she uses a conditioning oil, and it's bobbed around her face like a hat. She wears glasses, but the frames have little diamonds in them. Her nails are long and perfectly shaped and sometimes she's got little patterns on them too, like birds or flowers. Today she's got silver polish on her toenails.

'Bog roll,' I suggest. 'I bet you'd rather have bog roll, you just don't want to admit it.'

Mrs Franklin pretends to make a note on the pad of paper she holds on her lap, and while her head's bent she mutters, like she's talking to herself: 'Of course, the two are not dissimilar.' Then the edges of her mouth dart upwards in a quick little I'm-so-clever smile. The silly cow is always making smirky little comments to herself. I mean excuse me, it's *my* joke. But she can't even see the joke when I tell it, because she thinks I'm thick. So she turns it into this private joke where *I'm* the stupid one who doesn't get it that she's mopping up the shit in my head.

I'm in here every Tuesday and Thursday at 3.30 p.m., and I've been coming here for seven months now. But we never get anywhere. We basically just have the same conversation every week.

The Student Counselling Office is in the basement, so there's just one window high up where you can see everyone's feet walking past. The window's barred and it doesn't let in much light, so they've only gone and got a fluorescent interrogation lamp. As soon as Mrs Franklin shuts the door on me, I want to get out. There are two armchairs way too close together. Our knees keep bumping, which freaks me out. It gets really hot, too, so I can never tell whether I'm sweating because I'm nervous, or because I'm just boiling. I've rolled up my shirtsleeves and I've got my top button undone, but it's still really hot.

'Sarah,' she says now, leaning forward, 'Sarah, I want you to imagine you're standing in front of the mirror looking at yourself. You peel all the surface layers away . . .'

'You want me to take my clothes off ?' I frown at her.

'No, Sarah, not your clothes.' Her jaw's gone rigid. 'You know perfectly well I don't mean your clothes. I'm talking about metaphorical . . . about imaginary layers. What I'm trying to get at here is how you feel deep down, under your skin, underneath the exterior, the part you show everyone. I want you to peel off your outer layer and look at yourself and acknowledge what's there.'

'So I don't take my clothes off,' I say, 'I just peel off my outer layer. Is that what you mean?'

Some teachers nearly pee themselves with excitement when you ask whether you heard right. They think it means you want to learn something, when half the time you're just winding them up. But Mrs Franklin just nods.

12

'Okay,' I say. Then, after a minute, when she glances at me, I add, 'I'm peeling.'

I sit there without speaking. I look down at my hands, clamped together on my lap. My school skirt could do with a wash. I can see yesterday's ketchup dried into the grey of the material. It needs a good scrubbing, but that's not going to happen. I've got Jude's new mobile number on the back of my hand, just next to a patch of scaly pink eczema. I want to itch it, but then I realise I've got no nails to scratch with. I suppose I've been biting them, because there's no white at the top of my nail, they just kind of tuck under my skin. It looks like my fingertips have been amputated.

'Well?' She's sounding impatient by now.

I look up at her, but I'm thinking about the stumps where my fingers were.

'I was just peeling everything off,' I say to her. 'All the skin and that.'

'And? What do you feel? What emotion is left when everything else is peeled away?'

For a minute, just for like ten seconds, I actually think about it. And what I think is that I can't believe she's asking such a stupid question.

'What do *you* think?' I say.

'I want to hear it from you,' she says.

'I think, if you take everything else away, I feel . . .'

'Yes?' She's on the edge of her seat.

'Nothing.'

I look her in the eye.

'Nothing?' Her shoulders slump. 'Describe feeling nothing.'

13

'How can nothing feel like anything? That's why it's called nothing.'

'Well, personally, I don't think I ever feel nothing. There's always something.'

'So what is it now?'

She sighs.

'This is about you, Sarah. After all you've been through, I'm sure there are emotions there, and I'm also sure you know what they are. Are you angry?'

'What have I got to be angry about?' I ask her. Which is a bit of a trick answer, because she can't talk to me about any of the details of the murder, not when there's going to be a trial.

'You're not grieving?'

I could be angry. I could be grieving. Mum got killed, my sister's boyfriend got arrested for murder. My sister got sick because she's so stressed out. Now it's me and her facing Borys in court. I don't know how any of us can get through that.

I shake my head.

'You're not even a bit sad.' It's hardly even a question when she puts it like that.

'Well . . .' I tilt my head to one side as though I'm giving this more thought, and then I give her one word. 'No.'

She sighs and then it's her turn to shake her head. She scribbles something on her pad. She leans forward again.

'Sarah,' she says urgently, 'there's nothing wrong with feeling emotion. That's normal. It's not a sign of weakness. Even the bravest people sometimes cry. You can't just shut your emotions in a box and lock them up. Emotions are there for a reason.'

'What's the reason?'

She frowns. Her fingers go to her forehead, and she strokes the skin under her hairline with the tips of her long polished nails.

'The reason for emotion?'

'I'm just asking. It was you who said it.'

'Our emotions are what makes us human, they tie us to our friends and families, they are the way we communicate, the way we respond to the world around us, to people, to events. We can't cut ourselves off. And when you express emotion . . . it's . . . a form of self-expression, a form of relief . . . If you're angry, you have to let it out. The same with grief. If you keep it in, it eats away at you.'

'So you're saying if I feel those things, I've got to let them out for my own good.'

She smiles a little bit at that and speaks very slowly, as though what she's saying is really . . . really . . . significant.

'That's exactly what I'm saying.'

I nod thoughtfully and then speak even more slowly than her, like what I have to say is even more significant.

'And . . . I'm saying . . . I . . . don't . . . feel . . . any of . . . those . . . things . . . so . . . there's . . . nothing . . . to . . . let . . . out.'

She bites her lip.

'I don't mind if other people want to feel things,' I say, to make her feel better, 'that's up to them. It's just that in my experience emotions screw you up, and what's the point in that?'

'Emotions aren't something you can choose to have, Sarah,' she says quietly. 'I have to challenge you on this.'

15

But in my head all I can think is how stupid she is. If she really knew what emotions can do, she wouldn't want me to let them out, she'd be glad I keep them shut up where they can't do any damage.

'You can't get inside my head,' I say. 'It's nothing personal. No one can. *I* can't even get inside my head.'

She takes a sharp breath.

'Alright,' she says, 'let's talk about your shoes.'

'My shoes? What about my shoes?'

'They're always polished. Do you do that every night?'

I look at my shoes. They're scuffed now, but it's the end of the day. This morning they started out black. Not shiny, because once they're scuffed enough they never shine no matter what you do; they just look black and furry. Perhaps they'd look better if I had proper polish, but I don't. I use a scrape of oil or butter saved in a wad of bog roll from school dinner. It makes the leather soft and covers up the scratches a bit, but sometimes I get a whiff of rancid oil from my feet. Anyway, my shoes are way too small. When I put them on this morning, I had to squeeze my feet into them. My toes hurt all morning, but they gave up at lunch-time, like there was no point. Now I can't feel them, which is better, they're just like a dull warm ache.

'Your teachers tell me they think that deep down you want to do things the right way. I can see that from your shoes. You really take care of them.'

I don't see what my shoes have to do with anything, so I don't say anything, but my eyes feel like they're going to cry.

'Your teachers say there's nothing wrong with your brain . . .'

My throat is getting tight, like someone's tying something around it. I stare at the wall over her shoulder. I don't want to look in her face. Nothing wrong with my brain. Very good of them. Very kind. I had been wondering.

'Your brain could save you, Sarah,' she says.

'I need saving, do I?' It sounds angry. Anger is an emotion. That's not good.

'That's not what I meant, Sarah.'

'Isn't it? Only I don't think you're supposed to say I'm doomed, or things like that.'

'I didn't say you were doomed,' she says quickly, like she knows she really did and she shouldn't have.

Neither of us says anything for a minute, then she says, 'You know there's a school trip to France at the end of term, don't you, Sarah?'

I grunt. I don't know why she's talking to me about it. I can't afford to go, and she knows I can't.

'Your friend Sheena is going. Would you like to go if you could?'

It's like asking, would you like to eat a delicious meal if you could, or would you like to go and buy some really nice clothes if you could. Of course you would. And if you can't, it's really cruel to ask.

'No,' I say. 'Paris is boring.'

She gives me a look like she knows I'm bluffing.

'If we could get funding . . . and I'm emphasising *if*, so don't get your hopes up, would you be interested in going? It should be after the trial. It might make a really nice change for you.'

She looks at me like she really means it, like she's not just messing with me.

17

'I haven't got a passport,' I say.

'Oh,' she says, looking a bit surprised. 'That might be a problem.'

Like she's never even thought about that.

She may not think she's messing with me, but she is. Because if you make someone think even a little bit that something might happen, and then it doesn't happen, that's worse than not letting them hope in the first place.

Mrs Franklin's embarrassed now. She wishes she'd never mentioned Paris. She glances at the clock, and she's pleased by what she sees although she tries not to show it. It's twenty-five minutes past four. Our session's nearly over. I can feel her relief, and it makes me angry. She's supposed to want to help me. That's what she gets paid for. Someone pays her loads of money to care, and she just wants it over and done with.

I'm not hanging round any longer. I stand up.

'I want to ask you about Jude and Emma,' she says. She's waving me back to the chair, but I'm ignoring her, turning around, making for the door.

'Sarah,' she says urgently as I reach out to the door handle, 'you're going to have to walk into that courtroom very soon and stand there and give evidence . . . I have to be sure you can cope. If you can't . . .'

That sounds nice and caring written down. But that 'If you can't . . .' means it's a threat. She's not the only one waiting. They're like vultures sitting on a branch watching me with their beady eyes.

I pull open the door, and I'm out of there, head down, seeing my school skirt flapping around my legs as I run up the stairs. Running is hard when your feet feel like they've been chopped off at the ankle, but I can run fast. 'Sarah!' I can hear Mrs Franklin calling me back. 'What's the matter?'

There are other girls around now, in PE kit, red and sweaty from the sports field. Their eyes are scouring me, stripping me down, acid smoking on my skin. I'm running, but my feet are bursting out of my shoes, my finger-stubs are swollen to double size, my eczema is peeling off me like I'm being skinned alive.

I won't let them see me.

'Sarah Carnaby!' One of the girls calls out. 'Are you on the run?'

Another one hoots like a siren.

'They're coming to get you, Carnaby, they've got the sniffer dogs out . . . The dogs are sniffing your socks . . .'

'. . . oh no! The dogs are passing out . . .'

One of them makes a howling noise, like a dog. They fall about laughing.

I close my ears. I keep running.

Then I'm outside, and I'm on my bike and I'm cycling, and the sun is roasting my back through my school uniform. I'm concentrating on the road, where my front wheel spins fast, finding its way between the edge of the pavement and the wing mirrors. Stuck in traffic, the drivers have their windows wound down. I get blasts of talk radio and music as I'm racing past. I let it all in, all the noise and the voices and the beat, and it fills my head and my brain is singing loud enough to drown everything else out.

THREE

Me and my bike fight all the way up the stairs. If I look down, all I can see is the flights of empty steps zigzagging down to the ground. I try to keep my eyes on my feet instead. I count the steps out loud to keep myself company and to stop myself thinking about other things.

I hear soft footsteps running down the steps towards me. I stop and grab my bike closer.

It's Omar.

'Hey,' he says. There's no smile in his voice, but he doesn't joke around much these days. I don't see him do much magic any more, either, but his hands are always twitching like they're remembering.

He slows down, like he might have something to say to me. Then it's like he changes his mind, and he keeps on going. I listen to his footsteps until I can't hear them.

When I get to Level 8 I wheel my bike along the walkway. I know exactly when I'm passing Number 87, but I don't look at it. I've got into this routine where I just glue my eyes to the floor when I pass that door. If I lift my eyes up, anything could happen. I could turn to stone, or my head could come off or something. I don't look up at Number 88 either, where Millie lives. Mum used to call her a nosy cow and told us not to speak to her, and although

Mum's dead I still do what she said. Two doors along I'm at Number 89, which means I can look up again.

After what happened, me and Jude couldn't stay at Number 87 because it was a crime scene. So the council moved us two doors down to Number 89, and then we never went back. We asked the council if they could move us somewhere new, because we didn't want to be so close to where Mum was killed. But they seemed to think that two doors down was plenty far enough away to make a new start. Like there's a shortage of empty flats in Shepherd's Way. Like people are queuing up to live there, throwing hundreds of thousands of pounds down to outbid each other. We could've had our pick of empty flats. We could've chosen a flat with damp or a flat with smelly plumbing or a flat where the heating doesn't work. Any one of them would be good. But they go and give us a flat with all three, like it was a special offer. They must have looked at loads – no damp? That won't do. No smelly toilet? Not good enough. Heating? Ridiculous! When they found it they must have been over the moon. Walls running with damp so no wallpaper sticks, and even paint peels off, a toilet which stinks no matter how much bleach you pour down it, and heating that's not heating, it's freezing. Just right for us.

Jude and me were Scum before the black day, and so we're still Scum. And if they're right, and we were Scum before, then I suppose they're right that we're still Scum. It's not like what happened to Mum changed what we are. In fact maybe what happened to her made them think more than ever that we're Scum and always have been, because that kind of thing – being stabbed to death on

21

your couch by your daughter's boyfriend – doesn't really happen unless you're Scum to start out with. At least, not as far as I'm aware. I don't read about posh women being stabbed to death on their couch by their daughter's boyfriend, but perhaps it happens all the time, and they just cover it up. Or perhaps it happens to everyone about the same, like one in ten thousand women get stabbed to death on the couch by their daughter's boyfriend, but because there are loads of Scum and only a few posh people, there really are more Scum cases.

It's funny how fast things go through your head.

And how fast you can get from, 'I'm home' to 'I'm Scum'.

I unzip my pocket and get out my keys, but then I realise Jude's gone and left the door unlocked. Sometimes I wonder where her head is, it doesn't seem to live in the same universe as the rest of her, let alone the same body. I push my bike in, and prop it up by the door, dumping my school bag next to it. I breathe in carefully. The first breath back in the flat's always a shocker. It's like putting a pair of rotten socks in your mouth and chewing. When I look around I think maybe we've been robbed, because it looks as though someone's been flinging all our stuff around trying to find the treasure he knows is buried somewhere (there isn't any treasure, I'm just saying it looks like he's been looking for it). Sensibly, the robber's left the dirty dishes in the sink, because what would he want with dirty dishes? But then it looks like this every day, and does a robber break in every day? I don't think so.

I put on the radio then open the windows to let the damp smell out. If you don't open the windows it just builds up till Jude has an asthma attack. I go and put the kettle on. Then I get a bin bag from a roll I keep under the sink and pull on my pair of yellow rubber gloves. You can do anything if you're wearing rubber gloves. I should know.

Number 89 is smaller than Number 87. It's got just one bedroom, and the bedroom is the dampest of the lot, so we don't even use it. Jude spent one night in there and got really sick. So we moved the beds into the big room which is like a lounge and kitchen combined, with a sink and a cooker along one wall with a breakfast bar in front of it. But with the beds and the couch and Em's cot all in one room, it's really cramped.

I start picking things up. If it's clothes, I chuck them across the room to land on Jude's bed on the principle that she'll have to do something with them if she wants to lie down ever again, which I'm assuming she does. Jude used to go out a lot to nightclubs and that, but since Mum was killed she stays in all the time. She's been poorly, so she often has a lie-down. I lob dirty nappies and food wrappers and uneaten crusts into the bin bag; half-empty bottles of rotting milk get emptied and dropped into a bowl of hot water. Jude says everything's fine, she's totally in control, but then that's what the Prime Minister says, and look how that's working out for him. Jude's only got one little girl and another on the way, it's not as though she's a mother of ten. She says I'll understand when I've got a kid of my own. Well, for one thing, Em might as well be *my* baby, the amount of time I end up looking after her while Jude's busy being poorly or pregnant. And for another thing, I am never, ever, as long as I live, going to allow a boy anywhere near me. He can stand at the end of the street and beg and plead and wave his bits around all he likes, and I'll be saying, 'In your dreams!' If she thinks I'm going to end up like her, slave to a lump of squirming flesh with a mouth at one end and a nappy full of shit at the other, I'm sorry, she's got another thing coming . . .

All the time I'm tidying up, my head's shouting so loud it drowns out the radio in my ears. Then, when I've finished, the shouting in my head stops.

I think the one advantage of living in a crappy mouse hole is that it doesn't take long to clear it up.

I make myself a cup of tea and, just as I'm pouring sugar in, I hear Em screaming out in the hallway and then my sister's voice cooing nonsense.

'Em-em-em-em-em,' she's using her sing-song voice, 'Em-ti-tem-ti-to . . .' and so on. 'Em-ti-tem-tem . . .' A grown woman, pleading with a toddler. 'For Christ's sake, shut it, Em,' she's saying, struggling outside with the door and the pushchair. Shall I go and give her a hand? I ask myself. Or shall I leave her to struggle? Give her a hand? Let her struggle? Give her a hand . . . I've just cleaned up her mess, I'm not her bloody butler. But then there's Em, and by the sound of her she's hot and hungry.

When I open the door there's my big sister, skinny and pale, with beautiful blonde hair reaching down to her waist. She's wearing a sleeveless T-shirt, and her arms are like a flower garden, she's got so many tattoos. She's got a huge baby-belly, and she's leaning on the pushchair look-ing exhausted. In the pushchair, wearing a pink all-in-one, there's this mini monster, its face all red and purple, cheeks shiny with crying, snot caking its nose, a gigantic mouth wide open so that you can see its tonsils bobbing around, and eyes wide and staring. It's a toddler from hell. The noise is ear-splitting.

'You're scaring me,' I say to Em, pulling a scared face, hoping it might make her laugh. No chance. She's not going to fall for that one. I bend over and unclip her, and try to pull her out the pushchair. She takes a bit of yanking, because her fat little arms and legs are stiff with anger and her hands are all clutchy and pinchy. I hold her out to Jude, but Jude's had enough of her kid for a bit. She turns her back on the two of us, goes over to the bed, chucks the clothes back on the floor and plonks herself down with a groan. She lies on her side, because she can't do anything else.

Her belly's huge. We don't know if the baby's a boy or a girl, but I call whatever's in there Big Ben. She's got four more weeks to go, but she looks ready to drop any minute. Her stomach's hanging low, like it did just before Em. I don't want to think what happens when she goes into hospital to have it. She hasn't even asked me to look after Em, but what does she think's going to happen to her? And what about when she comes back to our bachelor pad with another little living thing?

'Are you all hot and bothered?' I ask Em. Not that I expect an answer from a year-old kid, but I'm hoping she'll quieten down because I'm being polite. Fat chance. She just shouts louder.

I put her down on her feet facing the edge of the bed where her mum's lying, so she can hang on to that. She always wants to be on her feet now, but without something to hold on to she just sways a couple of times and

25

then plops down onto her bottom, which we think is funny, but she doesn't. With her clinging to the bed and howling, I unzip her all-in-one and peel it off her. Underneath she's hot and damp. She stops yelling, at least, and starts heaving great pathetic breaths that make her little pink chest shudder. Every few seconds she gives a big sob, just to let me know I still need to be nice to her. 'She's all sweaty.' I turn to Jude. 'You're wearing shorts. Why did you put all this on her?'

'I took her to the freezer centre,' Jude replies. Then she adds, like she can't believe it, 'It's freezing in there.'

'What a surprise,' I say, 'who'd have thought it?' But actually she's right. Last time I went to the Co-op in a T-shirt I thought I might turn blue and freeze solid right there in the aisle, and they'd have to chop me up into steaks and sell me as a special offer.

Em's got a full nappy, so I change it while she's standing, and when I've done that I give her tummy a tickle, and she starts to giggle, her fat little knees wobbling with the effort of staying upright. She lets go of the edge of the bed with one hand, reaches towards me and says, 'Mama,' but luckily Jude thinks Em's talking to her.

'All nicey-nicey now, are we?' Jude says to her daughter.

Just then there's a knock on the door. We look at each other in a sort of triangle: I look at Jude, and Jude looks at Em, and Em looks at me. No one ever knocks on our door. I get up and go to the door. I check the peephole. Outside, a man and a woman I recognise are watching the door as though they think something horrible's lurking inside. And I don't mean Em's nappy.

I mean us.

'Get up,' I hiss at Jude, 'it's the SS.'

Jude groans and heaves herself upright.

I know what the SS are here for the moment they walk in the door. They're looking for only one thing, and that's Em. Once they've got her in their sights they glom onto her like aliens sent to pick up specimens of humanoid life and take them back to the mother ship. Peasgood pulls a folder from his briefcase. It's got Jude's name on a label on the front.

'What do you want?' Jude moves to stand in front of her baby like a bodyguard, feet planted on the floor, hands curled into fists.

Peasgood and Bocock stand in front of her, and it's like a stand-off in a Western. They're jumpy, their eyes roving around, ticking off lists in their heads. (In Westerns the cowboys aren't ticking off lists, they're looking for gunmen hiding in doorways, but like bog roll and counselling, it's not dissimilar.)

Syringes left lying around? No.

Empty bottles of vodka rolling round the floor? No.

Rats grazing in the fridge? No rats. At least, not this minute. At least, not actually inside the fridge this minute.

'Just a routine visit,' says Peasgood. He looks about seventeen, and he's twitchy, fiddling with his papers with bony fingers that droop from his wrist.

Peasgood looks like a proper bureaucrat. I don't think anything about him, he's got to do his job. But Bocock's something else. She gets right under my skin. She's like eczema in human form. She thinks she's God's gift. She's got really big boobs, and she shows them off so you don't know where to look. She dresses like she's going to a club, with her red hair halfway down her back and lots of mascara. She smiles so wide it almost cuts her face in two.

'Just checking you girls are alright,' she says, with a too-loud voice. 'Sarah darling, you know you've got an appointment tomorrow morning at the police station?'

'I know that.'

'You are going to be there, aren't you? We're trusting you to turn up. You know how important you are to this trial.'

She says it like I'm appearing in a theatre production or something, not like I'm going to put my sister's boyfriend in jail for murder.

When she smiles I can see how pointy her white teeth are.

I shrug. I'm not going to promise her anything. But she doesn't like that.

She frowns and turns to Jude.

'Judith,' she says, 'you're Sarah's guardian, we're relying on you to make sure she does the right thing. I think you got the letter about your own appointment, as well? Please turn up on time. This is a way to prove to me that I was right to let you all stay together.'

Jude just stares at her.

'She knows that,' I say.

Bocock ignores me, carries on talking in Jude's direction.

'This arrangement,' she waves her bare arms around our flat, 'you and Sarah and Em, and the new baby all being together in this small space, it's really not ideal. I want to get you out of this damp, for the baby's sake.'

'We're alright here,' I croak. Because I know what she's saying. She's said it before. She could move us. She'd *like* to move us. I don't trust her. I know she's looking for an excuse to split us up. Bocock keeps talking about how Jude can't look after me properly now, so how's she going to look after me when there's another baby, and how I'd be better off in foster care. Don't get me wrong, I want to move to a nicer place, but I don't trust Bocock as far as I can throw her.

'You're not alright here, though, are you?' Bocock says, like she's really sorry for us. 'The damp's getting worse, isn't it?'

She gazes pointedly at a patch of wall where the plaster has bubbled out. It's a big patch, but if she raised her head and looked at the ceiling, she'd see an even bigger patch. Actually she'd see that the whole ceiling looks like it could cave in at any moment. And if she opened the bedroom door, the mould might just surge out and wrap itself around her and suffocate her.

'We don't want to go,' I say, because Jude's still not saying anything. 'Don't threaten us.'

'I'm not threatening you,' she says.

'I know that,' I say. But actually I know from her face that she is. 'I'm just saying *don't* threaten us. I didn't say you *were* threatening us.'

Bocock is looking at me from under her eyebrows. I try to give her a cheery smile, but I know it doesn't come out right. I'm out of practice.

She turns on Jude.

'Judith, you're very quiet. Is everything alright?'

Bocock goes right up to her. Too close. It's like she's inspecting Jude, looking her up and down, hair, eyes, mouth, Big Ben bump. Like a doctor.

Jude nods. 'Yeah,' she says quietly.

'Is baby doing well in there?' She pats Jude's bump.

Jude flinches away from Bocock's hand and nods. Her eyes are miles away, looking at the wall over Bocock's shoulder.

'And you, are you eating well?'

Jude nods again.

'What did you eat last night then?' Bocock says.

Jude stares at the wall.

'Steak,' I say. 'And broccoli. She hasn't been well. She's been poorly, so I'm feeding her up.'

Bocock glances at me.

'Steak and broccoli,' she says, like she doesn't believe me. 'That's very healthy.'

'I know,' I say.

'I bet you do.'

'Money's no object to us,' I say. 'The important thing is a healthy diet.'

She's gazing at me, and I'm trying not to blink. It's like a game of chicken.

'Would you like a cup of tea?' I say.

She shakes her head. Not even a no thank you. How rude is that?

Peasgood says, 'No thanks, I just had one.'

He's looking flustered, like he always does. It can't be easy spending all day trying not to look at Bocock's chest.

He's sweating, and so's she, because the big window lets in too much sun on a day like this. So to break the staring contest with Bocock I fill glasses with cold water from the tap and go and hand them over. Bocock holds the glass up to the light, narrowing her eyes, looking for dirt.

She walks over to the sink and pours the water out, then stands there for a minute looking around her. Her nose is twitching, like she can smell something. Well of course she can. The place stinks. And I've missed a bit of pizza crust, it's sitting on the lino in front of the sink. To me it looks as though it's glowing red and pulsating. Maybe she can smell it. Maybe she's got a really sensitive nose, like a dog. Maybe that's why she got the job, because she can sniff things out. But she can't have seen it, because when she moves away she steps right on top of it, and I think I hear a mini squelch of high heel on Value margherita topping.

She turns around and faces us.

'Where will baby sleep?' she asks.

At first Jude doesn't say anything and I dig her in the ribs because if she keeps this up Bocock's going to say she's on drugs or something.

'Where's the baby going to sleep?' I hiss at Jude.

'With me, where do you think?' Jude says.

At which point, I'm wishing she'd kept her mouth shut. I've read about babies. I know the baby can't sleep with Jude in the same bed or she might smother it by mistake. Of course, Em slept with Jude for months in her bed before we got a cot, and she survived. But still, it's the wrong answer.

'We're getting a cot for it like Em's,' I pipe up. 'Jude just means the baby will be in the same room as us.'

Peasgood nods like that's an answer he likes.

'We can put you in touch with someone who'll help you get hold of a second-hand cot,' he says, making a note in his folder. 'Shouldn't cost you anything, and they check them out for safety first.'

'Okay,' I say, 'that would be good, wouldn't it, Jude?'

But she's all blank eyes and other universe again.

Then Peasgood puts his foot in it. Maybe he's just trying to change the subject to stop me and Bocock bickering, but it's like he completely forgets what's in his folder.

'Is the father going to be involved in the baby's upbringing?' he asks.

It's like everything goes into slow motion, Bocock frowning and grabbing his arm, and hissing in his ear, and Jude turning to me with a look of disbelief on her face, and then turning back towards Peasgood and opening her mouth.

'Is this a joke?' Jude shouts. 'How can he be looking after his baby if he's on remand in Wandsworth jail and he's going on trial for murder in two weeks?'

It's not often Jude looks like the brightest spark in the room, but Peasgood and Bocock just stand there blinking like total idiots. Peasgood closes his eyes like he can't believe what he just said, and passes his hand over his face, then clasps his folder in his hands behind his back and turns to face the wall, like he's in disgrace.

'What are you on?' Jude hisses. 'Why don't you both just get out of here?'

Her face is white, even her lips are white, and her hands are curled into fists at her side. She's making me nervous. If they leave like this, like *we've* humiliated *them* (even though it's *Peasgood* who's humiliated them) then we're the ones in trouble because Bocock will say Jude's not co-operating, and she'll make trouble, she'll split us up. She'll say Jude can't cope with two children, let alone three. She'll say the flat's too small and too unhealthy. She'll put me in foster care and maybe Em and Big Ben too. Bocock can do anything she wants.

'We're fine on our own,' I say to Peasgood, for all the world like he's not an idiot. 'But thank you for asking, Jude's just upset about the trial and that.'

Peasgood stares at me.

'Thank you,' he says to me.

'Oh for Christ's sake,' Bocock mutters.

'I'll go to the police station tomorrow morning,' I add helpfully. 'What time did you say?'

'Nine,' Bocock says, although she's gritting her teeth. 'A Miss Malik's coming from witness support to take you. She'll be here at eight-thirty.' She pauses, and I know there's more. 'Judith, you're going to have to prove you're up to this,' she says, 'and you're not persuading me that you are. I mean look at this place . . .'

She holds out her arms like it's *our* fault that the walls are sagging with damp and no wallpaper will stay on them, and that the smells of the whole of South London find their way into our toilet.

'I know,' I say, because I can see Jude's not saying anything. She's sat down on edge of the bed staring at the floor.

It's me who sees them out.

Once they're gone I need to keep counting us – Jude, Emma, me; one, two, three. And Big Ben still squished up in Jude's belly, that's four. You think I'm paranoid, but I wouldn't put anything past them. They take them when they're freshly born. One day they'll take them before they come out.

'What was that all about?' Jude says. But she says it flat

and dead, all her fight gone as quickly as it came, just like always. 'They can't just walk in here . . .'

'They can do whatever they want.'

She thinks about that for a while, but I know she just doesn't want to think about them splitting us up when she's about to have a baby. I think she's in denial. Instead, she starts to talk to me about my appointment at the police station.

'So,' she says, like she's trying to get her head around what's going on, 'are you going to go tomorrow?'

'I've got to, haven't I?' I say, but she doesn't reply.

I don't want to think about the police station. The only thing I can think about is Peasgood and Bocock. I try to tell myself the visit could've been worse. But I know that, unless a miracle happens, next time Bocock will take Em, or she'll say Jude can't keep Big Ben. Or she'll send me off to foster care. Or all of the above. She'll scoop us up and scatter us over London, and we'll all land in different streets, and we won't know where the others are, and we'll never see each other again. Bocock can do that if she thinks Jude can't cope, and we all know that Jude can't cope.

But what I think is, it doesn't matter if Jude can't cope, because if it means we can stay together then I can cope for all of us.

All evening I can't do a thing. It's like a storm is inside my head, great big black clouds gathering, pressing down on me. It's not just what happened with the visit, it's know-ing what's waiting for me at the police station the next morning. It's like there's a monster waiting there at the station with its mouth open, ready to gobble me up. And when I walk in, I'll walk right into its mouth, and I'll be dead.

My hands are all shaky, but I make macaroni cheese from a packet mix for us and turn the telly on to try and get rid of the way I'm feeling. Turning the telly on means finding a pound coin and sticking it in the meter on top of the TV. We used to get four hours for one pound, but then Mum got the fridge as well, so it went down to two hours for a pound. If you let the money run out the TV switches itself off. A man comes to empty the set every month. It's like renting and buying all at once. I asked Mum how long it would take us to pay the TV off so it's ours, but she didn't know. When Mum was killed and me and Jude moved, we took the TV with us to Number 89 and the man kept coming to empty it every month like nothing had changed.

I like telly. It's really good for getting you out of your head. When I'm in a bad way I watch some of the kiddies' shows, and sometimes I find them funnier than Em does. I'm not sure Em's even got a sense of humour except when you tickle her tummy.

Tonight, when we put our coin in the slot and turn on the telly, the news is on. There's an MP talking about 'efficiency savings'. I like the words. 'Efficiency savings.' That's what they'd call it if they cut Big Ben out of Jude's tummy and took him away before he was even born. It's what they'd call it if I dropped out of school. It's what they'd call it if we all jumped out the window and died because we couldn't bear living in our scum flat any more.

Then he says, 'We expect a full recovery in the fourth quarter.'

I laugh, because it sounds funny, and because I'm so wound up that I'm going to either laugh or cry.

Then there's a bit of news about us in Shepherd's Way, saying it's going to be knocked down now all the residents have been moved to new housing. Which is crap, because we're still here.

'We're still here!' I shout at the telly. 'Where are we supposed to go?'

Then there's a local councillor talking. It's like he heard me shouting at the telly. He says the journalist's wrong, and there are still some people living in Shepherd's Way, and the council's got to hurry up and rehouse them because the conditions aren't good and anyway they're going to knock it down so the conditions are going to get a whole lot worse. Like our damp walls are going to be dynamited, and then they'll be damp dust. That's not what he says, but it's what he means.

'I like him,' I say to Jude. 'He sounds like he wants to get things done.'

'Don't believe a word that comes out of his stinking mouth,' Jude says, like he's personally offended her or something.

Sometimes Jude gets really pissed off about things people say or do, even when she doesn't know them. It's like she thinks there are lots of people out there who've got it in for her. What I think is that most people are too busy watching their own backs to have it in for anyone else. It's just that when they're watching their own backs all the time, they're not listening to you or looking at you. They literally can't, because they're watching their backs. Like Bocock and Peasgood. They don't see Jude and me and how we are, and how much we love Em, and how we look after her. They just worry that something's going to go wrong and they'll be blamed.

'His stinking mouth?' I repeat what she says. 'That's not nice. He's got a lovely face.'

Nice curly blond hair and blue eyes: a baby face.

But she doesn't answer, and she's turned her own face away from the screen.

'I feel like I've seen him before,' I say, because I really think I have. I can't put my finger on when or where, though.

'On telly, you silly cow,' she says, and I say, 'Oh yeah!' and I laugh, and after a moment she laughs too, and calls me a silly cow again, but in a good way.

We carry on watching and the news starts talking about the stock market, which I don't find very interesting because me and Jude, we don't have a very big stake in the 'global economy', whatever that is.

After the news there's a film on. *Love Actually*. I've seen it a million times. I know it off by heart. But I haven't seen it for a year. And when the film gets to the bit about the kid with huge eyes who loses his mum, I can't take it. I mean I can take it, of course, I don't cry or anything, but I feel weird, like my stomach's been sucked out of me. My head's still bursting with thunder-clouds as well, so what with an exploding head and a gaping hole where my stomach should be, I don't feel too good. I pace around a bit, but there's no space to move in our flat, and I'm not going outside in the dark. Then I see my hairbrush and – I know this sounds really weird – I pick it up and take it to Jude, who's watching the film sitting cross-legged on my bed, and I say to her, 'Jude, will you brush my hair?'

At first she doesn't hear me, because she's watching the film. Then, when I say it again, louder, she looks at me like she's angry with me for interrupting.

'Just brush my hair, that's all,' I say.

'Why should I?'

'It's all knotty,' I say, 'it needs a brush.'

'Do it yourself,' she says, 'I'm watching the telly.'

I shake my head and hold out the hairbrush.

She stares at me for a minute, and I can't tell what she's thinking. Then she rolls her eyes and takes the hairbrush.

'Okay, come on then,' she says.

So I sit in front of her on the duvet. She's still cross-legged, with her knees pressing against my waist, and she brushes with long firm strokes, making sure the bristles dig gently into my scalp before she pulls the brush down through my hair. I have to bite my lip to stop myself crying.

'What's the matter now?' she wants to know.

'You're hurting me,' I tell her. She's not, and she knows it. She stops brushing, and for a moment I think she's going to yell at me. But then she starts again, more gently now.

'It's getting long again,' she says.

'I know,' I say.

Mum could get knots out without scissors and make it shiny just from brushing. So after Mum got killed, when my hair got knotty and Mum wasn't there to get rid of the knots, I cut my hair off. It was at school, like a week after it happened, and there was a pair of scissors in the art room, and I pocketed them and took them to the toilets in the break, and I went into a cubicle on my own and chopped all my hair off. I didn't even look in the mirror to do it, and I made a real mess of it. I scared myself looking in the mirror afterwards, and then I scared everyone at school. But now it's nearly seven months later, and it's down to my shoulders. It's growing back really fast. I let Jude cut my fringe when it starts growing over my eyes, and she can get it pretty straight.

'It'll be alright tomorrow with the police, Sare,' she says, and at first I think I imagined it, because her voice is so quiet in my ear. 'Just say what you said before.'

'I know,' I say, and then we don't talk about it any more.

We haven't really talked about it for all this time. Not what happened, or what Borys did, or what we're going to say in court.

When Jude complains that her arm's falling off and stops brushing, I lean back against her and she puts her arms around me and we just carry on watching the film, pretending that she's not hugging me to her, but she is. I can feel her solid Big Ben belly against my back, and sometimes it heaves and pushes me, and that makes me feel so happy that I don't dare move a muscle in case she realises and pushes me away.

In the film everyone gets a happy ending, even the little boy whose mother died. He races through the airport after the girl he loves, and he kisses her, and luckily she doesn't slap him in the face or have him arrested, and while he's doing that his dad has even found a whole new girlfriend who's going to be his new mum, and she's even a supermodel, which is a stroke of luck.

But later, when I'm lying on my bed in the dark, I still can't sleep. I start to talk to Jude, because she must be thinking what I'm thinking.

'I think something bad's going to happen,' I say.

Jude doesn't reply.

'I mean, I know something bad already happened, but I mean something else,' I explain. 'I think they might take Em away, or Big Ben when he comes out.'

Still Jude doesn't say anything.

'We could go somewhere else tonight. We could just do it, just go, then I wouldn't have to go to the police station tomorrow. We could just pack everything up and go, find a place to stay, somewhere they can't follow us, just till Big Ben's born. We could disappear. We'll find some other hospital, somewhere they don't know us. We can invent names, they'll let you register. They're not going to throw you out on the street in your state.'

There's no answer and I say, 'Jude?'

Still nothing.

Then there's a snorty snore and a kiddie fart.

I reach for my phone. If I listen to my music, it drowns out all the other stuff going on in my head. But it's not charged, and it's turned itself off.

I stare at the ceiling. I try whispering to myself, 'We're anticipating a full recovery by the fourth quarter.' I close my eyes, and tell myself the story from the film, and I pretend to be all the people in it in turn, the little boy who's in love, and the father who's lonely because he's lost his wife, and the girl who makes cups of tea for the Prime Minister and falls in love with him. I'm even the Prime Minister. How funny is that? But I still can't sleep. I've got

Items checked out to

O'Sullivan, Hollie

De profundis and other prison writings /
Oscar Wilde ; edited and with an
Late Due   **21 Jun 2017**

To renew your items:

Go online to libcat.wads8nr.com
Phone us at 847-555-9324
Opening Hours: Mon-Fri: 10am to 8pm
Fri-Sat: 10am to 5pm

We are going Paperless!

From 6th June, we are no longer posting
paid notifications. Ask a librarian for more
information

to make sure I wake up in time to go to the police station, or Bocock will have it in for us even more than she does. But the only way to get to sleep is not to think about the monster waiting for me at the police station, but if I don't think about it I'm afraid I'll forget and won't wake up in time. So then I worry more, and I can't sleep, but I know I'll fall asleep just before I have to get up and that makes me worry even more about not waking up. In the end I close my eyes, and I lie on my back, and I put my hands on my head and I press my nails into my scalp, and then I comb my fingers slowly down through my hair, and I think of my mum with the brush in her hand, and I'm floating and tumbling into a deep, deep well of sleep. Then suddenly I see his face, the local councillor from the telly. At least, it looks like his face, but it's distorted, like a cartoon, with a huge mouth and little eyes. It sounds funny, but it's not, it's scary. Then he's gone, vanished, and my brain starts closing down again and switching off all my worries. But even as I'm falling asleep a little bit of my brain flickers back to life.

I know where I've seen him before.

FOUR

At the police station the monster's waiting for me. It looks like a TV screen sitting on a metal table in a boring inter- view room. Alright, it *is* a TV screen sitting on a metal table in a boring interview room. When they show me into the room and give me a chair to sit on in front of it the screen is blank because they haven't switched it on. But it's still a monster and it still makes me feel sick to look at it.

The door opens and Inspector Ramsey comes in and pulls up a chair next to mine. I keep my eyes on the screen. He says hello to the witness-support woman, and waves her to a chair on the other side of me.

'Long time since it happened now, eh, Sarah?' he says.

'Seven months and one day,' I say. I don't need to look at him. He'll be on the screen soon enough, asking me questions.

'One day, eh? You're sure about that, are you, Sarah?' he asks, trying to make a joke.

'I'm sure,' I say.

'Yes, well, I can understand that . . . You know why you're here, don't you, Sarah?'

I shrug. I don't take my eyes off the blank screen. I'm afraid it might come alive any moment, and I won't be ready for it, and it will swipe my head off.

'You're here to remind yourself of the evidence you gave us when you were questioned after your mum was killed.'

'I know.'

'I'm sure you do. Now, have you talked to Miss Malik here about how you're going to give evidence in court?' he says.

'I don't know what you mean.'

He turns to the witness-support woman, who must be Miss Malik. I wasn't concentrating when she introduced herself.

'I tried to speak to her about the video link,' Miss Malik says, 'but it was clear her mind was elsewhere, so I'm afraid I gave up in the end.'

'I see. Well . . . Sarah, can you turn your head and look at me? I'd rather not talk to your ear.'

So I turn my head, but only a bit, so I can still keep an eye on the screen at the same time.

'If you like you can give your evidence by video link,' he says. 'You wouldn't have to go into the court or see the defendant, you could sit in a room on your own, and you'd see the lawyers asking you questions, and they'd see you, all on a TV monitor like this one.'

I'm hearing the words, but my skull feels like it's about to explode. There's no space in my head to make sense of anything, so I don't reply.

'You don't have to decide right now. I think Miss Malik is making an arrangement for you to visit the court, is that right, Miss Malik?' There's movement to the other side of me. She's nodding at him. 'So you can see the video link room and the court, and make your mind up then.'

'I know,' I say.

For a moment he goes quiet, and then he says, 'I expect you'd like to get this over and done with, wouldn't you?'

He doesn't wait for me to answer, just picks up a remote control from the table in front of us, and points it at the screen.

At once the screen lights up, and it flickers a bit, and then there's a face up there. It's a child's face, in shock; deathly pale with big round eyes under a heavy fringe of dark hair that's really long. When I recognise my face it's like someone's punched me in my throat and I can't breathe.

I'm staring into her eyes. I mean I'm staring into my own eyes. It's like I'm standing in front of a mirror and seeing myself with everything stripped off. I'm looking inside myself. I'm turning inside out. My skin's peeling off and the seething, bubbling stuff inside me is burning its way out.

I make a noise. I don't know what noise I make, but I know I make one, because a voice says to me, 'Are you alright?'

Inspector Ramsey shifts in his chair and clears his throat, pointing with the remote control. The screen freezes, and my face is still there, but it isn't moving. I don't want to look at it any more.

I've got to get the seething stuff back inside me where it belongs or it will burn me up.

I look around the room wildly. I'm desperate. What I need is something to hold on to. I spot a pen on the desk and I stretch out my hand and grab it. But it's not enough to hold me. The room is bare, like it was on that black day. If I lose my grip, I'll slip right back. I need something to anchor me here, now. I hear the door open and close.

Inspector Ramsey moves. His arm, his hands, appear in front of my face. He's holding something. A plate of biscuits. KitKats, still in their wrappers.

'Have a break,' his voice comes from behind me. 'Have a KitKat.'

Miss Malik picks up a KitKat and tears the wrapper halfway off it, and then holds it out for me. I don't know how long I stare at it. And then the seething stuff retreats a bit. It rolls back inside me, and in a little while I can't feel it any more.

I reach out for the KitKat and I put it in my mouth and its sludgy chocolate coats my teeth and the biscuit crumbles against the roof of my mouth.

After a few minutes Inspector Ramsey says, 'Shall we carry on?'

'Yeah,' I say, like nothing's happened.

I don't want to, but I have to look at the screen again, and the face appears, and this time I'm telling myself, 'It's not me, it's just someone who looks like me.'

And that's how I get through it.

'What do you mean you didn't realise she was dead?' a male voice booms from the speakers.

'It's what I said,' the pale face says.

'I think I'd have noticed if it was me,' Inspector Ramsey says.

The pale chin wobbles, but the lips open.

'*Was* it you, then?' the pale face asks.

Inspector Ramsey doesn't reply, but he must have shaken his head off screen.

'Then don't tell me what you'd do,' the white face says.

'There's no need to speak to me like that,' Inspector

Ramsey says on screen. There's a moment's silence, and then he says, 'I know you're upset.'

More silence. Then the girl says quietly, 'I thought she was asleep.'

'Is she often asleep when you get home from school?'

She shrugs.

'So you didn't want to wake her. What did you do?'

'I tidied up . . .'

'How long did it take?'

The child is rallying now, sniffing back the snot, wiping her face with the back of her hand, getting irritated by the questions.

'I didn't look at the time. It took as long as it took.'

'After you tidied up you tried to wake your mother?'

'I was hungry. I wanted to get chips.'

'She wouldn't wake up?'

'She didn't move, so I tried shaking her, and then I tried lifting her up by her shoulders. I thought she'd wake up if I made her sit up.'

The pale face crumples.

'But underneath her the couch was all bloody, and her shirt was all bloody . . . everything was bloody.'

There's a long silence.

'The thing is, Sarah, I'm struggling with the fact that you got home at just past four, but you didn't ring the police until past six.'

Inspector Ramsey lifts the remote control, and the image on the screen freezes again. He turns and speaks to me, dragging me into the present.

'The defence is going to raise questions about that timing,' he says. 'They're going to say you're lying.'

'I'm not lying,' I say it quickly. I can hear it as it comes out my mouth. Too fast.

'There's nothing you want to change?'

'I can't change what happened.'

'I mean, Sarah, do you want to change your statement in any way?'

'No.' I feel stupid for misunderstanding. 'If that's what I said, that's how it was.'

After the police station, Miss Malik drops me off at school, like she knows if it was left to me I probably wouldn't go. First because I've got too much going on in my head to sit through lessons. Second because I'm scared of how watching the evidence made me feel. Scared that it made me feel anything at all. You can't learn anything if you're scared. Third, because talking to Inspector Ramsey made me realise that the trial's really going to happen, and it's here, on top of me, in less than two weeks, not in the future any more. When I think about that, it's like I can't breathe properly. And if I can't breathe then it stands to reason I can't think about Shakespeare or global warming, or anything.

All I can think about is that I can't breathe.

By the time she drops me off at school it's really late, like lunchtime late. I'm too worked up to be hungry, but I know I have to eat or I'll feel worse later on. So I go straight to the canteen and fill my plate with pie and corn and baked beans. I don't want to talk to anyone. I want to sit alone and fill my belly. But someone calls my name, and when I look around there's Sheena waving at me. She's finished eating, and she's sitting sucking on a straw that's stuck in a carton of juice. There's a whole gang of them and they have their heads bent like there's something going on. When I reach the table, the others get up and leave. They know where I live, and they know about my shoes. There's lots they know that even the teachers don't know. They watch me and they see things.

They sniff around me.

They say I smell.

They would smell too if they lived in a bucket of mould.

They tease Sheena for being my friend, but Sheena doesn't care. She's quite plump, so if she didn't get teased about being friends with me she'd get teased about being fat anyway so she might as well be my friend. Sheena looks at my face and she doesn't ask me where I've been. She knows when I miss school it's because of what happened, and she knows I don't want to talk about it, so she doesn't ask. Which is a big sacrifice for Sheena, because she loves gossip more than anything.

She can't wait for me to sit down before she leans across the table and hisses.

'Did you hear about Mr Brent?'

'What about him?'

'He only hit Taylor.'

'He hit him?' I'm digging into my shepherd's pie.

'He hit him a little bit.'

'What do you mean, hit him a little bit?' I'm trying to concentrate on what she's saying. I reach across the table and punch her shoulder lightly. 'You mean like this?'

She punches me back harder, then laughs. 'No, I mean like this.'

I try to smile at her. I know she's excited about the

news, and I know she's trying to get me excited too. But my head's all over the place.

'How do you know?' I ask her.

'Taylor told his mum, and now his mum's complained, Taylor's telling everyone.'

'Will he be suspended?'

'He should be,' Sheena says. 'Teachers can't go around hitting us.'

'I know,' I say. 'But what was Taylor doing? Taylor's always doing something.'

'It was just verbal,' Sheena says. 'No reason to hit him.'

Her news isn't making me feel any better. Gossip is good, but there's gossip that makes you happy and there's gossip that just makes you feel like you felt already but more of it. So I'm feeling anxious, and the Mr Brent news isn't making me feel any better. The opposite, actually.

'Mr Brent's okay,' I say.

'Yeah,' she says, and she thinks about that for a while and then she says, 'but he shouldn't hit kids.'

I look down at my plate. I haven't been thinking about eating, but I've wiped it clean. All that's left is a smear of gravy. Sheena is looking at my plate too.

'I should've had the pie,' she says sadly. 'I had a ham sandwich, but the meat tasted like cheese, and now I think I might puke.'

Usually I'd force down a second helping of food, or hang around and gossip with Sheena, but I'm feeling hyper, like I can't sit still, like I've got to do something – anything, actually – so I can stop thinking about how I looked on the TV screen, and how I felt, and how the trial's going to be worse.

49

'I'm going to the computer room,' I tell Sheena. She raises her eyebrows at me, but she doesn't ask why although I know she wants to.

Actually it's a surprise to me too. That I'm going to the computer room, I mean. You'd think I'd have known what I was going to say before I opened my mouth, but sometimes I really don't know until the words come out. I must have been thinking about it while Sheena was telling me about Mr Brent although I didn't know that I was. Sometimes decisions are like that. They happen when you think you're doing something else. It's very tricky.

In the computer room, I sign on to my email account. School computers are only supposed to be used for work and for school email. Like I can email my teacher, but not my sister or my hypothetical boyfriend. Unless he's a student, like if my boyfriend were hypothetically Omar, in which case I could. Also, there are things you can't say on school email, so if my boyfriend *was* Omar, hypothetically, I could ask him about homework but not about anything personal. If he was my boyfriend I don't think I'd be asking him about homework. Anyway, that's not going to happen, even if I wanted it to, which I don't. I can't think of anything worse than having Omar as a boyfriend, because Omar's stupid, like the way he embarrassed Zoe Brown by pulling an orange out of her bum.

There are lots of emails from teachers about the work I haven't handed in. I ignore them.

Instead I google the local council, and I find the man on telly. His name is Michael Finch. He was born in 1980 and he's got a wife called Andrea who's a GP. There's an article about him in a local newspaper and it says he's 'a man of action', which is what he looked like on the telly. Like he could get things done. There's also an email link and I click on it and a box appears. So I write him a message:

Hello Mr Finch, I saw you on TV talking about Shepherd's Way. It was very interesting, because me and my sister Jude are living in Shepherd's Way still and our flat is really damp and smelly. My sister's got a little girl, but I don't think the flat's a healthy place for a kid. Can you help us get a new house with space for all of us because we don't want to be split up and my sister's having a new baby and we need to all be together somewhere that doesn't smell? Please tell me as soon as possible.

Then it's time for class again. So me and Sheena are sitting next to each other in history and I'm trying really hard not to fall asleep, because sometimes I don't sleep very well at home, and I come to school hungry then have a big lunch to make me feel full, so then of course I feel like going to sleep. Sheena's nudging me to keep me awake, but my eyelids are really heavy. So I'm not sure what Miss Stiffel is saying when the headmaster's secretary puts her head round the door. Sheena jabs me really hard in the ribs, so I lift my head from my arm, and I see her. She's looking very serious. She calls Miss Stiffel over and whispers something in her ear. Then she turns and looks in my direction, and beckons me out.

'What for?' I say, because I don't have a clue what it's about.

'Just come with me,' she says, a bit impatient.

There doesn't seem any point in arguing, because what am I going to do? Insist on my right to learn about the

51

causes of the Second World War? I don't think so. So I get up and walk out of the classroom, and I can hear them behind me, whispering about what I might have done now.

'What's it about?' I ask the headmaster's secretary again, the moment I'm in the hallway. She's set off walking right away towards the headmaster's office, and I'm keeping up.

'I'm afraid the police need to have a word with you,' she says.

I stop dead in my tracks.

'I just did that,' I say.

She frowns at me.

'I went to the police station this morning,' I say.

'Ah,' she says, 'yes. Of course you did. But something's happened. They want to talk to you, and to Sheena.'

I don't like the sound of that. I don't want them to talk to me or Sheena about anything.

When we get to the headmaster's office, she knocks on the door, and he calls out for her to come in, so we do. Inside the room, the headmaster's sitting at his desk looking worried, and there are two uniformed police officers sitting opposite him, one man, one woman. So the headmaster tells them my name, and that I live in Shepherd's Way, and the police officers nod and make notes, then they all shift around a bit and make me sit on a chair too so we're all in a circle around the headmaster's desk. They must know about Mum getting killed, because they look at me like people always look at me, which is sorry and embarrassed and even a bit scared. My heart's pounding. I don't understand. What more can they want from me? Is there something I don't know?

'Sarah,' the woman says, 'thank you for coming to have

a little chat with us. I want to ask you if you know a girl called Zoe Brown?'

I stare at her. I wasn't expecting that. What's Zoe Brown got to do with anything?

I nod. 'She's in Year 11 and she lives in Shepherd's Way B Block.'

'Were you friends?' the woman asks.

I shrug. I don't like that she's asking 'were' not 'are' – like 'were you friends?' Not, 'are you friends?'

I'm thinking Jude knew her and she's said some things about her but I'm not going to say anything about that. And I'm thinking Zoe was the one Omar did the orange from the bum trick to, but I'm not going to say anything about that, either.

'So you see her around Shepherd's Way?' the man asks.

I shrug again. 'Sometimes.'

'When was the last time you saw her?'

'I don't know.'

They all glance at each other in a circle that doesn't include me, and I can hear a siren screaming in my head, because that's when I know that something really bad has happened. Then the policewoman says, 'I'm sorry to have to tell you that Zoe's body was found this morning.'

I stare at her. I can't understand what she's saying. Zoe's body? Her *dead* body?

'Zoe?' I ask, because I don't think I can have heard properly.

'Zoe Brown,' the policewoman repeats quietly. 'Her parents have identified her.'

A memory whooshes out of the noise in my head. Zoe sitting at the same table as me at lunch and boasting to her friends that when she gets home she locks herself in her room so she doesn't have to talk to her parents. She's saying she lets her mum hammer on the door as hard as she likes, but she still doesn't open up.

'Are they sure it's her?' I say, thinking that her parents can't see much of her if she's in her room all the time.

They look at me pityingly and the woman officer says yes, her parents are sure.

We all sit there in silence.

They're looking at me all worried, like they expect me to burst into tears or something, but I can't cry. I didn't even cry much on the day Mum got killed. After that I felt like a dead person walking around in a bodysuit so everyone thought I was alive. Now I've got that dead feeling again just above my heart but this time it's a patch of dead, not dead all over.

'Where was she?' I ask.

'In one of the arches under the railway line,' the male officer says. 'Outside Denny's. Do you know it?'

I nod.

I know Denny's. You can see it if you sit in Sheena's mum's café eating a baked potato or something. It's just across the way. Carla, Sheena's mum, won't let me and Sheena go near the railway arches at night. She says it's dangerous under the railway track, but what she really means is Denny's is dangerous. That's why the police want to talk to Sheena then, because of the arches, because of her mum's café.

'How was she killed?' I ask.

They look at each other and then the woman says, 'It'll be in the newspapers later. She was strangled.'

54

They're watching me, but I've got nothing to say to them. I don't know much about Zoe's life, and what I do know I'm keeping to myself.

'Are you alright, Sarah?' the headmaster asks me.

I want to say why wouldn't I be? But the words don't come out.

'This is a lot for you to take in on top of everything that's happened,' he says. 'These officers will be talking to several students this morning. But we'd be grateful if you could keep this to yourself. We don't want everyone at school gossiping about Zoe. Not now. It's too late for all that.'

A few minutes later they say I can go and I find Sheena waiting outside.

'What's it about?' she asks. She's nervous but she likes a drama. I want to warn her so it's not such a shock for her but I only have time to say, 'It's really bad,' before the door opens and they call her and she goes in and the door closes.

I stand blinking outside the door. I can't go back to class. My legs take over, walking me up and down the corridor. Mr Hughes comes along and says, 'What are you out here for, Sarah, shouldn't you be in class?' I tell him I need the toilet, which is true, and then he says I'm going the wrong way. 'The toilet's that way.' He points back along the corridor, so I turn around and go to the toilet and when I come out he's gone.

All the time my legs are walking me up and down I'm thinking I can't believe it. Even though I didn't know Zoe that well, it's still really shocking. Even if I didn't speak to her, she was always there. In the corridor, or in the canteen, or around Shepherd's Way all dressed up on her way out. So getting my head around the fact that she's not anywhere any more is hard. And then thinking about how she got to be dead makes my head go dizzy, and for a minute I'm so scared my head feels like it's spinning and might almost come off completely.

Sheena's in there for ages and when she comes out she's as white as a sheet. It's like she doesn't see me. She's just standing there in front of me with her pudgy chin wobbling. Then she starts to cry. We're not kissy girls but I've got to do something so I actually give her a bit of a hug, and after a minute she starts to dry up.

She says, 'Do you think my mum's okay?'

So then we don't even talk about it. We go and get our bikes and we cycle out the back gate where there's less chance of getting caught. The fact is, looking at it now, we could just have rung Sheena's mum and checked she was okay, but nobody could expect us to go back to school after hearing about Zoe, so we don't.

When we get to the arches, it's crowded with strangers. There are police in uniform, and some who aren't in uniform so they look like normal people, and police cars parked up and down the street. There are photographers too, from the newspapers. A woman comes over to us and starts to chat, like do we live round here? And do we know the girl whose body was found? And how do we feel about a girl being found dead? She sounds like she's all sympathy but her eyes are cold.

'How do you *think* we feel?' says Sheena.

'I don't know, tell me,' the woman says, and she reminds me of my shrink because she only wants something she can write down.

The number of people who can make a living out of asking stupid questions.

'What does it matter how *we* feel?' Sheena says, like she thinks the woman's an idiot, which she is. 'It's *her* that died. Ask *her* how *she* feels.'

I don't think Sheena's making sense, but I know what she means. After a while the woman gives up and goes away frowning like, the youth of today, what are they coming to, they won't come up with one good quote when you want one.

We can't get through the cordon to Carla's café, but we can get close enough to see it's all locked up, and so's Denny's across the way.

We stand and watch. So many people there just for Zoe. I hope somewhere she can see us all. I hope she's pleased there's so much fuss. Then I stop hoping about her because thinking about her makes my throat get tight.

From behind us a woman elbows her way through the crowd and when she gets to the cordon I can see she's carrying a bunch of flowers. She reaches under the cordon and puts the flowers on the pavement. A few minutes later, there's another bunch, with a note saying, 'We'll never forget you.'

'I think we should write something for her,' Sheena says. Her chin's wobbling again. She's really serious.

I'm not keen, what with all the cameras around.

But Sheena gets a pen out her bag, and one of her exercise books, and she tears a page out.

'What shall we write?' she says.

I shake my head. It's no good writing what I'm thinking. What were you doing in the arches at night, Zoe? Was anyone out looking for you? Didn't anyone tell you to be careful?

Sheena is scribbling something. When I look, she's written, 'We hope God's taking good care of you in Heaven.'

I'm a bit surprised because I didn't know Sheena believed in God, but after she puts the note down she gets all weepy and tries to hug me.

I push her off.

'We should go home,' I say.

She nods and sniffs, and asks me if I want to go back to her house for tea, and I say yes, because even when someone's got killed, you've got to eat.

When we get to Sheena's flat, which is about five minutes' cycle ride from the arches, we go and find Carla in the kitchen. Her flat's not posh, but it's always warm from cooking, and it doesn't smell of damp, it smells of toast and baked beans, and big fat chocolate cakes that come out of the oven and get butter icing squished all over them.

'We heard about Zoe,' Sheena says right off to her mum's back. 'We went to the arches, but we couldn't find you.'

'You went to the arches?' Carla swings round to face us and her hands are on her hips, like she wants us to know she means business. They're big hips, and she always wears her hair tied in a knot on top of her head, so she's tall too, and right now she's angry as well. 'A girl's been murdered, and you go sightseeing?'

'We didn't . . .' Sheena starts to say.

'You go to a place where a girl had the life squeezed out of her?' She's not just unhappy, she's furious. Her voice is getting louder, and she's saying her words really short and sharp.

'Whose idea was that?' she demands, looking from one to the other of us.

Sheena and I look at each other.

'We didn't do anything wrong,' Sheena says, 'we were—'

'Don't you talk to me like that, young woman!' Carla barks at Sheena.

I take a step backwards. This is between Sheena and her mum. It's not for me, this kind of stuff. No one tells me off about where I've been. I can go anywhere.

'Not so fast, Sarah,' Carla's snapping at me now. 'I may not be your mother, but you're going to hear this from me anyway. There's a psychopath out there, and he's killed a girl hardly older than you. Sheena, you don't go anywhere except to and from school without telling me first where you're going. And Sarah, you've got to warn Jude. She mustn't go near Denny's . . .'

'She wouldn't!' I protest.

Carla stands gazing at me. She bites her lip.

'Well, she'll have two kids soon,' she says. 'So perhaps she'll change her ways.'

'She never would!' I protest again, and Carla sighs and shakes her head.

'All I'm saying,' she says, 'is that you and Jude have to look out for each other now, watch each other's backs.'

She turns away from us and busies herself at the sink.

Sheena and me look at each other like we don't know what's going on. Carla's not usually dead serious like this. Usually she's funny.

'I'm sorry,' she says, still with her back to us. 'I'm sorry. I know you're good girls.'

Then she turns round, wiping her hands on her apron, and she's crying, which I've never seen her do before.

'She was lying in the gutter when I got there to open up for breakfast this morning,' Carla says. 'There I am thinking she's drunk, and I go over and have a look, and then I see she's not drunk because her head is twisted . . . So I call the police, and I spend the next hour with them giving them a statement, and all the time I'm thinking about her lying there, and how it could have been you . . .'

She's sobbing now, and she opens her arms and Sheena goes straight to her and gets wrapped in her mum's huge chest.

It's embarrassing watching them hugging like that.

I don't know what to do with myself.

Then Carla opens her eyes and sees my face over Sheena's shoulder, and she lets Sheena go and she says, 'You too, Sarah, I'd hate for anything to happen to you. That's why I shouted at you.'

'It's okay,' I say, but I still don't think she should've shouted at me. I'm nothing to her.

'Let's have some food,' Carla says, wiping her eyes.

She makes us a really nice tea, with bacon and tomato and eggs, like it's her way of saying sorry for shouting. But none of us is in the mood for eating, so although I'm hungry, I'm looking at all this good stuff on my plate and it's going cold and fatty, but there's nothing I can do about it, I just can't eat it. It's like Zoe Brown is standing in the room with us, like we can each see her there watching us and listening to us, and enjoying our food would be rude when she's dead.

We talk a little bit about school, but soon we can't help talking about Zoe. Sheena wants to know all about the police and taking the body away, but Carla doesn't say much. She's got a look in her eyes like there's stuff she's not telling us. I'm thinking she must have touched Zoe to see she was dead. It makes me feel like I know how Carla's feeling because I did that too, with Mum.

'Did you see her around the arches before?' Sheena's asking her mum.

I don't know why, but her mum glances at me.

'I saw her,' Carla says, 'more than once. When I was at the café late . . .'

She stops talking and rubs her eyes with her hands, like she's thinking about whether to carry on or not.

'I saw her going into Denny's,' she says.

'You're always telling us it's dangerous. So why didn't you stop her, Mum?' Sheena says.

Carla looks at her daughter.

'I did speak to the police about Denny's,' she says. 'I didn't want a club like that opposite my café, and I told them what I saw; young girls going there. I wanted them to close it down.'

'Really?' Sheena's staring at her mum. 'You did that?' Then she says, 'You did the right thing, Mum.' Like she's really proud of Carla.

Although I think the police have got better things to do than stop girls going out at night.

But Carla's watching her daughter with a funny expression on her face.

'I wasn't thinking of Zoe, though, I was thinking of the café, and now I'm ashamed of myself. I should have given her name to the police. I should have gone and seen her parents. I should have told them. Finding her like that, it's my punishment.'

With the last few words her voice goes all wobbly and she pushes back her chair so it scrapes on the floor and she turns away from us and tears off a piece of kitchen paper to dry her eyes.

'I'm sorry,' she says to us. Then she laughs in a weepy way. 'Come on, Sarah love, I'm going to walk you home.'

But then Sheena says she's not staying at home on her own, so they both walk me home. We're all nervy even though it's not really dark yet, checking around us and listening for footsteps and that. There are more police around than usual, and I suppose they're patrolling the area around Denny's just in case. I push my bike, and Carla asks me lots of questions about Jude, and Em, and the baby coming. It doesn't sound nosy from her, it's just making conversation on the walk home. I tell her what she asks about because she knows how it feels to be embarrassed about what you've done. I don't feel like she's judging me, even if she did shout at me. Sheena's mad excited about the baby coming, she won't stop talking about it. Even Carla thinks Sheena's going on about it too much.

'You talk about a baby like it's a puppy,' she says to Sheena.

Sheena says a baby's cuter than a puppy, and Carla says, 'You should have seen yourself when you were born, I don't think cute was the word. Ugly as sin, perhaps.' And Sheena shrieks and they both laugh and I'm thinking Carla is good at making us forget what's happened.

Then Carla starts to speak all seriously about how you can never take your eyes off a baby for fear it will hurt itself or get lost. 'Babies are so vulnerable,' she says, 'a mother has to protect her baby with her life, her baby is her number one priority above sleep, food and her own comfort.'

It's like she's giving me a message for Jude. This is your duty. Your baby is more important than anything, you have to keep it safe. I know that's what Jude intends. She's a good person. She should be a good mother. She loves Em, and she'll love Big Ben. But she hasn't been well, and I don't know if she's capable of doing what Carla says.

They go with me all the steps up to Level 8 so I don't have to be on the dark staircase on my own. When we get to the door of the flat I don't ask them in because I'm embarrassed by the state of it and also because I don't know how Carla and Jude would get on. Carla's like the opposite of Jude. She's had a lot of bad things happen to her but you wouldn't know it because she manages everything really well.

When I'm turning to go in Carla steps forwards and hugs me. She's like a big warm overcoat, and I'm clinging to her. Then I realise the hug is probably over already and I'm hugging too long so I let her go really fast. I say 'bye' really quick and hurry into the flat without looking at them.

I wish I hadn't hugged Carla so long.

I feel embarrassed.

Then I think that even if I hugged too long, Carla would never laugh at me.

FIVE

When I walk in, Jude's lying on the bed rubbing her tummy and moaning, and Em's standing in her cot holding on to the frame and screaming her head off. Even if I wanted to tell Jude about Zoe, this is not the right time. And I don't want to tell Jude. I don't really know how well she knew Zoe. Jude can be very secretive about her friends. It's possible Jude got along okay with Zoe, in which case Jude will be upset, and I don't want her upset if I can help it.

I pop a dummy into Emma's mouth, but she spits it out right away so she can carry on screaming. I rinse out a bottle and I dig around for the milk powder. My hands are busy, and I'm thinking about ways to shut Em up. I'm still feeling sick from what happened to Zoe. But I know the only thing to do is to block it out and keep focusing on what's in front of me. Or, in this case, what's slobbing on the bed behind me.

'What's up with you, you lazy cow?' I say to Jude, over my shoulder. 'Deaf cow actually, if you can't hear the racket she's making.'

'I'm having contractions,' she groans.

'Contractions?' I wheel around to get a better look at her. She's lying on the bed, like I said, but now I see she's clutching her belly. Her face is dead white. Her blonde hair's all spread out on the pillow, and the tattoos on her arms make it look as though she's being swallowed up by a garden. She's got no make-up on, or jewellery, and she looks really young, like a little girl, and I can feel it like an earthquake inside my own belly: soon there will be four of us, four children.

I remember when Em came back from the hospital so tiny, anything could have done for her. A little flat like ours is full of danger – there's hot and cold and germs and boiling water and electricity and windows that open wide eight storeys up . . . It's like Carla said: You have to keep them so safe, babies. You have to be watching out for them all the time, never taking your eyes off them . . . Carla would know what to do.

I run out the flat and onto the walkway, leaning over the balustrade and shouting Sheena's name. If she hears me, if they come back up to help, I know we'll be alright . . . I stop shouting and listen for an answering shout . . . But there's nothing, just a big eery silence . . . I turn back into the flat.

I look at Jude lying there, and I know I should be feeling sorry for her and cooing 'you poor darling', and mopping her brow and calling an ambulance or a taxi or something but I'm actually just looking at her and feeling so angry I want to slap her stupid, sweating face.

I grab my phone and try to call Sheena, but the number's dead, like she hasn't charged it. I throw the phone down in disgust.

'Jude, what've you done to us?' I'm shouting. 'What're we going to do? We can't cope with another baby.'

'Too bloody late now,' she moans. 'Get me to the hospital, or I'll be having it right here.'

I give her a good look. She's panting, clenching her fists, her head lifting from the pillow in pain. She'll never make it as far as the bus. I think about ringing for a minicab, but they won't want her waters breaking on their seats and it would cost more cash than we've got. So I call 999, and a crabby woman who sounds as though I've woken her up from a nap tells me an ambulance will be with us shortly.

'Pack me some stuff, will you, Sare?' Jude says. She's calmer now the pain has passed. She gives me a small smile but the smile just irritates me more. She may think when she smiles like that that she looks like the Mona Lisa but it makes me want to vomit.

'Pack you some stuff?' I can't believe it. 'You've known for nine months that you're going to have a baby, I mean it's not as though this day was never going to come, once it's up there it's going to come out one way or another, and you haven't packed a—?'

But it's too late, there's another contraction. Her whole body's snarled up in it and here I am having a go at her.

Anyway, it's nine months too late. I hurry round the flat picking up clothes off the floor, finding a Lidl bag to put it all in. When I glance back at the bed I see Jude is lying there curled on her side and texting someone. She's texting as fast as she can, like she knows another contraction is on its way and she needs to send her text before it gets her. Then I see the pain sweep over her, and she stops texting, and she drops the phone and clutches herself and moans. I don't know whether she pressed Send before the contraction hit, and I don't care. I've got to pack up Em's stuff too, and make the bottle I was making when all this started, and stick it in Em's mouth, and tell her that she's about to have a night out at the hospital. Because where else is she going to go? She can't stay home alone.

I hear a siren. That freaks me out, because it's like the day Mum got killed all over again. Then my head fills with Zoe, lying dead. Have they found another girl killed?

There are footsteps running on the stairs, and then banging on the door.

At first I can't move. I'm paralysed.

Then they bang on the door again, and shout 'Ambulance,' and I make myself go and open it and let them in. Like before. And I point to my mum, only it's Jude this time. And they rush over to her and crowd around her, like last time.

Em starts to cry, and that breaks the spell. I go and pick her up. She's looking all suspicious, her little eyebrows in a V over the top of her bottle.

'Can you believe that? Your mum's making more noise than you,' I say to Em. Her eyes fix on mine and I give her a bright smile that's totally fake.

One of the ambulancemen is looking around.

'You live here too?' he asks, and I nod.

'And the kid? It lives here?'

'It does,' I snap at him.

'Is it hers or yours?'

'What business is it of yours?'

He looks startled.

'I want to make sure there's someone to look after her,' he says. 'I can't just cart her mother off and leave a kid behind.'

'Okay,' I say. 'I get it. I'll be looking after her.'

He exchanges a look with the other paramedics. I don't like the look of that look. I should've kept my trap shut.

They're examining Jude and then they're moving her onto a stretcher. Jude is beside herself, begging for an epidural.

She's scaring me with the noise. I turn, so Em can't see her mum's face all contorted. Em's warm little body makes me feel better.

But then I think, what will happen if Jude dies?

When we reach the hospital I want to go into the labour ward with Jude, and first the nurse says I can but then Em starts to kick up a fuss in her pushchair, crying and shouting, and she changes her mind.

'Well, what am I going to do with her, then?' I ask as I watch them wheel Jude off down the corridor.

'Isn't anyone else with you?' the nurse asks. 'Is your mum coming in?'

I give her a look and then I turn the pushchair round and we walk off down the corridor. I don't want to leave Jude on her own but I've got no choice. I'm a bit relieved because I wasn't there when Em was born and I don't think I want to be there when this one's born either. I've seen labour on the telly, and I'm not keen on seeing all the grunting and shrieking. I'm sorry Jude's got to do it, but she got herself into it so she'll have to get herself out of it.

There's a room calling itself a waiting room, so I go in and sit on one of the chairs, but Em soon gets antsy. There are toys in there, but they look grubby, so I won't let her have them, and the other people in there keep giving us dirty looks. When Em starts wailing a man says to me, 'Can't you keep that child quiet?' And a woman says, 'Look at her, she's just a child herself.' And the man mutters, 'Dirty slag.'

Any other day I'd have told him to say that to my face. But I'm too scared to care. And maybe he'd have done it. Maybe he'd have said it again to my face. You can never tell.

I go back to the desk where the nurses are, and there are two of them now and they tell me that Jude's waiting to go into theatre because the doctor's decided she's going to need a Caesarean.

So off I go, pushing Em all over again. The corridor stretches into the distance, I've no idea where it goes, but that's alright. I start walking with Em and it's not long before she settles down. All along one side of the corridor is one long photo of the city at night, and on the other side a mirror, so it's like walking along a corridor between two glittering River Thames, past two floodlit Houses of Parliament, two glowing Big Bens. Em falls silent, and I think she must be looking at the buildings, but when I look down at her I see her face is lifted to the row of square yellow lights set into the corridor ceiling and her eyes are flickering as we go underneath.

'You feel sleepy,' I say to her. 'Your eyelids are heavy, you want to go to sleep.'

Her eyes glance from the lights to my face that's upside down to her then back to the lights. She really does look sleepy and I think of Omar hypnotising Martin at school and getting suspended. Then I think of Omar pulling an orange out of Zoe's bum and then I think of Zoe and that she's lying dead and cold in a drawer somewhere.

I can't stop now. I keep moving, lifting my eyes to the lights in the ceiling, like Em, and I count the lights. One, two, three, four . . . one, two, three, four . . . Perhaps that's why soldiers count as they march, to stop them thinking of what's just up ahead . . . that they might die, or their sister might die, or they might lose all their family . . . I think if I carry on counting I can keep myself at scared and not progress to hysterical. I've got the steady rhythm of my feet on the ground and strangers walk by and I like that. They keep me company but they don't hassle me or bother me. I don't know how long I march through the fake city. Thames, Houses of Parliament, Big Ben, Thames, Houses of Parliament, Big Ben . . . it's like I'm floating through a tube with the waters of the Thames lapping around me. My head gets woozy.

Above me the lights are flashing and flickering . . . Flashing and flickering . . . I get a sudden flash of Jude in the operating theatre, of blood and knives . . . blood seeping into a couch . . . a body slumped in the gutter . . . flashing and flickering and cutting . . . I think of Borys, whose baby's being born this very minute. Borys and a knife. Zoe and a strangler. Borys and my mum, and her bleeding body, and the murder trial that seems, right now, like a dark distant terror, shapeless and nameless compared to the terrors I've got on my plate right in front of me.

After a while my legs get wobbly because I'm hungry. It's dark outside already, and I haven't eaten since Carla's and I hardly ate there. After all the walking, I'm back near the labour ward. So I go and ask the matron there whether there's any news about Jude. She's just come on duty, so she hasn't seen me before, and she gives me an interrogation – am I next of kin? Does Jude know I'm there? What's Jude's surname and her date of birth? At first she tells me there's no one there by that name. Then when I start to cry she checks again and tells me there's no news and that Jude's still in the operating theatre.

'Why's it taking so long? Is she alright?' I ask.

The nurse's mouth makes an I-do-this-a-dozen-times-a-day smile.

'We'll let you know if we have any information,' she says.

'But I'm her sister,' I insist, 'and this is her kid. We've got a right to know if there's a problem.'

The nurse glances at Em, who's fast asleep with a little smile on her face and her head thrown back, looking like she couldn't care less whether her mum is alive or dead.

'I'm afraid I don't have any information for you right now,' she says, 'these things can take a while.'

'I need to get something to eat,' I say.

'There's a snack bar down the corridor.' The nurse indicates a general direction. 'Don't worry,' she adds, 'your sister's in good hands.'

I find the snack bar and I see how much I've got in my pocket. I should've raided the TV money before I came out but I wasn't thinking what with Jude crying and shouting. So I've got four pounds. I buy a sugar doughnut and a cup of hot chocolate. I just need to sit here and eat and get some sugar into my body. Into my head too, because when I'm hungry I can feel myself not thinking straight. I don't know why everyone's always saying you shouldn't eat sugar. I'm a big fan of sugar. Your brain needs sugar, it uses loads of it. That's a fact. That's why supermodels are brain dead. So now I'm thinking doughnut might make my brain calm down.

I find myself a table. Someone's left a newspaper on it with a headline, *Local Schoolgirl Murdered*, and a picture of Zoe. When Mum got killed she didn't get her photo in the paper. Perhaps it's only schoolgirls who get pictures.

I don't know if it's because of the picture or because I'm hungry but suddenly I'm shaking. I'm trying to carry my tray and shift the pushchair and sit down all at once and I trip and drop the tray and the doughnut goes on the floor and the hot chocolate goes over the lot of it.

I don't swear about it. What's the point? I just sit down and look at the mess at my feet. I know I should clear it up but I don't have the energy. I watch it. The hot chocolate's sinking into the doughnut, turning the sugar dark brown and making the doughnut into gunk. It crosses my mind that I could just get down and lick it off the floor but that would be disgusting.

The woman behind the counter sees what I've done and starts to tell me off.

'You made the mess, you can clear it up yourself,' she says.

In my head I'm answering her back – she wouldn't talk to an adult like that, it's just because I'm a kid.

'Get her another one,' a man's voice says behind me.

I turn around.

I hadn't seen him but he must have followed me in. He's got blond shaggy hair like a boy and he's wearing a suit.

He's the one from the TV, I think. Then I think I'm hallucinating because I'm so tired. He's just a man, not that man.

'Get her another one,' he says again to the woman behind the counter who's standing there with arms crossed in front of her, giving him a look. There must be something about his voice because she pours another hot chocolate although she's not happy about it. She puts it on the counter.

'And a doughnut. Come on, show a little compassion,' he tells her, and his voice isn't bossy, it's like he's jollying her along. He's getting up and going to the counter to collect the drink for me. She's not making a move for the doughnut but he reaches into his pocket and puts a pound in the tip jar, and she drops a doughnut on a plate and hands it to him. She still doesn't like us.

'Thank you,' he says to her, 'that's very kind. And some paper napkins? Thank you.'

He comes over to where I'm sitting and he moves the paper and puts the mug of chocolate and the plate with the doughnut on it down in front of me, and says quietly, 'There you go.'

He's just like he was on the TV, nice-looking and sweet. A man who gets things done.

He squats down and wipes up the mess on the floor with some paper napkins. I take a bite of the new dough-nut. Anyone who can bring me hot chocolate and a doughnut and mop a floor is my hero.

While he's bending over he takes a good look at Em.

'She's a beautiful child,' he says.

I look at Em. She's looking cuter than normal, her little red lips pressed together so she hasn't got her gob open yelling, and her face pink with sleep. Almost angelic.

He stands up to look for a bin and goes and puts the dirty paper in there.

I'm so out of it I don't even say thank you, I just say, 'You're Michael Finch, from the council, aren't you?'

And he smiles like he's very, very tired and says, 'That's me, for my sins.'

'I wrote you an email,' I say.

He says, 'Did you?' but actually he doesn't look surprised. Like he knew who I was before I said about the email.

I say, 'I wrote to say me and my sister Jude live in Shepherd's Way, and our flat is damp and it's no good for the baby.'

He doesn't say anything for a moment, then he says, 'That was you, was it?'

I'm thinking what a coincidence that I can send him an email and then out of the blue I meet him in a hospital coffee shop. But he doesn't say anything like what a surprise, or what a small world.

He doesn't seem to want to say anything at all. So I gabble on. I reach for the newspaper and point at the picture of Zoe, and I say, 'That's Zoe Brown, I knew her. She lived in Block B, and look what happened to her. It's not a good environment for kids, all sorts of things happen . . .'

He glances at the picture of Zoe, then he sighs deeply, hangs his head so he's looking at the table and says, 'I know, it's a terrible environment. I'm afraid, long term, that new housing is the only answer. Shepherd's Way is virtually uninhabitable, we've got to get people out, there's no point in just moving residents around inside the building. Look,' he lifts his head and looks straight at me, 'I can't promise anything, but I'll try.'

He pushes his chair back and stands up. 'I've got to get home, or my wife will be wondering where I am,' he says.

'I just dropped by to visit a friend and he was in a bad way, so I stayed longer than intended . . . Can I ask you to send me another email? With all your details? We'll see what we can do.'

When he goes I feel confused because this nice thing happened in the middle of being scared for Jude and scared about Zoe. All it takes is one nice person, and everything seems better. And then I remember I didn't tell him that even in a new flat we've all got to stay together and that's the most important thing.

This time when I go up to the maternity-ward reception desk, the nurse is looking serious. 'Ah yes,' she says, and I recognise her tone of voice at once. It says there's a big problem but if you say it like it's a small problem then there's a chance the little sister won't realise just how big a problem it is.

'Your sister's had her baby,' she says. 'But she's lost quite a lot of blood. You can see her, but you mustn't distress her.'

'She's lost blood?' I'm shouting. 'Is she alright?'

'Mum's okay. Baby's in an incubator. He was in Mum's tummy for longer than we'd like.'

He. Big Ben was just a joke, I never thought he'd come out a boy. What are we going to do with a boy?

'Has your sister had any bleeding in the past few weeks?' The nurse is frowning.

'No,' I shake my head, because it sounds like she's accusing me or Jude of something. But even as I'm saying no, I'm remembering dried blood on Jude's knickers in the laundrette.

'The placenta was blocking the cervix,' the nurse is saying, 'so Baby couldn't come out naturally.'

Placenta previa. After half of Year 11 got pregnant, they put *What to Expect When You're Expecting* in the school library. I took it out for Jude when she fell pregnant with Em, but she wouldn't read it. 'What *should* I be expecting?' she asked me. 'A bloody elephant?' So I read it instead. It wasn't all the stuff about giving birth that made me feel sick, it was the stuff about husbands making their wives dinner, and painting the nursery with white puffy clouds and stencils. But once I'd got over the shock of that, it did occur to me that with the number of things that can go wrong, it's a miracle any of us are born alive.

'She's lucky,' the nurse says grimly. 'She could have died.'

My legs almost give out. Jude could be dead. And all because she didn't care about her placenta. That was so like her. There are too many things that can go wrong in life without being careless with your placenta on top of everything else.

The nurse is still talking, being rude about Jude, about how can she look after a baby if she can't look after herself?

'I'll look after her,' I say, and the nurse gives me a funny look.

'Do you know what you're saying, love?' she asks, a bit gentler.

'A new baby can't be much different from this one.'

She gives me another funny look, like she's sorry for me.

'Go on in,' she says. 'She's in room 12, but if she's sleeping you need to let her rest. We'll let her know you were here.'

I push the buggy past the desk, and I can feel them watching me all the way down the corridor. When I open the door and go into Jude's room, I turn and see them with their eyes still glued to me.

There are two empty beds in there, and another woman fast asleep. Jude is propped up, eyes closed, her blue hospital gown falling off her shoulder and a drip stuck in the back of her hand. She looks like a vampire's stuck his teeth in her neck and drained all the blood out. With her skin so pale, I can see red blotches on it a bit like my eczema but not the same. There are big black bags under her eyes. She's awake, but dozy.

'Sare,' she whispers. I touch her hand, and she clutches at me, but her hand's got no power in it, and it falls back onto the bedcover. 'Where's Em?'

'She's here, look, she's fast asleep. We'll be fine. You mustn't worry about us. You're the one . . .'

'I'm still here,' she murmurs. 'What have they done with him?'

'The nurse said he's in an incubator . . . Jude, what are we going to do with a boy?'

There's a long silence.

'I don't know what you mean.' she mutters after a bit.

If she hasn't thought about it then this probably isn't the time.

'Nothing,' I say. 'I expect he'll be the same as Em.'

She thinks about that for a minute.

'Em with a willy,' she says weakly, and we both giggle.

77

She moves in the bed, and the sleeve of her hospital gown rucks up around her shoulder, and my eyes go to the inside of her arm, which is showing. This bit of her arm isn't tattooed because she was scared it would hurt more than the rest. Her skin is so pale you can see through it but it's ugly, pockmarked with little dark bruises that have little blue trails to them. I glance at the other arm but it's caught up in the blankets.

After a while I suggest, 'We could call him Ben, the same as when he was in your tummy.'

'Yeah,' she says. 'Okay.'

She closes her eyes and I think she's gone back to sleep but then I see that she's crying. Tears are oozing out the sides of her eyes and rolling down the side of her face onto the pillow.

'What's the matter?' I ask, a bit panicky.

She whispers something and I can't make it out because her mouth's so wobbly. So I make her say it again and this time I hear it.

'I want Borys,' she's saying.

I'm so shocked I step away from the side of the bed.

'Don't say that, Jude.' Like I'm begging her.

But she whispers it again, 'I want Borys,' and the tears keep rolling down the side of her face.

I think I should pat her arm or something to make her stop crying, but I can't. I can't go near her if she's going to say things like that.

For a long time, I just stand there looking at her like she's a stranger. Then I realise the tears are drying up and her breathing is calming down. I tell myself she's just had a baby and that screws with your head. She doesn't know what she's saying. I should feel sorry for her.

Em's shifting in her buggy like she's about to wake up. I look around. There's nothing to tidy up, except for a few medical bits that I don't dare touch. Perhaps if Jude is stuck in bed she won't be able to make a mess, but I wouldn't put money on it. That's when I notice the flowers. It's a big bunch of pink roses. I don't understand why they put them by Jude's bed because no one's going to send her flowers. I stand in front of them and look at them. They're a bit saggy, like it was the last bunch in the shop. There's a label, and I turn it over and look at it. It says, 'Time for a holiday. You have to get out of here.'

The message sends a chill through me. A bunch of flowers should say 'Congratulations!' or 'Get Well Soon!' And perhaps 'Time for a holiday' is supposed to sound sympathetic, but when it's followed by 'You have to get out of here', it doesn't sound so nice.

There's no name, either. Still, it doesn't matter what the message means, because it can't be meant for Jude. She doesn't know anyone who'd send her flowers.

'We're off then,' I say quietly to Jude. It seems wrong to just walk out but I don't know what else to do. On the telly when people are unconscious in hospital their relatives lean over and kiss them on their forehead and that's how you know they love them and don't want them to die even if they've been shouting at each other in the last scene. I can't remember when we've ever kissed each other but Jude's asleep so she won't know. I lean over and press my lips against her forehead. Her skin is clammy. I wipe my mouth with the back of my hand.

Outside the room I look up and down for another exit but I can't see one so there's no choice but to walk past the nurse's desk again.

'See you tomorrow,' I say casually.

They glance at each other and one of them says, 'Who's going to be looking after the little girl while Mum's in here?'

'She's mine,' I say quickly. 'I'm her mother.'

'You told me—' one of them starts to say, all sniffy, but I interrupt.

'You heard wrong. We'll be back tomorrow.'

'How old are you, love?' Another one has a go. 'Shouldn't you be in school tomorrow?'

'Inset day,' I say, shrugging.

I'm already walking away from them. My heart is beating fast and the siren's screaming in my head. I have to stop by the lifts and wait.

Behind me, one of the nurses calls out:

'So it's all right if we call social services, is it?'

I don't look round. I raise my hand behind my back and give them the finger. The lift door opens and I push Em inside.

SIX

Next day, I don't go to school. I've got to look after Em and take her to see Jude and her new baby brother in hospital, but I can't tell school that. It's nine a.m. which means Sheena's in a history class now. I text her to tell Mrs Stiffel that I'm sick. She texts me back: **stiff sik 2! r u 2 2gether?!? haha.** I switch off my phone. I don't want anyone from school phoning me, not even Sheena.

Em's a good girl when she's with me on her own. She doesn't make any fuss. She stands hanging on to the couch and chuckling, jigging up and down, her fat little knees bending and straightening, while I'm getting her breakfast. Then we get on the bus to go to the hospital. People look at us like they always do when I'm on my own with Em, like they think she's mine and I'm too young to have a kid. I like it when she acts nicely so I can show them that I take care of her properly.

We pass the arches on the bus. There's a yellow crime board by the side of the road, and I turn and strain to read it as we drive by, and I catch sight of Zoe's name. They must be asking for information from the public. I suppose Carla has told the police about seeing Zoe at Denny's by now. I remember Carla telling me to warn Jude, tell her she shouldn't go there, and I shiver.

When we get to the hospital they won't let us in straight away because the doctors are doing their rounds. So it's like the day before, off we go walking round the corridors. Only this time it's different because I know Jude's safe so I don't have all that adrenalin racing round me. I feel really tired. Just putting one foot in front of the other is taking all my energy, and I stop to buy a packet of sweets in the shop.

When Em has a little nap in the pushchair, I find a seat in a waiting room ('ENT day clinic', whatever that is) and I sit for a little while with my earphones in, listening to my music, and that makes me feel a bit better.

After a bit I push Em back to Maternity, and this time they let us in. All the nurses are giving me icy little glances, and I wish I hadn't given the nurse the finger the night before. I can't see that particular nurse on duty today, but it's the kind of thing that gets around. A nurse tells me Jude's been moved to a side room where she's on her own.

When I get in the room the curtains are closed except for a strip down the middle, where the sunlight's coming in. In the half-dark I can see Jude lying propped up in bed. Her hospital gown's pulled up so I can see her belly which is still all puffy, and lying against it there's a tiny baby wearing his nappy and nothing else.

I rush over and I don't even notice that he's crying in a little high-pitched voice, I just notice that he's got his eyes wide open and he's staring at me with gorgeous great big eyes. He's got soft cheeks like butter and dark blond hair like strands of gold. I'm in love. Just in love.

Then I remember and I whisper, 'Hang on a sec.'

I dig my phone from my pocket and snap a photo and send it straight to Sheena because I promised. Sheena loves babies. Or she thinks she does. She doesn't know anything about them. She thinks they smell of strawberries. All the time.

I put the phone away and gaze down at him.

'He'll do,' I say, and I can't help grinning, despite everything.

'Yeah,' Jude says. But there's something about the way she says it that makes me do a double take.

'You alright?' I ask her.

Her eyes meet mine and I'm shocked by what I see there. Sometimes Jude has dark moods and that's when you don't want to be around her. She's all I've got. So when her eyes look like this, all blank and empty, like there's no one home, that's when I get scared.

'His crying's driving me mad,' she says, and I can see she's on the edge of tears. 'He won't sleep, all he does is cry. He doesn't know how to suck and he's getting himself more and more worked up.'

I look at him more carefully. He doesn't look comfortable. His little fists are making tiny jabby boxing movements. He's mewling in a high-pitched voice.

'It sometimes takes a while to establish feeding,' I say, remembering what it said in *What to Expect When You're Expecting*.

She's shaking her head and tears are leaking from her eyes. 'He won't suck at all,' she says, 'if he'd suck, he'd calm down.'

'Did the doctor see him? What did he say?'

She doesn't answer me right away. Even with her lying there crying I can almost see her thinking what to say to me.

'He just says to make the room dark and let him lie here with no clothes on, as if that's going to help.'

83

'Really?' I never heard a doctor saying taking your clothes off is a cure for anything. But it must feel nice for Jude to have her baby snuggled against her skin like that. Or it might be if he'd stop crying.

'Can I pick him up?' I ask.

'You can have him,' she says without a smile.

I pick him up carefully. I had lots of practice with Em but I've forgotten, so his head flops around for a moment until I remember and slide my palm underneath his head and then he's alright. I look down at him lying in my arms. I don't remember Em feeling like this, all trembly and hot. His big eyes are gazing at me but his little face is all scrunched up because he's so unhappy, and he's crying in a shrill, sharp way. For a moment I wonder whether this is just how boys are, all frustrated and wanting something they can't have, but I can't believe Omar ever looked like this. A baby Omar would be lying there waving his hands round and grinning like he wanted to show his mum his latest trick.

A nurse comes into the room. I don't really take any notice of her. I assume she's going to fiddle with something or take Jude's blood pressure or something. But instead she just stands there and watches us like she's spying on us. In which case I think she might as well be helpful.

'The baby's all sweaty,' I say. I'm trying to be polite after the thing with the finger the night before. 'He's shaking all over. Is he alright?'

She comes over and takes the baby from me and lays him in the cot, checking his nappy and then his temperature. She's very gentle with him and I think for a minute that maybe I'd like to be a nurse because you can be around babies and sort things out for people but then you get to go home and put your feet up too. When she's finished she glances at me and then speaks to Jude in a kind voice.

'You've seen the doctor, haven't you?' she says to Jude.

'The doctor doesn't know what he's talking about,' Jude says. She sounds really unhappy.

'Oh, I'm afraid he does,' the nurse says softly, 'he sees this a lot.' Again she glances in my direction and I feel as though something's going on that I don't understand. 'And I know this is a difficult time for both of you, but you'll both come through it.'

'What's going on?' I ask Jude. 'What is it?'

She's crying now, not just leaking tears but great big sobs shaking her.

'Don't do that, love,' the nurse says, sitting down on the edge of the bed. 'Think of the baby, you'll just upset him more.'

'It's all my fault,' Jude gasps, and cries some more.

'I very much doubt that, love,' the nurse says and puts her hand on Jude's shoulder.

We all stay there a while in the half-darkness. My phone vibrates in my pocket, and it's a message from Sheena about how cute his baby nose is!!! How cute his baby cheeks are!!! How cute his baby chin is!!!!

After a time Jude calms down and she lets the nurse help her. The baby's really not very good at sucking and he still doesn't seem happy but after a while he drifts into a light sleep and Jude closes her eyes too. When I think she's asleep I say to the nurse, 'What's the matter with him?'

But she says, 'I can't tell you that, my love, you'll have to talk to your sister about it when she's feeling a bit better.'

'Is he going to get better?' I ask.

'Yes,' she says, 'he'll get better, but maybe not for a little while. He may need some medication, and in any case he's going to need a lot of love and attention.'

I don't know what to say about that.

I look around.

'Do you know what happened to the bunch of flowers that was by her bed yesterday?' I ask her.

'Your sister's been moved, so they might have got left behind,' she says. 'Are you sure they were hers?'

I shake my head and say I don't think so.

And she says, 'If they belonged to a patient who's already left the ward then they'll have been thrown out.'

I'm on my way out of the hospital when Sheena texts me to say do I want to bring Em round to her mum's for tea? But I don't feel like company after what the nurse said about Ben and I don't want to talk any more about Zoe Brown so I text no thank you. Then I take Em home and make her some some tea and put her to bed and I dig out a pound coin from the jar so I can watch television. But when I switch it on, it's the news, and it's about Zoe, so I can't get away from it. They show her mum and dad at the door of their flat, and her mum's in tears and her dad's got his arm around her. He says what a lovely girl Zoe was and how they'll always miss her. And there's a police officer requesting information from the public, but I'm not listening to him, I'm just thinking about her parents, and I'm thinking, so why did you let her go out to Denny's? Why didn't you stop her? And then, although I try to stop myself, I think of Mum, and how she didn't stop Jude. She didn't just not stop her, she *wanted* her to go out . . . she *made* her . . . I switch channels. I find the stupidest show and I watch it until my brain is numb, and I fall asleep on the couch with my clothes on.

Next morning when I get up I don't even think about going to school. It's just not going to happen. I text Sheena that I'm sick again and she texts back something about Mr Hughes, who's Head of Year 9, asking her lots of questions about me, and Sheena trying to lie and getting caught out and she's sorry but maybe they know I'm not really that sick. I'm too irritated to text her back. Sheena's a hopeless liar.

Just as I've got Em in the buggy and am about to walk out the door, someone rings the bell, and when I open the door I find it's the two police officers who came to the school. They look a bit surprised to see me, and they say they didn't know that's where I lived, and do I have anything more to tell them than what I said at school (which was nothing)?

I think about saying that Jude knew Zoe better than me, and perhaps she could help. But in the end I leave Jude out of it and tell them I still don't know anything.

When I've closed the door I find myself standing there thinking about Jude and Zoe. Were they friends? Jude was older than Zoe, but they used to hang out together before Jude met Borys, in the days when she was out every night. After that, I don't know what happened, but I think they must have fallen out, because once I heard Jude call Zoe 'a stupid slag'.

So I haven't moved from in front of the door when the bell rings again, and this time it's Mrs Franklin, the school counsellor.

'You're not at school,' she says when I open the door.
'I know.'

'Oh my!' Mrs Franklin exclaims, catching sight of the buggy. 'Is this Emma?' She pushes her way past me into the flat, kneels down in front of Em and has a good coo.

'She's adorable,' she says.

'Yeah,' I say. 'You haven't seen her when she's in a snit.'

'And Jude?'

'She's had the baby.'

Mrs Franklin looks up at me doubtfully.

'Does that mean you're looking after Em on your own?'

I can read her face. If I say yes, Em will be gone by the end of the day.

'No, course not,' I say. 'Social services sent someone, she's just gone out. But I'm not going to leave her alone in here, not with all our stuff. You can't trust them.'

She glances around her, but the fact is that I keep the place tidy and clean, and it's tidier and cleaner since Jude's been gone.

'Social services gave us a bit of a clean-up,' I say. 'I always give them a ring when I need a maid.'

She smiles, but she's still looking doubtful. She's not sure I'm telling the truth but she's going to choose to believe me because it lets her off the hook, that way she doesn't have to go and make a load of phone calls about me.

'I should wait,' she says, but I can see she doesn't want to. She keeps glancing at her mobile phone like she's waiting for a text. That makes me angry. She's paid to make sure I'm alright but she's got something else going on, someone waiting for her somewhere. I can fob her off with a single stupid lie, the kind a ten-year-old could see through. I thought they hired people to care but *she* doesn't care or she'd know I was lying.

'Sarah,' she says eventually, 'if social services are looking after Em, you need to be back at school tomorrow. You know that, don't you? You can't let all the things that are going on distract you from your school work. You're going to have to take time off for the trial in ten days' time, that's bad enough.'

'I know,' I say.

She looks at me doubtfully, and I shrug. 'What?' I challenge her. 'You don't believe me?'

'No young woman should be on her own at a time like this,' she says. 'Not after what happened to Zoe.'

But it doesn't stop her going and leaving me on my own.

When she's gone, I take what's left in the jar of coins for the telly, and I push Em to the playground in the park, and I sit on the edge of the sandpit while she plays. She gets sand in her hair and sand all over her dress and in her nappy. There are mums with their kiddies in the playground and they sit on benches chatting while their children play. One little boy hits Em because he doesn't want her in the sandpit with him and she starts crying but his mum doesn't notice because she's so busy gabbing. When he raises his arm again I grab it to stop him hitting her again but of course his mum sees that and gives me a mouthful so that's when I get Em and her things and get up and go and I just walk, pushing Em in front of me.

The news stands have got more photos of Zoe so I stop for a minute to have a look at the front page. It says the police think she knew the person who killed her, but I don't know how they can tell that just from looking at a dead body. That's like guessing. They say she was strangled, nothing else, no cuts or stabs or anything, just strangled, and that perhaps it didn't take very long. I don't think that's going to make her parents feel any better. It doesn't make me feel any better. Dead is dead.

In a little back street near Victoria there's an internet café, and it makes me think of meeting Mr Finch in the hospital café, and him asking me to email him again about the flat. So I take Em in, and buy my time, and she sits on my lap. When I open up my mail, I'm surprised because he's emailed me already, and I haven't even sent my message to him yet.

It was nice to meet you, Sarah. I've been thinking about your problem, and I think I've found a way to help. We have a vacant flat. It's not a new development, but it's better than where you are now. Can you and your sister meet me at Flat 6B, Queen Elizabeth Drive, at 3pm Thursday? It's the only time I have free this week.

When I read his message, I'm like, open-mouthed. Then I read it again, and I can hardly believe it. I didn't really think he would help us. And even if he did, I didn't think he would be so quick. I read his email again and again, but it says the same thing every time. I don't want to get excited, because really good things don't usually happen even when you think they're going to.

First I think, never mind that Jude can't go, I'll go on my own. Then I think about Thursday and I realise it's Thursday today, and it's already two o'clock in the afternoon. Then when I'm thinking I've got to go and find Queen Elizabeth Drive right away, Jude rings me to say I've got to go and get her.

'They're letting you out already?' I'm frowning, trying to remember what *What to Expect When You're Expecting* said about that.

'I've got to get out of here.'

'What does the doctor say? Shouldn't you stay in bed a bit longer?'

If she stays in hospital, I might just be able to get to Queen Elizabeth Drive to see the new flat. Finch might wait for me. If he does, I can look at the flat, and say yes, this looks good. If Jude will just stay in hospital a few more days, when I take her home I can take her somewhere nicer, somewhere better.

'I'm not staying here,' is all she says.

'I can't come now,' I say. 'I'm busy . . .'

'Just shut your mouth and come and get me!' she says, and the line goes dead.

Em and I get to the hospital on the bus. When we get to the maternity ward I don't recognise any of the nurses at the desk. When I find Jude she's hauled herself half out of bed and she's got her clothes lying around her and she's trying to pull them on.

'What's the hurry?' I ask her.

She's all jittery.

'Keep your nose out of this,' she says.

I watch her struggling, but she's got no muscle power because of the operation so she just can't do it. I give in and help her pull her shirt over her head.

'How can you go home when you can't even put your clothes on?' I ask her.

A nurse comes into the room behind me.

'You can't go home in your state,' she says. It's not the

nice gentle nurse from the day before. This one's like a schoolteacher and I know Jude's not going to take to her.

'I bloody can,' Jude says.

'We'll see about that,' the nurse says and huffs out of the room.

Jude's in such a state that at first I don't realise the baby's in a state too. He's lying on his back in his cot and he's fretting like the day before with that high-pitched cry. I think that cry's going to send us all mad.

'Jude, can't you stay one more night?' I plead. 'The baby's not well, you need to look after him.'

'I can do that just as well at home,' she says. 'All they tell me is to keep feeding him and holding him. He doesn't need hospital for that.'

'They can keep an eye on you both here, though.'

'I don't want them keeping an eye on me. I found her going through my stuff.'

'Who?'

'That nurse. She was going through my stuff.'

I stare at Jude. I have no idea what's going on. Is Jude going mad? When you carry your belongings around in a Lidl bag, mostly people don't want to nick them.

'No one wants to nick your stuff, Jude,' I say. 'It must be a misunderstanding.'

'I know what I saw.' Jude's getting angry now. 'I'm not staying here to be treated like a criminal.'

I stare at her again. So it's not about nicking her stuff, it's about looking for evidence, like when a criminal gets searched. What does she think they're looking for? I don't know what to think. I'm wishing I'd ignored her. Without me, she couldn't have gone anywhere. She'd have had to stay. I could've gone to Queen Elizabeth Drive and got us a new flat, but now it's too late.

'Come on,' she nods grimly towards the cot. 'You take him.'

When I pick Ben up he calms down a bit. He's not hot and sweaty like he was the day before.

'You can keep him if you like,' she says carelessly.

I give her a smile but she's making me nervous. Anyway I've got to push the pushchair. So I pass the baby to her and say, 'You're the one who got yourself pregnant.'

But she pulls back.

Then I realise the nurse is back in the room and she's watching us play pass the parcel with the baby.

'They'll take him away from you if you carry on like this,' I hiss at her, and when she starts to argue with me I say, 'I'm not joking,' and I push her out of the room ahead of me, pushing Em's buggy at the same time.

We move at a snail's pace. Jude shifts her feet a few inches at a time and she keeps having to stop and lean against the wall.

'Hang on!' one of the nurses calls out behind us, but when I swing around I find her standing in front of me holding out a plastic carrier. 'Your goodie bag,' she says, 'you might as well take it.'

I stare at her. She's very young. I don't think she knows what's going on. Then I take a look at the bag. It's chock full of nappies and other stuff that we can use. I don't know what to say, so I just take it from her and hang it over the back of the buggy.

We get to the lift but we have to wait forever, with Jude leaning against the wall.

'How are we going to get you home if you can't walk?' I hiss at Jude. 'You should be lying down, you'll do yourself an injury.'

But tears are rolling down her face and I can't argue with her any more. We've just got to get ourselves home.

I look back at the nurse. She's on the phone.

At last the lift comes and it takes us down to the ground floor. Outside it's warm and the sun's beating down. Jude looks as white as a sheet. I'm seriously worried about her. I wish I could say let's sit down while I ring for a minicab, but we haven't got the cash for it so instead we get ourselves to the bus stop. It's got a roof, and plastic bum-moulds, so I get Jude to prop herself on one of those. It's not like you can lean back and put your feet up but it takes a bit of the pressure off. There's a man there with a boy with Down's syndrome and an old man with a cane. They make a bit of space for us, eying us and our babies and our carrier bags. It seems to me that it doesn't much matter if you polish your shoes for school, babies are the thing that show you for what you are. If you've got the money you can pop your baby into its car seat in its four-by-four and get rid of its nappies in pink plastic bags that smell of air freshener not baby poo. The rest of us lug all the crap around in plastic bags and have to manoeuvre the whole bloody lot onto a bus where we spend the whole journey getting in people's way and them looking at us and seeing the carrier bags and the baby and staring. When the bus comes I have to practically carry Jude onto it. A man with a turban takes one look at Jude and stands up so she can sit down with the baby, who just carries right on crying. There's a slot on the bus for a buggy, but there's already a woman and a buggy there.

94

She's not happy to see us and our carrier bags but she wiggles around to make a bit of space.

I glance at Jude. She's dead white but sweaty too, there's damp glistening on her forehead and over her lips, which are blue. Did the doctor even see her before she signed herself out?

I can feel everyone's eyes on me. And it's not just the carrier bags and Em and the unhappy baby. They're all working it out. They're not stupid. They can all see Jude can't look after a baby in this state.

They can see it's down to me.

The bus is hot and people's eyes are burning into me. I start to sweat. I feel sick, like I'm going to throw up. I've probably gone green. I can feel people pulling away from me. They probably think we're on drugs, the two of us, probably wondering what we're going to do. But they probably don't expect what happens next.

Jude bolts. At least, she bolts like someone who can hardly move.

This is how it goes. I'm watching her and sweating. We're stopped at a bus stop and the man next to Jude stands up to get off the bus. Jude has her head leaned against the window and she's just staring blankly at the passengers in the aisle. Then her head jolts up from the windowpane and I see something happen to her face. Her eyes widen and suddenly go from being dead to being alive but it's not good alive, it's confused and scared alive. I follow where she's looking, and I can see who she's staring at but not the whole of his face.

Just as the bus doors are closing, Jude staggers to her feet and makes a break for it. With the baby in her arms she has to use her shoulders to push her way to the door, and you can see she's got no weight to her, and the only thing that's making people move out of her way is that she's so obviously desperate to get off the bus and they don't want to hurt her by standing in her way.

'Jude,' I shout after her, 'what're you doing?'

She's got one leg out the door, and then the door closes on her, so she's pinned there, one door hard up against her back, the other one down her front at the middle, with the baby's head caught smack in the door. There's a big gasp of shock, like everyone on the bus gasps at the same time. Jude starts to swear and the baby starts to cry, and the bus engine is revving up again, and passengers grab at the door to try to pull it open, and someone shouts at the driver to open the doors. But before he does that the passengers have somehow pulled her back inside. Someone stands up again so she can sit down again, and she collapses onto the seat.

'You stupid girl!' a woman shouts from the back of the bus.

'What did you think you were doing?' a man says angrily.

Everyone's hating her, and me by extension. I can't believe what she just did. I want to go to her. I'm going to give her a piece of my mind, too. What was she thinking? But I can't get to her through the crush of people. I can just see her hanging her head. Her shoulders are shaking and the baby is still crying.

I crane my neck around to get a better look at the man who started all this. He's looking out of the window as though nothing's happened. He must be the only one on the bus who's not looking at me or at Jude. Then he glances up – I could swear he knows I'm watching him – and catches my eye.

Fear shoots through me.

I know him. The frizzy greying hair, the pale blue eyes, broad bulky shoulders.

He's not where he should be, here on a bus. Where have I seen him before? And when?

The memory is hiding from me.

Then the bus is pulling in, and before I know what's happening he's swinging himself up from his seat and pushing through the other passengers towards the door.

For just a moment he's standing there, right in front of Jude. He reaches out and taps her on the shoulder. She looks up at him with an expression of dread. He smiles, and I can see sharp white teeth. Then, in the blink of an eye, he's gone, out the door and into the street. As we pull away, I concentrate hard so I can remember him for next time. His clothes, his hair, the way that he walks, turning right into Charlotte Street. Then he's gone.

The bus stops right outside Shepherd's Way and somehow Jude and the baby and me and Em and the bags all get off and stand there. And that's when I look up at the block of flats and realise we're never going to make it up the stairs to Level 8.

'We've got to go back to the hospital,' I say. 'We can't live on the street.'

Jude starts to cry, and what with the baby crying too, I have an urge walk away and leave them to it, but I don't of course.

There's a block of concrete that's supposed to be like a bench and so we shuffle over there and sit down on it. I don't know how long we sit there with the baby still strapped around Jude and Em on my lap dozing off. At last the baby has gone to sleep, and it's bliss to have the peace and quiet. It's actually a lovely day with a blue sky and a bit of a breeze, so although we're sitting there like we're homeless with one baby, one toddler, and a bagful of nappies and nothing else, completely desperate, with Jude still snivelling, the sun is on our faces and the wind is on our skin and it's actually quite nice.

I think about the email from Mr Finch. I don't have his telephone number, so I can't tell him why I didn't go to meet him at the flat. I'm worried that he'll think I'm rude or not interested. I don't want to tell Jude about it in case he's already given the flat to someone else.

There aren't many people around, and none you'd want to ask for help. There's a drunk in a worse state than us huddled in a corner of the forecourt by some steps, and a couple of girls hanging around looking like they're waiting for a bad idea to come along. I'm getting hungry. I didn't have any breakfast, and now I've missed my lunch too.

By the entrance to Block B I can see another yellow crime board and some lads standing reading it. After a little while, I see the two uniformed police officers who came to the flat walking out of Block B towards Block C. I hope they don't see us. I don't want them talking to us. I don't want them asking Jude about Zoe. I haven't even *told* her about Zoe yet.

'I can take Em and Ben up first, then come back for you,' I say at last. 'We'll try it in a bit when we've got our energy back.'

But I don't think I can get Jude up there on my own, and if we get stuck halfway with Em and Ben on the eighth floor and Jude on the first floor then we're in an even worse state. That's when I get upset and cry a bit too so we're both sitting there blubbing. But then after a while sitting in the sun I stop crying. I begin to feel like there's no point in struggling any more, there's nothing we can do, we just have to sit here and wait.

So we wait. I think about the man on the bus, and I'm angry with myself for being too scared to ask Jude about him.

'Jude,' I say, 'who was that man on the bus?'

She doesn't reply. So I repeat the question: 'Who was that man on the bus?'

And she says, 'I can't believe you don't remember.'

'That's why I'm asking,' I say, 'because I don't remember . . . I know I've seen him . . .'

And then I do remember.

'It was Uncle Keith,' I say.

Jude doesn't reply, but I turn to look at her face, and I can see from her expression that I'm right.

'He looks older,' I say. 'He's fatter, and his face is redder, and his hair is grey.'

She turns her face away.

'Why did we call him uncle?' I ask her. 'He wasn't our uncle, he wasn't anything to do with us. He was just Mum's boyfriend, and then . . .'

I frown. The memories are leaking out of their hiding place . . . *Uncle Keith knocking on the door . . . Jude holding back, digging her feet in . . . Mum's hand in the small of her back . . . pushing her . . . pushing her out . . .*

Omar's dad walks up to us. He looks like he's just got back from work, because he's carrying a jacket over his arm. I get up off the concrete block with Em in my arms and I don't wait for him to say anything.

'Mr Jones, can you help us? Jude just had her baby but she can't walk up the stairs.'

He doesn't say anything. He looks carefully at us, at the bag of nappies, and at the tiny baby scrunched against Jude's chest.

He pulls his mobile phone out of his pocket and dials, then speaks into it.

'Omar,' he says, 'are you at home?' He listens for a minute and says, 'Leave that now. I'm on the forecourt here and I need your help with something.'

Then he puts the phone back in his pocket. He walks a few steps away and gestures with his head that I should follow him. Jude doesn't even notice.

'They let her leave hospital like this?' Mr Jones asks me.

'I couldn't stop her,' I say. 'She wouldn't stay. She thought they were searching her bags.'

He shakes his head. There is a dark look on his face, and he starts to say something which begins, 'Your mother . . .' but he stops and shakes his head again, as though there's no point. Then, as if he's speaking to himself, he says, 'And then there's the trial . . . on top of all of this, there's going to be a trial . . .'

He looks at me, and says, 'So many trials for you, Sarah, one trial on top of another . . .'

'I'm alright,' I say.

'Yes . . . well, you are a strong young woman. You have no choice . . . But you must call the health visitor as soon as possible. You need help. Things can't go on like this. Jude should be back in hospital. You should be in school.'

I nod, but he can see I'm going to cry.

'What is it, Sarah?' he asks me.

'They'll split us up if she can't cope,' I say. 'She's the only one of us over sixteen.'

Mr Jones puts his hand on my shoulder.

'You are too young for this,' he says. 'They should find someone to look after you, so you can concentrate on school . . .'

I pull away from him, but I need him to help us, so I can't shout at him.

That's when Omar appears, and just seeing him makes me feel better. Surely he won't say the same things as his dad, about how this can't go on.

He nods at me.

'Hey, Carnaby,' he says.

'Omar,' his father scolds, 'what are you doing calling Sarah by her surname? That is not polite. She is our friend, and she is called Sarah.'

Omar grins sheepishly.

'Hey, Sarah,' he says.

'Hey,' I try to say, but my voice doesn't come out.

His eyes take it all in: Jude and the baby, and Em and the plastic bags, and my face. I think he can probably tell I've been crying. His face says it all; he's thinking the same thing his dad is. It hits me how much the same they are. The sort of sameness that's not just because of genes, but also because they spend so much time together. Otherwise they wouldn't nod their heads the same way and smile the same way and hold their shoulders the same way. That can't be genes, that's watching without knowing you're watching and copying and not even knowing you're copying.

Once Omar's there everything happens very quickly. Mr Jones waits with Jude while I go up first with Omar. He carries Em, wrapping his long arms and hands around her. She looks a bit shocked, like she might cry, and we laugh at how she's staring at his nose. But he pulls a face at her and she gives him a coy little smile like she's flirting with him. I strap the baby carrier to my chest, and put Ben inside it. The feel of his little body pressed against me makes me feel better and scared all at once. Then Omar takes the hospital goodie bag and puts it over his shoulder, and I pick up Jude's carrier bag, and we climb the stairs. We don't talk much, except that Omar says, at about Level 5, 'Is your sister going to be alright?' and I say, 'I don't know.'

When we reach Level 8, I unlock the door and go inside, and I'm ashamed for Omar to see the damp bare walls, but he follows me in. While I'm unstrapping Ben and lying him on the bed and putting Em in her cot, I can see Omar is having a good nose around.

'Is your place like this?' I ask him.

He shakes his head. 'It's bad,' he says, 'but not as bad as this. Anyway, we've found a new place, we're moving out.'

I stare at him.

'Not yet though,' he says.

'We might too,' I say, 'there's a flat free in Queen Elizabeth Drive.'

'Good,' he says. 'You should move out of here.'

Then he says, 'Look . . . about Jude . . . I didn't want to say anything, but—'

'Then don't,' I say.

He frowns. 'But you don't even know what I'm going to say.'

102

'Maybe I do,' I say, 'and maybe I don't. Just don't say it.'

We stand there not speaking for a minute, and then he says he'd better go down and help his dad, and he turns towards the door. Then he turns back.

'You've got to look after yourself,' he says. 'After what happened to Zoe Brown and everything . . . Jude and Zoe . . .'

'I know . . .' I interrupt him.

He's looking at me really intently.

'I'm serious,' he says. 'You've got to be careful about who you speak to.'

'I know,' I say again.

When he's gone, I sit on the bed with Ben and try not to think about Jude and Zoe. Instead I think about Omar leaving. I won't miss him, of course. That would be weird. But if the new flat doesn't work out, soon we'll be the only ones left. Like I said, the ones with the functioning brain cells all leave.

After a while, they're at the door, Omar and his dad, with Jude in-between them, her feet scarcely touching the floor, they've got her so well supported. They lower her onto her bed, and she doesn't even say thank you, she just heaves herself onto her side. Next to her, the baby is already twitching and moaning in his sleep.

Omar's dad stands there looking down at her and breathing heavily from the effort.

'How are you going to cope?' he mutters to me angrily. 'This is no way to give a child a start in life.'

'I know,' I say.

'And you're as much a child as they are . . .' He sounds angry, and I know I've messed things up but I don't know what to do about it.

'Come on, Dad,' Omar says, 'let's go.'

But his dad just stands there looking around at our flat. When Omar's dad gets angry about things he doesn't let them go. He's been angry ever since the council started running Shepherd's Way down. He says it's no wonder that there's crime, no wonder people want to move out when the council don't maintain it, and let the place go to rack and ruin. He says we didn't need regenerating, we were doing fine. He's fought the council and the developers, getting up petitions, starting campaigns, he's even been on the radio talking about it. And when no one listens he just gets angrier. I know he gets angry about things you should be angry about, but him being angry now just makes me feel even worse. It makes me feel embarrassed, like I should've done something different, and then it wouldn't be like this, making him angry.

'Come *on*, Dad,' Omar says again, and he puts his hand on his dad's shoulder and gently pushes him towards the door, and perhaps Omar's hand really is magic, because his dad calms down right away. But before he goes he makes sure I've got his phone number, and Omar's.

And then he says it too. 'You've got to take care,' he says. 'Make sure you lock your door. And call the health visitor.'

I don't know what he sees in my face, but then he adds a warning that sends a chill right through me. 'If *you* don't call her, Sarah, *I* will. This can't go on.'

SEVEN

When they're gone I assess our situation. Jude lies on her bed with her back to me, and the baby cradled between her and the wall. The warmth of the day has lulled Em to sleep in her cot.

I open the window wide and kick off my shoes and lie down on my back on my bed. The noise from the street outside is muffled in the heat. A breeze is moving the ragged curtains. I should feel at peace, at least for a few minutes. Soon enough one or other of them will wake up and need something. But even lying on my bed I feel as though I'm falling through a hole. They say babies bring hope for the future but this one has brought something else. I'm not saying it's his fault. I'm saying that he's arrived and everything's changed. Nothing's alright any more. I thought I'd got a handle on things. I thought as long as I kept pulling on my yellow gloves and polishing my shoes, we'd get through. But if my life was a spaceship – which it isn't, but I'm just saying if it *was* – it would be about to vanish into a black hole.

Someone knocks on the door.

I sit up on my bed. On her bed, Jude twists to face me.

'Don't answer it,' she hisses.

I stare at her.

'Sarah, Judith?' I can hear Bocock's voice. 'Judith, are you in there? We need to make sure you and the baby are alright. You shouldn't have left hospital like that, you weren't ready.'

I stand up, but Jude reaches out and grabs my wrist as hard as she can.

'Don't,' she hisses again.

'Come on, Jude, we know you're in there,' Bocock wheedles. 'We know you've had your baby. The hospital says he needs some special care, you shouldn't have brought him home yet, you're not well enough, and he's not well enough either. You want the best for him, don't you? You want him to be safe and well?'

I'm pulling against Jude's hand and I'm frowning, mouthing that we have to open the door. Not opening the door means we're not cooperating, and that's the end of us. And what they're saying about the baby needing special attention is scaring me. But Jude shakes her head at me. Her eyes won't let me move a muscle.

They knock again. Any minute Em or Ben or both are going to wake up and start crying. Then they'll break the door down.

Then suddenly they go away. We can hear their footsteps retreating. We listen for a minute to be sure, then Jude grins weakly at me and puts her hand up all shaky in the air. I stare at it. I don't know what it means.

'High five,' she says. 'We won.'

I press my hand lightly against hers but I don't think we've won anything.

'Are you going to be alright?' I ask her. 'You look awful.'

For a moment she doesn't say anything. Then she says, 'Thanks a million for that,' and we both start giggling in a bit of a hysterical way.

'Jude?' I say after a few minutes.

'Yeah?' She sounds exhausted.

I just remembered she still doesn't know about Zoe.

But then I look at her lying there, so white and drained, and I think I can't tell her now. I'll tell her when she's stronger. So I just say 'nothing,' and then she whispers the word 'nothing' too, like she's echoing me.

She's quiet for a long time but I can tell by her breathing that she's not asleep.

Then she says, 'Sare?'

And I say, 'Yes, I'm here.'

And she reaches out her hand to me and I take it and hold it in-between my hands. Her fingers are cold and bony in mine.

'Whatever happens, Sare, you've got to promise me you'll take care of yourself. Don't trust anyone. Only trust yourself.'

'I know,' I say.

What she's said scares me because it sounds like she's going somewhere. Like she's going to die. And looking at her lying there, she looks like she could. So I say, 'I can trust you, though.'

I'm waiting for her to say, 'Of course you can, Sare,' so I'll know she's not really going anywhere, or dying.

But she doesn't, and then I realise she's asleep and I let go of her hand, and I lie down myself and close my eyes.

*　　*　　*

107

Em's crying, and I wake up feeling heavy with sleepiness. When I check the time on my phone it's only eight. It feels like the middle of the night but it's still light outside. I lie there staring at the damp patch on the ceiling and my brain's struggling to wake up. When it does, it realises that with everything going on I haven't given Em her tea so her tummy's empty and that's why she's fussing. I look over towards Jude, but she's totally out of it. Her jaw's open, her tummy's rising and falling with deep sleeping breaths. There's sweat on her forehead and above her lip which I suppose is because it's so hot. Carefully, so he doesn't wake up, I pick up baby Ben from the bed where I'm afraid Jude might smother him, and I lie him in Em's pushchair which flattens right down so it's almost like a cot. He's sleeping too, but I can see him begin to worry at Em's noise and whatever I do I don't want him to wake up. He's twitching, his little head turning from side to side like he's struggling not to wake up. I drag myself off my bed and stumble around looking for food, opening the cupboard and then the fridge. There's nothing in the flat. Not a single jar of apple or mashed veg, and no leftovers I can feed a one-year-old. I stand and stare at her. She's sobbing now, standing up in her cot and clinging to the bars, her mouth turned down, giving me that look like I'm personally torturing her.

There's nothing for it, I'm going to have to nip out to the shop. And then I realise I'm going to have to take Em with me or she'll wake Jude and the baby. The baby's in the pushchair, so I just pick up Em and carry her, although these days she weighs a ton. Down one hundred and sixty-eight steps. I don't like it in the evenings, especially not since Zoe's death, even though it's still light outside. So I

108

just concentrate on putting one foot in front of the other as fast as I can and getting out of the building. I run to the corner shop, clasping Em to me. Jigging her up and down shuts her up a bit. I pick up a jar of baby pasta in sauce and put my coins on the counter and Rashid takes them and waves at Em and we set off again. Then we run all the way back, although by the time we have to climb the stairs I'm totally out of breath. Em's getting dozy again now and I can see what's going to happen. Before we get back to the flat she's going to forget she was ever hungry. She'll fall fast asleep in my arms, and all the running and the stairs and the getting scared will have been for nothing.

We're nearly at Level 8 when I hear it. Someone's rapping on a door up above us. It could be any door, but I stop stock-still on the staircase and listen. I'm trying to make sense of the noises. They knock on the door again, louder, and someone shouts, 'Come on, open up, love!' and at last someone opens it, so it can't be our flat because Jude wouldn't open the door.

But now I can hear a baby crying, shrill and insistent. It must be Ben. I've never heard another baby cry quite like that.

There are low voices, but they get louder, as though Ben's crying is getting everyone worked up. 'Be reasonable, love . . . You both need to be in hospital . . . you're not in any fit state . . .'

Then the voices fall quiet, and there's just one voice – Jude's voice – thin and high.

'Go on, take him then . . . Just leave me alone . . . Take him, I don't want him . . .'

My blood runs cold. I mean it really does. I never thought it could, but it does. I can feel it running round

109

my body like liquid ice, freezing my veins. It runs from my hands up my arms and into my chest and my heart literally stops. Then it starts going again but I'm still cold all over.

I need to go and explain. I need to get there, to tell them we're alright. Jude's just screwed up because she's had a baby. That always messes with your head. They can't take him just because she says so. I'll look after him until she's better. I need to climb the steps so I can go and tell them but my feet won't move.

Em's wide awake now too, and she lets out an almighty howl. I clamp my hand over her mouth but it's too late, they've heard. If they've taken Ben, we're next on the list. Jude might give us away, too. I can't trust her.

I turn and run back down the stairs still clutching my jar of baby food in my hand and holding Em so close to me that she's part of me. My feet have never moved so fast.

No one comes after me. Or if they do, they give up.

I wait on the ground floor in the dark bit under the stairs where I never go. I can't see anything, and for an instant I have a flash of Zoe Brown in a dark alley, and someone fastening their hands around her neck . . . I whimper, and I shake my head to get rid of the image of Zoe fighting for breath . . . Trembling, terrified, I peer out from my hiding place, and I see them come down the stairs, three men in police uniform and a woman I think might be Bocock. She's holding a bundle against her chest.

The bundle must be Ben.

Silently, I cry into my sleeve.

They get into a car and the car pulls away.

My legs collapse beneath me, and I sink to the ground. I don't know how long I kneel there with Em crying against my chest. My arms are locked around her, my head bent and resting upon hers.

Everything has changed. It's like an earthquake. I can't move, because the earth's not solid. It's turned to liquid. If I move, I'll drown. My only hope is to stay still until the world's stop shifting around me.

I drag myself and Em back up the steps. I'm stumbling – I can't see my feet because I'm blinded by tears. I'm not scared any more, though, because nothing can happen that's worse than what Jude just did. Back inside the flat I lie Em down in her cot. Jude is lying on the bed staring at the ceiling with dead eyes. I stand and gaze down at her, but I can't say anything to her. I don't even ask her why she opened the door, why she told them to take Ben. I hate her for what she's done, but I know why she did it. It's like when she handed Ben to me in the hospital and said, 'You can have him.' Deep down she knows she can't cope with another baby. She knows she should never have left hospital. She knows it wasn't safe. I want to say, 'Why don't we go back to the hospital, then they'll give him back,' but I know she won't go, and I know they won't give him back. Not just like that. Not now.

The pushchair's empty. It's like Ben was never there.

My knees go from under me again. I can't stand.

I make it as far as my bed and I lie there blinking and shivering. I feel like someone's cut my hand or my foot off or something.

When I stop shaking I start to speak. And it's really strange because although my brain's racing around in circles, the words are coming out of my mouth direct from my belly.

'You've got to go away, and you've got to take Em,' I say. 'They'll come back for her.'

Jude may be a stupid cow but her brain's been doing the same as mine.

'What about you?' she says.

'I can take care of myself. If we stay together they'll find us and they'll split us up and we'll never see each other again. This way if they don't get hold of you and Em we can find each other again. It doesn't matter what they do with me, I can get out of anything.'

There's a long silence, and then I say. 'Is there somewhere you could go?'

She doesn't reply. I look at her. She's curled up on the bed, facing away from me, and she's got her stupid phone, and she's texting again. Who can she be texting at a time like this? I remember what she said in hospital. 'I want Borys.' But Borys hasn't got a phone in jail, and anyway, what would she say to him: 'Borys, I just gave your son away'?

Tears are running away down the side of my face onto the bed now. I don't know how she can text at a time like this. She's such a stupid cow.

And that's the last thing I think before I fall asleep.

EIGHT

It's funny, although I'm asleep I know she's gone. So when I wake up I'm already in a panic. I shoot up off the bed and stand there looking around me into all the corners.

I can't see Jude.

I can't see Em.

My brain sucks up the clues.

The pushchair's gone. The plastic bag we brought back from the hospital's been emptied on the floor and Jude and Em's clothes are all over the place like someone went through them in a hurry.

Jude's gone and she's taken Em.

Time for a holiday. You have to get out of here.

That's what it said on the flowers in her hospital room. But she can hardly move, so what holiday could she be going on, and anyway, who would send her flowers? I think of her texting before she went to sleep. Who was she texting?

Someone's banging on the door. I float over to it. My feet aren't on the ground any more. I open the door. There's a uniformed police officer there, thirty-ish, looking impatient.

'Judith Carnaby?' he says.

'I can't find her.'

'She's got an appointment with the police,' he says. 'We've sent a car.'

I stare at him. I remember Bocock saying something about an appointment.

'She can hardly walk,' I tell him, 'she's just had a baby.'

He ignores what I've said, like the only thing he can see is that he's being inconvenienced.

'She should have phoned us if she's not coming,' he says.

'Don't you get it?' I shout at him. 'She's gone, and I don't know where she is, and she's going to hurt herself. The reason she's got an appointment with you is she's a witness in a trial that starts in a week. If you're the police you should go and look for her.'

'I'm just a driver,' he shrugs. 'You'll have to call the station if you're worried about her.'

He turns and starts to walk off. Then he hesitates and looks back.

'I'm sure she'll turn up,' he says.

And that's that. Off he goes.

'And if she doesn't, then what? If she's not here, she can't be a witness,' I shout after him. But he doesn't turn around.

I go back into the flat and look everywhere I've already looked. I even look under the bed although I know she isn't there. I know I told Jude to go, but I never thought she'd do it without telling me. Why didn't she tell me? Does she think I'd let on where she is?

I don't have a clue where she is.

Not one clue.

Time for a holiday. You have to get out of here.

I try to calm down. I try to think.

Say, just for argument's sake, that the flowers *were* for her. Say the message was an order, an instruction . . . Say the message meant, *You have to get out of hospital now* . . . Well, that's exactly what she did. And then she gave Ben away. Why did she do that? Did she know she was going away? Did she think it was better if she didn't take him? Was she protecting him?

Or am I just finding ways to excuse what she did?

I'm just playing with words. Words and a bunch of flowers. A bunch of flowers that wasn't even meant for Jude in the first place.

Phone, I think. I can phone her and ask her: 'Where are you, Jude?'

I snatch up my phone and dial her number.

A ringtone plays from the pile of clothes on her bed.

I dig it out.

She's only gone and left her phone behind. I hurl it back down on the bed.

'Stupid cow!' I'm shouting. 'You stupid cow, Jude. How am I ever going to find you now?'

First her placenta, then her baby, now her phone. Can't she look after anything?

I pace around the flat angrily. I pick up the phone from where I threw it down and stick it in my pocket. Then I pace some more. I know it sounds stupid but I'm still looking for her in the flat. I can't believe she's gone. How can she have gone anywhere, the state she's in?

Then I see it. A small pile of cash sitting on her pillow. There's a scrap of paper torn from a notebook beside it and on it she's written: Luv U. Sorry. J xxx

115

I count it and it's seven pounds, which is probably everything she had in her pocket.

I stuff the cash in the zip pocket of my hoody. I read her note again and again, but it just takes me round and round in circles. *Luv U. Sorry, J . . . Luv U. Sorry, J . . . Luv U. Sorry, J . . .*

I'm breathing too fast and then I'm punching at the wall and kicking her things. I'm going stark staring mad. First there was a baby and he vanished, but he was hardly there in the first place. Then a whole full-sized sister and her monster pink toddler just go and vanish too. It doesn't make any sense. It's mad. They were all there and then they were gone.

Jude can hardly walk, she can't have gone far.

I think of Zoe lying dead in the arches.

Jude can't walk as far as the arches and, anyway, why would she want to?

Still, I should've warned her, like Carla said.

She'll be sitting on a step with Em or on a concrete bench in the shopping centre. I've got to get out of the flat because there's one thing for certain and that's that she's not here.

A funny thing happens while I'm running down the stairs to look for her. My head comes off. My body still keeps going and my feet are hitting the steps, down, down, down, down, down. But my head's gone. Sarah's not there. Her body's there but there's no head on top of her neck.

Sarah's searching. Even without her head, her body knows what it's got to do, and it's got to go looking for Jude and Em. Her body reaches the bottom of the stairs, then it goes all the way up again to double-check, then down. Outside, her legs take her walking in circles. She runs down alleyways and turns round and comes back out. She's walking blindly, heading straight into people so that they have to dodge out of her way.

Omar's at the shop buying bread, and he sees her.

'Sarah,' he shouts. And when she doesn't stop he jogs after her and touches her arm and she spins around, swings, and swipes him in the face.

'What did you do that for?' Omar says angrily, shielding his eye. 'I just want to talk to you.'

'Go away,' she mumbles. There's a loud rushing noise where her head should be.

'What's the matter?'

Omar reaches out with his long fingers to touch her, but before he can reach her, her hand darts out and her fingers rake his face. She's got no nails, so she doesn't draw blood, but he shouts in shock and she screams at him. She doesn't know where the noise comes from. It's like an animal, like a pig being stuck.

She turns and runs away from him straight out into the traffic. Brakes are screaming and she's standing in the middle of the road stock-still with drivers swearing at her out their windows.

Omar is shouting at her. 'What's *wrong* with you?'

Her legs walk for miles. They take her through the tunnel under the Waterloo line, and the roar in her head could be trains overhead, or it could be fear. Then her legs propel her onto Westminster Bridge but she can't feel her feet touch the ground. There's a man in a kilt playing the bagpipes and other men coated in silver paint and wearing toothy-grinning masks and cardboard crowns and tourists posing with the fake queens and shouting to their friends in languages she doesn't understand. She stops and leans out over the balustrade. Below her the water is muddy green. Slivers of pale sky glisten between patches of frothy bubbles. If she jumps in, the water will jump up and then it will close over her headless head and no one will know she was ever there. She can taste the muddy water in her mouth. It's trickling down her throat, it's driving out the air from her lungs . . .

There's a voice behind her. 'Don't do it, love, he's not worth it.'

There's a joke in his voice, he doesn't really think she's going to jump. She doesn't hear the joke; she just knows someone's going to hurt her. She spins around to fend off his attack and when he sees her face so scared, he realises that he's the one who's misunderstood. He takes a step towards her and she takes a step back, towards the water.

'Alright,' he says, lifting his hands in surrender. 'Alright, love, I'm not going to touch you.'

Her legs walk her to the abbey. She's in the middle of a crowd. She's surrounded by excited, noisy people. A helicopter beats its way through the sky above her. Her feet spin her around and into a church, whisking her along the aisles then stopping dead in front of a figure carved into the wall. A headless man. In front of the headless man there's a carving of a woman and her two daughters and one of them is carrying something in front of her, and it's a skull. Sarah's feet spin her round and out of the church.

Outside, she hovers in the crowd. Something's pulling at her leg. She looks down to see a blond-haired boy with his face turned up towards her. He's grabbed a handful of her jeans and he's pulling on her leg. She shakes her leg to get rid of him but he just grabs harder. She wants to tell him to get lost, but she's got no head, so she's got no voice, so she's stuck with this kid glued to her. Where are his parents, why don't his parents look after him properly? There are people who shouldn't be allowed to have kids, they're so irresponsible. Someone could just walk away with this kid or do him harm. That would teach them. She puts her hand down towards him, and in that way that kids do, all trusting, he lets go of her jeans and slides his hand into hers. His hand is hot and tiny. It feels like it belongs in her hand.

'William!'

A woman's voice.

She appears in front of Sarah, drops to her knees, pulling the little boy towards her, tearing his hand out of Sarah's.

The woman stands up and the little boy is clinging around her neck now. Little traitor. Just a moment ago he was swearing undying devotion to Sarah and now look at him, clinging to his mummy.

'And who are you, might I ask?' The woman turns on Sarah. 'Where were you taking him? You were taking him away from me, weren't you? Oh my God!'

Her voice is rising. People are turning to look. A police officer turns his head and watches.

'Are you crazy, lady?' A voice speaks from behind Sarah and a hand grabs her arm.

Sarah flinches. Her muscles bunch, ready to hit out. But the voice is familiar and so is the long hand.

The kid's mother is surprised. She looks up at Omar. He's taller than her and his face is grazed like he's been in a fight. She doesn't want to mess with him, and anyway she's got her kid back.

Sarah lets Omar pull her away from the woman.

'She wouldn't hurt a kid,' he says over his shoulder to the lady, 'she was just helping him find you, you should say thank you.'

The woman gives Sarah one last dirty look over the kid's head, and turns away. The policeman turns back to his traffic.

Sarah's feet are dragging, they're not under her control.

'Come on.' Omar yanks on her arm. 'Don't hang round here.'

He leads her in the direction of Shepherd's Way, and as they walk without talking, Sarah feels like her head is settling back on her shoulders where it should be. She feels her feet making contact with the ground.

Then she starts thinking . . . *I* start thinking . . . I should be embarrassed, because I hit Omar. He's still got marks on his face. But he doesn't tell me off about it or anything. He just walks beside me and I think he's okay really. He doesn't say anything for ages and I don't say anything to him but it's alright.

'What's going on?' he says when we're walking past the Imperial War Museum. 'Why were you acting like that?'

'I wasn't acting like anything,' I say.

He turns off to the left, into a newsagent, and I think he's given up on me, but he comes out with crisps and Coke and chocolate.

Then, while we're stuffing our faces and walking, I tell him that Jude gave away her baby and now she's gone. I tell him how sick she looked and how she could hardly walk, so how can she have run away?

120

'It's like she just vanished,' I say. 'One minute she was there and then she was gone.'

'Maybe she went back to the hospital,' he says.

'No way, not without telling me.'

But then I'm thinking maybe she did. Maybe I should check with the hospitals. But she could hardly even walk . . .

'Or maybe someone came and picked her up,' he says.

I frown. I think about her lying there texting. I pat my pocket, and her phone's still there. But when I get it out my pocket, it's died. Jude's hopeless at keeping her phone charged. It's like keeping a clean nappy on Em, or giving her food before she gets hungry, it's all too much for Jude.

'Who would come and pick her up in the middle of the night?' I try to get my head around this idea.

'I don't know.' Omar sounds uncomfortable, like he didn't intend to get into this conversation. 'Like a friend or something, a friend with a car.'

I've got pictures in my head. I see a car pulling up outside our block, and a car door opening, and Jude appearing from the shadows and climbing in with Em in her arms. It creeps me out because in my head I can't see who's driving the car – it's like one of those driverless cars that comes alive all on its own, but that's in films not in real life.

'I'm scared because of what happened to Zoe,' I say. 'What if they find her like that?'

Omar doesn't say, 'Don't be silly, why would she end up like Zoe?' What he says is: 'Tell the cops, then.'

But the police driver didn't care even though she's supposed to be a witness. I don't think any of them will care until she turns up dead. The fact is, no one came and dragged her out screaming, or I'd have woken up. She left me a note, she left me the seven pounds. Which means she chose to go. And she didn't think she'd need the seven pounds.

'She'd have told me if someone was coming for her.' I'm thinking aloud.

'Maybe she thinks you know where she's gone and who she's gone with.'

'What do you mean? Why would I know?' I say.

Omar's running his tongue over his lips, like the conversation makes him uneasy about something. Or like there's something he's not telling me.

'Maybe she's been kidnapped,' he tries to joke, but it falls flat and he shuts up for a minute or two. Then he says, 'Wherever she is, she'll be back.'

'I hope so,' I say, and Omar laughs at me for the way I say it, all gloomy like I don't believe it. When he laughs it makes me feel like he's right, that it's the only thing that makes sense, and she'll come back. I'm feeling silly now about letting my head go off like that. If Omar's right and Jude's coming back then I should be waiting for her at home. Otherwise she'll come back and I won't be there, and then we'll be in a fine mess. But on the other hand Bocock will come back for her. So even if she comes back and I'm waiting for her, we'll have to go away again.

I follow Omar back up to Level 8 of Shepherd's Way to the door of Number 89. He stands there, waiting for me to go in. And I want to go in, but I can't do it because I know she's not in there and what if she doesn't come back? What if I'm sitting in there all on my own and none of them come back, not Jude and not Em, and definitely not Big Ben. Even the thought of it makes me breathe really fast.

'What?' he asks, because I'm just standing there panting in a panicky way. 'Haven't you got a key?'

I get the key out my pocket and show it to him because I can't speak.

'So open the door,' he says. He wants me to put it in the lock, so I do, and I push the door open, but then I just can't do it, I can't go in.

I let out this howl which is like the most embarrassing noise I've ever made in front of Omar.

'Sarah,' he says, like I'm making him nervous. 'Sarah, you've got to calm down.'

But I can't calm down. I just sit down where I am on the concrete floor of the walkway, and I carry on bawling.

'Sarah, come on,' he says, 'get a grip. Someone will hear you.'

Someone will hear me and think he's hurting me, is what he means.

He squats down beside me, then reaches out and squeezes my shoulder. He leaves his hand there and his fingers feel warm even through my T-shirt and it's like his hand's got special powers that are burning through my skin. I know in a minute he'll move his hand away and that makes me cry even more because if he could just leave it there for the rest of my life I think I might be okay.

'I can't go back in there,' I wail. 'I'll go mad all on my own.'

'You're right,' he says, 'you shouldn't be on your own. Just in case. You can come back with me to my dad's.'

'I've got to be here so Jude and Em can find me.'

'Yeah,' he says. But he looks worried now, like he was lying before about her coming back and now he's sorry he got my hopes up. So then I'm howling all over again.

He lets go of my shoulder and he's looking all around him like he's looking for inspiration but I could've told him no one ever found inspiration on Level 8. What I want to do is to beg him to come into the flat with me and wait with me until Jude gets back, but I know it's impossible. The trial's a week away and he's a witness too. We shouldn't even be talking to each other, the lawyers wouldn't allow it, they could say we told each other what to say in court, or he threatened me, or something, and then they could tell the jury not to listen to anything we say.

He's knocking on the next door along, Number 88.

'You can sit with Millie for a bit,' he says. 'She'll look after you.'

'No,' I say, and get to my feet to grab his arm and stop him knocking. 'No, don't . . .'

But it's too late. Millie's at her door, peering out over the security chain. She's our neighbour, but we've never got on. She and Mum had a shouting match once about the clothes Mum let Jude wear, and letting her out to go clubbing at her age, and Mum called her a nosy bitch. After the row I steered clear of Millie. Anyway, she looks like she might smile when she sees Omar, but then she sees me and decides to scowl instead.

'I thought you two were supposed to be in court?' she says.

'Mill, can you watch Sarah for a bit?' Omar asks, all friendly with his showman smile, all teeth and dimples, like he's going to do a trick for her.

She takes off the chain and opens the door and steps out onto the walkway and gives me a good looking over. I don't know why she's looking at me like that. I've never paid her much attention, and it's a long time since I've seen her up close. She doesn't come out of her flat much, but once in a while I've seen her in the distance in the Egleton Shopping Centre. She likes her chicken and chips. I can see that from the size of her hips. She's having trouble walking because she tips from side to side like she might topple over.

'What's the matter with you?' she asks me.

'Nothing,' I say.

'Her sister's gone and taken Em,' Omar says, 'and she doesn't want to be in the flat on her own. She shouldn't be on her own anyway, just in case.'

Just in case what? Just in case things get even worse? Just in case I end up lying dead in the arches like Zoe?

'Well her sister's not coming back, so what's she going to do?' Millie says. 'She can come in if she likes, but she can't wait forever.'

'She *is* coming back.' I manage to find my voice. 'I told you, she can't walk, she's not well enough to go anywhere.'

Omar and Millie exchange a look, and that makes me mad.

'You told me she'll come back.' I round on Omar.

'I was trying to make you feel—' But Millie interrupts before he can finish what I know he's going to say.

'Omar, you go off home and tell your dad what's happened. Sarah, you come inside and have a cup of tea, and wait for your sister.'

She turns back towards her front door. I look at Omar, but I know he can't help me any more than he already has, which is a lot. He nods at me and hesitates, like he might say something, then turns and walks away.

I turn around. My front door is still open, but I can't do it. I'll die in there on my own.

'Come on if you're coming,' says Millie.

So I pull the door to our flat closed, locking it, and follow Millie inside her flat.

Which is like stepping into a parallel universe.

I mean, she lives next door, and the flat is identical, but it's so different from ours. It's all pretty little things, like knick-knacks, vases, clocks and statues, nothing more than about six inches tall but all lined up on the mantelpiece over the electric fire and on the coffee table and on the shelves. Her windows have curtains and the curtains have flowers on them, and she has two proper armchairs and on the back of them and on every flat surface are these white knitted mat things, and then I see there are knitting needles and one of the white matty things on the needles, so I know she makes them herself. The flat even has its own smell which I think is a hairspray smell, sharp and chemical and sweet. It's the same smell as Millie. When I look up at the ceiling there are patches of damp but you don't notice them because there's so much else to look at.

Millie goes into the kitchen to make tea and although I follow her I can't actually get into the kitchen because she fills it with her big swaying hips.

So I go back and sit in one of the armchairs. But I think it's not safe for her to leave me here with all her things. They're so small I could put one in my pocket.

When she comes back, she's carrying proper flowery cups and saucers on a tray and there's sugar in a little flowery bowl and milk in a little flowery jug and a proper teapot. She puts it down on the coffee table and then she

126

sits herself down in the armchair, and I'm glad I've left the bigger one for her, because she fills it up completely. Once she's sitting down she puts her feet up on a little padded stool in front of her, and she breathes a big sigh.

'So, Sarah,' she says to me, speaking slowly, 'would you pour the tea?'

I nod like I'll do it, but I've only ever put a tea bag in a mug so she tells me what to do, like pour a bit of milk into the cups then pour the tea from the pot on top of it then put in a spoon of sugar if you want it then take the spoon out and put it on the saucer. All the time she's talking to me, she's breathing heavily. I put a cup of tea on a little table by her chair and I take one myself and put a spoonful of sugar in it. When I sit and take a sip it tastes like heaven. Millie watches me.

'What will you do if she doesn't come back, Sarah?' Millie says. 'And why would she come back if she thinks she might end up like Zoe Brown with her neck broken in the gutter?'

I shake my head furiously.

'Jude knows . . .' Millie insists. 'Jude knows who killed Zoe, and that's why she's run away. She's frightened . . .'

'You're wrong.' I speak over her loudly so she can't carry on talking. 'Jude's not like Zoe. You just hate all of us, you don't know what you're talking about.'

'Oh don't I? Well, let me tell you I have nothing against you or your sister,' she says. 'I pity you.'

'Everyone always pities us!' I exclaim. I'm getting fed up with everyone's pity. It never seems to turn into anything useful like money or a new flat.

Millie snorts, and it sounds like she's laughing.

'You think I pity you because your mother is dead?' She laughs. 'Lord no, I pity you for being her daughters.'

I curl over in my chair, burying my head on my knees, pressing my hands to my ears. I don't want to hear this.

'I never met a woman with a crueller tongue than Dianne,' she says, as if it's okay to say that to me.

I can't even speak I'm so tied up inside. My intestines are twisting and churning. My belly wants to burst out of my mouth. But my head wants to hear what she's going to say next.

'She's my mother, and she's d—'

I try desperately to interrupt again, but Millie talks right over me.

'. . . a woman has babies, and she is obliged to look after them. Even a cat or a dog will feed their young, even a rat! But oh no, not Dianne. You two were an encumbrance and an expense. She liked nice things, and when she had money, she spent it on herself, but she did nothing for you. She didn't cook for you, or make sure you had clothes to keep you warm. Even when she could have fed you, the two of you were always hungry . . . there's no need to look at me like that, Miss Carnaby, I'm not telling you anything you don't already know . . . your sister making an exhibition of herself with those men . . . you so thin and your skin so grey from having no food . . . no one could blame you—'

When I interrupt, it is almost a shout.

'Mum did her best.'

But Millie can't let it go.

'Your mother only ever did her worst,' she says. 'I'm not saying who did it, but whoever it was killed your mother did you both a favour.'

That's when I jump out of my chair and I start to shout at Millie, how she's a stupid old cow and she doesn't know what she's talking about, and her house smells. And I pick up the teacup and I hurl it at the mantelpiece where it smashes into a little horse made of china, and both of them smash into a million pieces, and Millie shouts out in alarm and then pulls herself up out of her chair and lowers herself to the floor to pick up the pieces.

She looks up at me from where she is on all fours.

And then she says, 'I saw you.'

I stare at her. She's an old woman and she's on her knees, and I could kick her until she shuts her stupid mouth and stops saying any more of her lies.

'I saw you,' she repeats.

I could shut her up for good.

But I don't. I run out of her front door and slam it behind me really hard. So hard that the noise echoes up and down the walkway.

I'm shaking so much that I can't go anywhere. I can't walk, and I can't run any further. I sink to my knees on the walkway. I close my eyes. I want to wipe it all out of my head. Everything she said about Mum. Everything she said about Jude and Zoe.

I don't know how long I'm there.

I'm wiping everything she said out of my head.

If I think back, I'm finished. I've got to think forwards. I've got to keep going.

What I need is a place to be still and to watch for Jude. If I can find Jude and Em, then everything will be alright. I lift up my head and right away I see the empty window at Number 93. I know it's empty.

Number 93 is going to be my watchtower.

NINE

I manage to climb up and squeeze through and onto a kitchen counter on the other side. I graze my legs a bit, but nothing serious. As soon as I'm in the smell hits me and I gag. I push the window open more and try to breathe the bit of air that comes in there. I'm not interested in the rest of the flat, I just want the window. I sit cross-legged on the counter by the window, watching out for Jude and Em.

It's not as if people are coming and going along the walkway, so most of the time I don't even worry about anyone seeing me. I just watch. Then Omar appears, and I slide off the counter in a hurry and out of sight. I don't think he sees me, but I can't be sure. I can just see him by peeking my head above the counter. He goes and knocks on Millie's door and stands there with his head hanging while she says something to him. Probably she's telling him I broke her stuff and shouted at her. I'm glad I did that, she deserved it. Omar looks miserable. Then she shuts the door on him, and he slopes off in the other direction.

Then someone else appears from the far end of the walkway and I duck out of sight again, but not before I've seen that it's the man from the bus. The man Mum used to call Uncle Keith. I have a sudden vision of a wad of cash in this man's hand. A wad of cash passing from his hand to Mum's . . .

I get up my courage to peek above the window ledge and he's disappeared. My heart beats really fast. He must be in our flat. Which means he's got a key, and Jude's the only one with a key, except for me.

I wait, and at first I can't see him, and I get scared that he's watching me from somewhere I can't see him. But in a little while he walks out of our flat, and on the way out he doesn't stop to shut the door behind him.

I don't want to go anywhere near him. But if he's got Jude, I've got to go after him.

I wait till he's out of sight and then I slip out through the window the way I came in. I run to our flat. Once I'm in, I'm horrified. It was a mess when I left the flat because of throwing things around looking for clues Jude might have left before she disappeared, but it's even more of a mess now. Things are chucked all over the place. The pile of laundry's been tipped up and the beds stripped and the sheets left on the floor. The doors of the kitchen cupboard are open and the drawers all pulled out. I can't believe it. Then I think, did he get what he wanted? It doesn't look like it. It looks like he couldn't find whatever he was looking for so got really frustrated.

But there's only one thing of Jude's that I've taken and that's her phone, and why would he want that?

I grab my bike and race down the stairs at my end of the walkway. I think I might stand a chance of beating him but I'm slowed down by the bike and I'm expecting that by the time I reach the ground floor he'll already be half a mile away.

So when I get there and I see him standing talking into his mobile phone it feels like I'm getting lucky. I hold back by the stairs, and he never looks in my direction, which is lucky again. Then he ends his call and walks towards a car, and my heart sinks because I can't keep up with a car. Still, I get on my bike and follow him out of the car park as he turns right onto the main road and then off into a side road. Because the road is narrow and there are lots of parked cars all along it, I can keep up. And when he parks in Charlotte Street, ten minutes later, I'm right behind him.

I hang around while he gets out of the car and locks the doors with a remote, then heads for Number 23. Charlotte Street is a curved street of terraced houses, red brick with bay windows, old but not posh. The houses have peeling paint on their window frames and doors, and some of them have overflowing rubbish bins, or cracks in their windowpanes. Still, this is South London, so there are trees planted by the edge of the road and their branches shade the pavement from the sun and birds chirp up in the leaves.

Once he's gone inside I go and stand outside Number 23. I look up at the windows. On the third floor someone twitches a curtain aside and for a millisecond I think I see a woman and a baby but it's so quick I don't really know what I've seen.

I can't move. I just stand there staring up.

If it was Jude, she'd wave at me. Or she'd open the window and call to me.

She wouldn't hide from me.

Except if she's not hiding, how come she hasn't told me where she is?

I can't help myself. I go up the steps to the front door and there's a row of bells to push. I'm deciding whether or not to push the buzzer when the door bursts opens and a young man comes out, nearly barrelling into me, pushing past and running down the steps. The door's about to swing shut behind him but I catch it in time and slip through. Inside the hallway, there's a pile of envelopes and fliers on the floor, and a door off to my left, marked 23A. There's a sign with a black arrow pointing up the stairs to 23B and 23C. It's really quiet. I stand there for a minute pushing the post around with my toe. Then I squat down and take a closer look at the envelopes. The ones for 23A are all in the name of Simon Pettifer, and there's a Miss Raskin in 23C. Which leaves 23B. The ones that are addressed to 23B mostly have Keith Butcher on them. But there are two addressed to Chloe Vaz. Before I think about what I'm doing I've picked up the letters for 23B and stuck them down my front. I stand up, push the remaining post around a bit with the toe of my trainer and then, before I can change my mind again, I climb the stairs.

My heart is pounding.

I don't want to come face to face with Keith Butcher.

But maybe Jude is here.

Two flights later I find myself outside 23B. It's a blue door.

I don't even know if I saw a woman.

I don't even know if it was Jude.

I don't even know if it was this flat.

I turn around and start to go back downstairs.

Then I hear a kid start to cry.

I stop and listen.

It sounds just like Em.

A woman's voice soothes the child. She sounds like Jude. I turn around.

The first time I press the bell I can't hear it making any noise inside the flat so I press it again and this time it sounds really loud. The door opens and Keith Butcher steps out into the corridor. He's really close to me. I can smell his sweat. I'm trying to stand there like I'm not afraid, but my knees are going to give. Up close he seems huge. From where I'm standing I can see behind him into his flat. There's a corridor behind him and at the end of it I can see a woman and a child pressed against the wall peering out.

It's not Jude.

All the hope goes out of me.

But I'm so frightened I can't move.

'What do you want?' he says.

He doesn't recognise me.

I don't expect him not to recognise me now I recognise him.

'Come on,' he says. 'You don't go ringing on my bell and not telling me why.'

'Where is she?' I manage to say.

'Where's who?' He's grinning, and turning to grin at the woman. Perhaps he's going to call her to meet this funny kid who's asking strange questions. Then suddenly he's not grinning any more. He's turning back towards me and saying, 'Well I never. Little sister Sarah. You *have* grown up, haven't you? Let me get a better look.' And his shoulder muscles are bunching, his hands darting out to grab me. But in that millisecond when I glimpse his face turn from grin to something else, somewhere deep in my brain, electrical charges start screaming, 'Run for your life!' I feel his hands moving through the air towards me and I hurl myself down the stairs. I'm falling more than running, as my feet touch the stairs and slip and slide all at the same time. But still I'm moving fast and in a downwards direction, which is the right way, and when I get to the ground floor I grab the door which is still a bit open and I hurtle out and leap down the steps and jump on my bike and pedal for my life.

When I get back to Shepherd's Way, I leave my bike on the ground floor, trying to put it out of sight so no one will nick it. Then I run back up the stairs to Level 8, climb back in the kitchen window of Number 93 and into a back room, so that if anyone comes looking through the kitchen window, they won't see me.

My heart's still pounding.

I sit down on the floor and curl into a ball, whimpering.

As soon as he was there in front of me, the memories began flooding me.

I'm ten years old, and Keith Butcher is at our front door talking to my mum.

'You can't waste an asset like her,' Butcher says to Mum. 'Got to take advantage in this life.'

'You'd know all about that,' my mum snaps at him.

But she calls Jude, and Jude comes to the door.

Jude, aged fifteen, is all dolled up in Mum's lipstick and mascara. She looks like a model. She doesn't know what's going on, and doesn't want to go. She's been bribed by Mum with the promise of new clothes. Mum has to push her out the door.

As he turns to go, Keith Butcher passes Mum a wad of notes behind Jude's back, like he doesn't want Jude to see. But I see.

'Where's she going?' I ask, age ten. 'Why aren't you going too?'

'None of your business,' Mum says and turns away from me, but not before I've seen the jealous look on her face.

Jude comes back late, after I'm asleep. Someone's given her a new necklace, and a bottle of perfume . . . Next day, when she's scrubbed the make-up off, she tells me she's in love.

In love . . . Oh, how can she have been so stupid?

I scramble to my feet. I can't allow myself to think back. I have to think about the future. I have to find Jude.

If I focus on what I'm doing – the envelopes as I pull them from inside my shirt and tear them open – then I don't have to think about where I am and I don't have to think about what just happened. If I keep moving, I don't have to think about Keith Butcher at all.

My hands are shaking and scraped raw from my fall down the stairs in Charlotte Street, but I try to concentrate on what's in front of me.

There's an electricity bill for a Keith Butcher at flat 23B. It tells me nothing except that he's lived there at least a couple of months, and that he uses 450 units of electricity on average a month, mostly in peak hours, but slightly less overall in the past thirty days. He pays his bills on time.

As for Chloe Vaz, she's got a letter from her mum in Norwich and a red-letter demand for payment on her credit card which is three thousand pounds overdrawn. I feel bad about stealing the letter from her mum, especially as she sounds a bit down (her cat just died, and she's got new noisy neighbours). She says she's tried ringing Chloe but Chloe never picks up and perhaps Chloe could give her a ring sometime. Good luck with that, I'm thinking, your daughter's too busy running up credit card bills. Still, maybe the letter would give her a bit of a kick up the conscience. I fold the letter and try to put it back in the envelope but the flap's all torn where I ripped it open. Even if I take it back she'll know someone's been spying on her. Perhaps if I glue it back down and write, 'Sorry, wrong address,' on it, or something like that? But I cast one eye quickly round the squat, and I know I'm not going to find a glue stick here. Not unless it's stuffed up someone's nose.

There's another envelope addressed to Keith Butcher. So I open it up and I take out the letter. I start to read but I can't believe what I'm seeing.

It's about Keith Butcher's pension. His *police* pension.

He's been a police officer for twenty-six years.

Did Mum know he was a police officer?

I know I should go back into Number 87, and try to work out what he wanted in there, but it's getting dark, and I'm scared to go in on my own. I decide I'll wait till the morning. Then I look around me at the squat as the sun goes down outside, and the corners of the rooms become gloomy and I realise I'm quite scared to stay where I am, too.

I stand there staring round me, and I think I should go to Sheena's house. Carla will feed me. It's warm there and clean. Carla will ask me what's going on and I can tell her . . .

But I can't! Carla said you have to protect babies with your life. She said you can't let them out your sight. How can I tell her that Jude gave away her baby? I'm hot with the shame of it. I'm sweating. I can't tell Carla what's happened ever. I've got to wait here for Jude and Em, and then we'll go and tell Bocock that Jude's alright now and she's changed her mind and we'll make them give Big Ben back.

Soon I need to go to the toilet. I find the bathroom but it's pitch-black. No windows, no electricity, no light. I'm frozen because I'm thinking about Zoe. I can't move. If I got into this flat then anyone could get into this flat. Anyone who's on the run. Anyone could be waiting in the dark bathroom . . . I can hear myself whimpering like a puppy.

'Don't think about Zoe any more,' I hiss at myself, out loud, and that scares me too, like when your arm goes to sleep because you're lying on it funny, and you wake up thinking there's a strange hand in your bed and you grab it and it's yours! Hearing my voice hissing at me is like that, like there's someone else hissing at me.

After a minute of thinking really hard that I mustn't think about Zoe I'm still thinking about her and I'm still scared, but my muscles can move again.

It smells foul in the bathroom. I'm glad I've got my shoes on in case I step in anything. I feel my way around, pulling my fingers quickly back from sticky, furry places. The smell is strongest by the toilet, and by the sink. I find the tap and turn, and there's a trickle of cold water. I wait, but it doesn't warm up. My eyes are getting used to the dark. I can see myself dimly in the mirror, dark hair and the palest face I've ever seen. I scare myself. It's like I'm seeing a ghost. By the loo, my fingers find a soft round roll of bog paper. Whoever it was who left it, I forgive them everything, even if they made the stink.

Afterwards, somehow, I fall sleep on the couch.

In the morning it's the light that wakes me up, and for a moment I just lie there letting my eyes wander over the place. Whoever lived in here before left a curtain. It's filthy, and hanging off the rail, and the rail's half off the wall. I don't even want to think about who's been sleeping on the couch I'm on before me. There's a rotten, sweet smell under my nose, and a gritty feel to the fabric.

I'm rolled up like a ball. Even my brain's all curled up, like it's too dangerous to let any thoughts escape. My fists are buried in my belly, and I'm clutching Jude's dead phone. My toes are all scrunched up too, and my knees are folded into my stomach. I'm really small like this, not too much skin touching the couch. And if I don't move, I can't put a foot wrong. But I've got to move because I've got to watch for Jude. I can't believe I've let myself sleep. What if she's come back, and she doesn't know where I am?

Even though I've been asleep and woken up, and a whole night has passed, what Millie said about my mother is still making me feel sick, like I've eaten something bad.

When someone bangs on the door I nearly jump out of my skin, even though I'm half expecting it.

Quietly as I can I put my feet on the filthy floor and tiptoe to the front door. I look through the spyhole to see who's there.

It's Omar, head down, looking at his feet.

I watch him. He doesn't know I'm just on the other side of the door.

He raises his head and looks straight at me.

'Hey, Sarah,' he shouts, just loud enough to be heard through the door.

I feel like he can see me, even if he can't.

I can still feel his hand on my shoulder, and when I think about it, my tummy feels hollow. I put my hand flat on the door, like I can touch him through the wood.

'Come on, Sarah.' He's not shouting this time, but his voice is raised, like he knows I'm pretty close by. 'I've got something to tell you.'

That means he knows where Jude is. What am I waiting for?

But something's making me hesitate.

He turns away from the door. He's giving up. He can't give up before he's told me.

I start to panic. I wrestle with the locks on the door . . . I came in through the window, I never thought I wouldn't be able to get out through the door, but it won't shift.

I run back into the kitchen and climb onto the counter, and as I do that I'm shouting, 'Omar! Wait!'

And then I'm on the kitchen counter pressed up against the window and I see them all on the walkway. Omar, and Omar's dad, and Bocock and Peasgood, and two police officers – one man, one woman.

I just stand there, blinking like an idiot, with my hands pressed against the glass.

Omar's looking at me, but when he sees my face he looks away. His dad's standing behind him with his hand on his son's shoulder. Bocock is smirking like she's so frigging clever, and she's outsmarted me. Peasgood is looking nervous, and saying something to the police officers, who're beginning to move towards the front door.

I stare at Omar.

How could he do this to me?

I can hear them at the front door, messing with the locks like I did. The difference is, they'll have tools with them. And if they can't open the door, they'll break it down. I scramble down off the counter again and rush round the flat trying to find an escape route. But there's no nice back door leading onto a green pasture that I can run off into, no convenient fire escape. The flat backs onto the back of Shepherd's Way, a sheer drop of eight floors. I open the window wide and lean out, and the next-door flat has windows close by, and they're broken, and for a millisecond I can see myself climbing out of this window and clinging by my fingernails and swinging my feet into the next window, kicking out the broken glass, and dropping into the flat below, just like they do in films.

But only for a millisecond. I'm not suicidal.

I turn around, and they're already there, lined up behind me, all looking like they think I'm going to jump. And I almost wish I could, so I could screw up their lives like they're screwing up mine.

'Come on, Sarah,' says Peasgood. He's looking petrified. 'You can't stay here, it stinks. You'll catch something.'

He's wearing jeans and a T-shirt that says, 'Trust Me, I'm a Jedi' across his chest. He hasn't shaved. I think this was supposed to be his day off.

'Traitor,' I say, spitting the word at Omar. He looks like he wants to say something, but then he changes his mind. Good decision, Omar. I don't care who it was who decided to stab me in the back, Omar drove in the knife.

'Sarah, we'll keep a lookout for Jude,' Omar's dad says. 'If she comes back we'll make sure she knows where you are.'

'What about them?' I point to the police officers. 'It's *you* should be looking for her. She's sick, and she can't look after herself, and she's gone.'

'We'll certainly be filing a report,' the woman says. I look at her, and realise she's the one who questioned me at school after Zoe Brown was killed. I take a deep breath. 'Jude knew Zoe,' I say. 'So you've got to find her.'

'I understand,' says the policewoman, 'don't worry, we'll look into it.'

'They used to go clubbing together,' I say. 'I think they had a row. Maybe Jude knows all about Zoe. If you find her, you can ask her.' But the police officer doesn't respond.

I stand there, and they stand there. They don't dare come closer in case I turn around and jump out of the window. I think I'll stand there all day and make them sweat, but my knees are feeling shaky and my tummy rumbles. I haven't eaten anything for a long time.

'I'll only go with you if you promise to take me to Ben,' I say.

They all look at each other like they don't have a clue.

'Jude's baby. The one you stole,' I say. 'You've got to let me see him. I'm his family. It's not like we're all dead or something.'

Bocock makes a funny sound, like a controlled explosion. Peasgood looks worried.

'We can't promise anything, Sarah,' he says. 'The courts will make their decisions based on what's best for the baby.'

'His name's Ben, and his family's what's best for him,' I shout, but I'm feeling really wobbly now. 'I could take you to the international court of human rights.'

Omar's dad steps up to me.

142

'They took the baby?' he asks me.

'Isn't that what you wanted?' I shout at him. 'Was it you who called social services? Well, they did what you said. They came and took him, and now she's gone too.'

'No.' He shakes his head. 'No, that was not what I wanted. Not at all.'

He turns to Bocock and Peasgood. 'Is this the best you can do?' he asks them angrily. 'Do you steal babies in the night because the mother is in trouble? Why don't you help the mother?'

'Our priority is the safety of the child.' Bocock's spitting, she's so pissed off she even has to speak to this man. 'We've tried to help these two many times, and they just won't cooperate.'

'They won't *cooperate*?' Mr Jones says in a mocking, angry voice. 'They won't *cooperate*? Well *now* I understand why you have to take the baby. I can't abide people who won't cooperate myself. When they don't cooperate, I always take their babies.'

Omar puts a hand on his dad's shoulder, but it's no good, he's in full flow.

'Go with them,' Mr Jones says to me, waving me away. 'Go with them, you can't stay here. Leave it to me. I will nag at them and worry them and bite their heels until I find out where the baby is, and I will tell you.'

I look at their faces. Bocock is rolling her eyes, Peasgood is biting his lip. Omar just doesn't want to be there.

'I'll try to help,' Peasgood says, and because he says *I'll* try . . . *I*, not *we* . . . and because his face looks like he means it, I start to cry. And because I start to cry, they close in and grab me, and there's no point in fighting any more.

143

TEN

They've laid on an entire minibus for me, like I'm a one-person school trip or something. I sit down as far back as I can get and huddle up with my arms folded around me. I look out of the window. I can see Bocock talking to the police. They must be saying goodbye, because after a couple of minutes the police walk off, heading for a patrol car. As Bocock's climbing into my minibus Mrs Franklin runs up, all flustered, like she's been rushing.

'Sorry, tube delays,' she says to everyone as she clambers into the van. 'Sarah, love, sorry, they just called me this morning. I got here as soon as I could.'

Peasgood climbs into the driver's seat and turns the key in the ignition.

Someone taps on the window by my elbow and it's Omar.

He's mouthing, 'Sorry,' but I turn away from him, pretending I didn't even see him.

'Seat belt!' Bocock says, from across the aisle.

I ignore her, and Mrs Franklin leans over and plugs it in for me. She has to lift my arms to get the belt around me but she doesn't pinch or grab, just moves them gently then sits down herself, taking the empty seat next to me.

'We've found you a foster mum,' Peasgood says, when we're on the road.

There's no way I'm going to reply to that.

'A foster dad too,' he goes on, 'even a foster sister, a whole foster family.'

'Are they all Jedis, like you?' I ask coldly, and he shuts up.

I stare out of the window, my forehead rammed up against the cool glass.

Mrs Franklin tries next.

'Sarah, I know how hard this is for you. Shepherd's Way was your home. Everything you've ever known was there. I can only imagine how you must feel.'

I turn my head and look her in the eye, and she looks away. Then I remember.

'My bike,' I shout. 'We've got to go back. I need my bike.'

'We're not going back,' Bocock says firmly, 'you should have said earlier if you wanted to bring anything with you.'

'You kidnapped me!' I shout. 'How was I supposed to think about my things?'

'Can't we go back and get her bike?' Mrs Franklin asks, but Bocock ignores her.

'You'll thank us one day,' Bocock says. 'With the trial coming up in a week, we need you in a secure environment. Don't get me wrong, I'm not surprised you liked living with your sister. What teenager wouldn't? No rules, no boundaries, just get up when you want, leave your stuff everywhere. Your foster home will give you focus, structure. You and your carers can sit down together and work out a set of rules to create a constructive framework for your stay. That may sound intimidating, but believe me, a framework's what you need.'

'Sarah's quite a grown-up teenager,' Mrs Franklin murmurs. She reaches out to squeeze my hand but I snatch it away from her.

'I'm sure she *thinks* she's very grown up,' Bocock says, 'but does she understand the concept of Rights and Responsibilities?'

She rolls her 'r's.

'I think she just might,' Mrs Franklin says lightly. But Bocock has turned to frown at me.

'Well, Sarah,' she barks, '*do* you understand the concept of Rights and Responsibilities?'

I shrug.

'You see?' Bocock raises her eyebrows, tips her face slightly to the side, and gives Mrs Franklin a nasty smile. Then she turns back to me.

'You have a responsibility to reply when I ask you a question,' she says, like she's talking to a five-year-old.

'And I've got a right to remain silent,' I spit back at her.

Mrs Franklin laughs out loud.

'I don't know why you think it's funny,' Bocock snaps.

'I'm not laughing because it's a joke,' Mrs Franklin says, 'I'm laughing because I'm enjoying Sarah standing up for herself against you. I'm celebrating Sarah's independence!'

'Her independence? *Her independence?* None of these little shits have any idea what true independence is. Believe *me*, I've heard every snotty little word your type comes up with. Endless excuses. Victim talk, that's all it is. Christ, I wouldn't be her foster mother no matter what they paid me!'

At that Mrs Franklin leans across the aisle and says something very quietly in Bocock's ear, and Bocock turns her head away angrily.

After that everyone inside the minibus goes quiet for a long time.

I get a text from Sheena.

> luke suspended 4 hacking clares hstry sa
> he changd wrd century 2 fart 16x

Outside the bus, men and women are doing their normal things. I'm watching them walking in and out of shops, carrying bags of groceries. They're calling their husbands and wives on their phones, or they're texting them, and some of them have their kids with them. It's only me who's got this life where everything's a disaster. Out there they're all thinking about what they're going to eat for tea or where they can buy a packet of fags or whether they're going to be late for work or what's on telly tonight. None of them is thinking that their entire family has just vanished and until they find them they can't even be thinking about what's on telly or what's for tea. My phone vibrates, and it's another message from Sheena.

> can I c bb 2day?

I stare at the little screen. What can I text back?

> sstr gv bb away
> ddnt prtct hm wth hr life
> all bcos of me
> i tuk my i off hr

There's no point. She wouldn't understand. I'm inside the black hole and I'm on my own.

I must have fallen asleep, because next thing I know they're prodding me and saying my name. At first I don't open my eyes, because I don't want to see their faces. In my dream Jude is there and Em and even my mum, and I know that when I open my eyes they'll all vanish all over again. But even though I keep my eyes shut, with all the noise and the prodding Jude and Em and Mum start to fade and I just have to let them go, although it aches in my chest when I do.

I open my eyes and it's as bad as I feared. Bocock's face is six inches from mine shouting my name like I'm deaf, and her boobs are wobbling up and down with excitement. I push her away.

Mrs Franklin's got hold of my hand again. She's stroking it like I'm a dog or something. I snatch it away. I'm not that dozy.

The minibus is parked, and out the window I see a street of do-your-head-in-boring houses like little pale brick boxes. I look right and left and can see it's not just one street, it's a whole estate of do-your-head-in-boring houses.

Bocock, all business-like, picks up her bag and gets out of the minibus and Peasgood and Mrs Franklin follow on, assuming I'm behind them. Which I'm not. Peasgood waves the key at the minibus and the locks all click into place. Then Bocock realises I'm still in the van and she prances round to my side and taps on the glass and beckons me out furiously. Mrs Franklin is making pleading faces, holding out her arms to me as if she wants to give me a hug, like that's really going to persuade me. I'm not getting out of the van. My head's done in enough without boring it out of existence. Bocock snatches the key from Peasgood and the lock clicks open but I bash my fist against it so it goes down again, and although she's pulling on the door she can't unlock it.

So she's standing by the car getting more and more pissed off and tap-tap-tapping away on the glass and pulling on the door handle and I'm sitting in the car ignoring her, when a woman comes out of the pale brick box we're parked in front of. She looks just like the box. Square and completely do-your-head-in-boring. She's not old, but she's wearing an old-fashioned skirt and blouse with an old-fashioned dyed-blonde bob and glasses. She stops a few steps behind Bocock and watches for a minute. Then she comes over to the minibus. She smiles and waves at me, mouthing 'hello', like it's totally normal for me to be locked inside the bus and totally normal for me to ignore her. Then she says something I can't hear to Bocock and the others.

Then they all turn their backs on me and walk into the house! Mrs Franklin's the only one who so much as glances back at me.

What kind of fostering is that? What kind of a fake mother just turns and walks away like she couldn't care less?

I wait about five minutes but they don't come out again. I don't know what to do. I don't want to go into the do-your-head-in-boring house but I also don't want to sit all afternoon in the do-your-head-in-boring bus. Apart from the fact it's do-your-head-in-boring it's also very hot.

I unlock the door and open it, stepping out onto the pavement. I stand there and look up and down. I could run. They clearly haven't thought of that. Except that I'm so hungry I wouldn't get further than the end of the road.

I start to walk up the path towards the house. My heart feels heavy, like it knows there's nothing waiting for it inside the pale brick box. But at least there might be food.

I ring the bell and it plays a disgusting tinkly tune.

A girl opens the door and stands back to let me in.

'In there,' the girl says.

I find myself in the doorway to the lounge, where the rest of them are all sitting having a cup of tea. There's a cake on the table, and biscuits. Mrs Franklin's on one side of the table and Bocock on the other, and I can feel the tension between them. Mrs Franklin's talking to Linda, the blonde woman who came out the house to greet us, so I suppose she's the one that's my foster mother. I catch the word Paris, and I think I can't believe she's still on about the school trip that I'm never going to go on. Talk about living in la-la land.

'Sarah, I'm delighted you've decided to join us,' Bocock says when she sees me standing there.

I'm so hungry I can't stand up any more but there's nowhere for me to sit. Like actually I'm the one they're all here for but they've forgotten about me already.

Mrs Franklin shifts up on the couch to make space for me. I sit next to her with my hands under my thighs to stop her grabbing them. No one offers me food.

Linda starts to talk then, but I don't know what she's saying, I can't take anything in except that she's Linda and her husband is Donald, but he's out. And there are children who come in and out of the room called Susan – the girl who opened the door to me – and Sam.

I can't wait any longer so I take a biscuit from the table and then another and another . . . and I stuff them in my mouth. The quicker I can swallow the quicker I get to feel food in my tummy. I don't think anyone's watching but then Linda says to Bocock, 'When did she last eat?'

And Bocock doesn't say anything for a moment, and then she says, 'You heard the question, didn't you, Sarah? Answer nicely. When did you last eat?'

I think back but it's hard to know exactly when I last ate anything and I'm not sure if chocolate counts or not. Walking back to Shepherd's Way with Omar he bought us both Snickers bars and crisps and cans of Coke.

I shrug. I can't waste energy trying to explain how difficult it is to answer that. So I reach for another biscuit.

'Well, I think it's lunchtime,' Linda says, and her voice is breezy on top and all tight underneath. 'If you ladies and gentlemen would excuse us?'

Bocock, Peasgood and Mrs Franklin all look at each other like they're not sure what's going on. Then they put down their teacups and Peasgood takes a plate of chocolate cake off Bocock's lap and puts it on the table and they all get up and shuffle out of the room.

I see Mrs Franklin standing talking to Linda in the corridor, and I'm sure I lip read the words 'school trip'. You've got to hand it to her: she doesn't give up.

When she's finished speaking to Linda, she comes back into the lounge to say goodbye to me.

151

'Sarah, I feel awful, we should have made sure you had something to eat,' she says as she spots the empty plate in front of me.

'It's okay,' I say through a mouth full of biscuit.

'No, but . . . Linda says you can borrow their computer if you need to. You've got my email, right?'

I nod. I've got her email, but I haven't got her mobile number. She wouldn't risk that.

'You will email me if you have any problems, won't you?'

I nod. And because I've got some food inside me I give her a bit of a smile, just enough that she knows I don't blame her.

I blame Omar.

ELEVEN

I sit there while Linda goes to make lunch. I can hear her moving around in the kitchen but I don't want to go in there before there's food or I'll have to talk to her. A man comes into the room and looks at me. He's big and bulky, round, not square like his wife. He's got a round face with a round nose in the middle of it and not much hair.

'Hello,' he says, 'you must be Sarah.'

I nod.

'I'm Donald,' he says.

I nod.

'Settling in alright?' he asks.

I nod again and he looks at me for a minute, says, 'Okay then,' and he disappears back out the door.

Now I've got the biscuits inside me I'm feeling a lot better. Actually I'm feeling exhausted. I don't want to fall asleep on their couch, so I stand up and move around the room. They've got wall-to-wall carpet and a couch that matches two armchairs and an electric fire with fake logs for the winter and family photographs all over the place on the walls and on the mantelpiece.

I pick up one of the photographs to get a better look. It's Linda's daughter, Susan, in her school play. She looks strange in her costume, like some kind of animal. I look at the frame. It looks like real silver.

'Sarah?' It's Linda. I don't know how long she's been watching me but I feel really embarrassed, like she must think I was going to steal the photo frame.

'Lunch is ready,' she says.

Nobody says much over lunch, which is spaghetti bolognese, and much better than we get at school. I worry about getting sauce around my mouth, because I know I'm eating faster than anyone else. I'm not really hungry after the biscuits, but I'm not going to pass up food like this. I feel like they're all watching me but mostly they don't ask me questions. They do a bit of talking among themselves, and they make sure I know what they're talking about, it's like they've all discussed it and decided that I mustn't be left out. The girl, Susan, is eight, and she's into gymnastics. The boy, Sam, is six and likes football. But he wears thick glasses, so I can't believe he's ever going to be David Beckham. He's the only one who stares at me, and his eyes look super-big behind his specs.

Then when their dad's on the telephone and their mum goes out of the room to get something, they close in.

'Why are you living with us?' Sam asks me.

'Didn't you have other children coming to stay?' I ask, and he shakes his head. Great, I think. I'm their first. I'm the experiment.

'Well, don't ask me, I didn't want to come here,' I say.

'I thought you hadn't got anywhere else to live,' says Susan in her prissy voice. 'And no parents, so we should be sorry for you. And nowhere to live except dirty smelly places,' she pauses for breath, 'which is why you smell funny.'

Just as she says the last three words, her mum comes back into the room.

'Susan! Don't be so rude! I'm really sorry, Sarah, I apologise for my daughter, she's got no manners.'

I shrug.

'It's alright,' I say, 'she smells funny too.'

Susan stares at me, and her chin starts to wobble like she's going to cry.

'Sarah, that's enough!' Linda says, but worried, like she doesn't know where this is going.

'She started it,' I point out.

Linda's face is bright pink. I can see she's got hold of her daughter's hand, and is squeezing it like that way she can control what comes out of her mouth.

'I'm going to have a shower,' I say to Susan. 'You should probably have one too.'

The girl sniffs a bit, and she's about to say something, when Linda says, 'Susan, show Sarah where the bathroom is.'

Once I'm in the bathroom Linda knocks on the door with clean towels for me. When she's gone I lock the door and take off my clothes. I look at myself in the mirror. Last time I looked in a mirror this big I was a little girl, all skin and bone and straight up and down. Now I'm about to turn fourteen, and I've already got breasts and a waist and everything. I don't want this body. It's no use to me. I'm in somebody else's house in somebody else's body. None of it feels like me.

I lie a long time in the bath. There's a lot to soak off, all the sweaty fear and the smelly abandoned flat. Lying there in the bath looking at the yellow-tiled walls and the bottles of shampoo and conditioner and moisturiser all neatly lined up along the edge of the bath. I can't believe I spent the night on a stinky sticky couch at Number 93, but at least I wasn't being ordered about by somebody there. I was free. It was a filthy couch, but it was my filthy couch. I think about them all coming to find me. I think of Omar and his expression when I saw him through the window, and how he let me think he was the only one there, and how he didn't warn me about all those people he'd brought to catch me. I want to tell him what I think of him. I think of Sheena in school and her mum Carla, working in the café opposite Denny's and thinking about Zoe lying in the gutter. I think about Borys in prison, waiting to be tried in court for murdering Mum, and I think of Jude and Em, and I wonder where they are. Here in this foster prison, I can't do anything about any of it.

When I get out of the bath I have to get dressed in my grotty old clothes again. Susan's right. They smell. I pull on my hoody and I make sure Jude's phone is still in my zipped-up pocket, and her seven pounds. The phone's still dead, of course, but I'm going to bring it back to life.

On the landing Linda is waiting for me. She takes me to a small room just wide enough for a single bed and a wardrobe. On the windowsill there are bookends and in between them books for children. There's a *High School Musical* poster on the wall and a poster that has writing on it. It's a poem and its title is *Desiderata*, which I don't understand. It says I should be placid but it also says 'Be yourself'. I don't know whether Linda knows it's contradicting itself. And it says I should avoid 'loud and aggressive persons', which I reckon means Bocock. I like it where it talks about people who are 'vexations to the spirit'. It makes me think of Millie, and the evil things she said about Mum, and how I wanted to kick her when she was down on the floor. And it makes me think of Omar now he's betrayed me.

The room's got carpet on the floor and a sheet that matches the duvet and the pillowcases. Linda shows me that in the wardrobe there are hangers and she's left two drawers empty for my things.

'I haven't got any clothes,' I say. 'And I haven't got a charger for my phone.'

'Do you want to go shopping, then?' she says.

'Alright,' I say. Then I worry about who's going to pay. But Linda's already saying Donald's going to look after the kids while I go with her to Tesco's. Then she asks what kind of phone charger I need, and she goes away and when she comes back she says Donald can find me a phone charger later, and I say thank you, but really I'm thinking I want one right now. Then we go downstairs, and I get in the car with her, and we drive off.

'Is this your first time fostering?' I ask Linda, thinking about what Susan said to me.

She looks embarrassed.

'Yes,' she says. 'It's our first time, can you tell? It's yours too, isn't it?'

I shrug, but I know it's stupid to shrug, because either it's my first time or it's not, but I don't want to let her know I don't know what I'm doing. I want her to think she's the one getting everything wrong, which she is.

We park in Tesco's car park and go inside and Linda puts food in the trolley as we're walking through the aisles,

157

asking me what I like first so she gets something I'll eat. Then we go to the clothes and she tells me to choose what I'd like. But I can't just do that. I stand there not knowing what to do.

'What's the matter?' she asks me.

'I've got no money,' I say.

'That's okay, I'll pay,' she says. Then, when she sees I don't understand, she says, 'They give us an allowance for looking after you, it covers your clothes and your food and so on. What do you need?'

I can't speak for a minute because I don't know where to start. I haven't got anything with me, not even a change of knickers, no pyjamas, nothing. I don't know where to start and I'm worried I'll look greedy.

It's like she reads my mind.

'Come on,' she says, 'how old are you, fourteen?'

'Not for a couple of weeks,' I say, and she says we'll have to have a party. I don't say anything, but I know I'll be back living with Jude by then.

She starts to go along the aisle. She picks out two packs of underwear for age 13–14, and holds them up in turn. 'Spots?' she says. 'Or stripes?' I still don't know what to do, so I just stand there, embarrassed. Then she says, 'Come on, Sarah love, which is it to be? We can't spend all day choosing knickers.' So I shake my head at the spots and nod at the stripes, and she drops the pack into the trolley. She does the same with pyjamas, a vest bra thing, and tights, so I don't have to pick them out, I just have to nod and in they go.

By the time we get onto real clothes I feel okay about picking out a couple of T-shirts, one with a photo of a dog on the front, and some skinny jeans and a blue hoody identical to the one I'm wearing but without the holes.

'How about clothes for court?' she suggests. 'You'll feel better if you look smart.'

'I've got school uniform,' I say, and then it hits me. 'But it's back at the flat. Am I even going to school? Don't you live miles away?'

'Oh you'll go to school,' Linda says, 'a bus will get you there in twenty minutes. And Nicky Bocock said she'd bring your uniform over. But I don't know when she'll get round to it, she didn't look like a woman who's going to put herself out, so let's stock up anyway.'

So then in goes even more, two white blouses, a skirt.

I've never shopped like this in my life. You need pyjamas? They're yours! Knickers? Yours! School skirt? It's your lucky day! It's like I've won the lottery.

When I see Linda sticking all the stuff into the trolley, I can't get Bocock's voice out of my head. *I wouldn't be your foster mother no matter what they paid me.*

Then a thought strikes me.

'My school shoes don't fit.'

'Alright,' she says, 'let's get you some shoes.' So we go and look at the aisle where there are hundreds of pairs of shoes hanging up.

'Which ones do you like?' Linda asks.

I reach out for a pair of black pumps, but they're not my size, and when I look on the rail there aren't any the same style in my size.

'What about these?' Linda picks up a pair in my size, but ugly, with a fat bow on the front.

I don't want to say no, but she sees my face and says,

'Let's go to a shoe shop, then, they'll have a bigger selection there.'

At checkout, when we pay for the clothes and the food, I ask Linda for some phone credit and she gives me a little glance and then says yes. She puts fifteen pounds on my phone. I don't want my credit to run out before I've found Jude but I can't say that so I take what I'm given.

So we get back in the car and drive off and park all over again and go to a shoe shop where we have to take a ticket and wait to be served and all the shoes are on display. There are other children in there trying on shoes. One of the mothers is down on her knees and she's got her fingers inside the shoe with her kid's foot and she's moving her fingers to and fro to see if the shoe's too tight. She takes forever to decide whether it's fitting right. I can't believe it. You'd think she was buying a new house or a new car or something, the time she's taking.

When it finally gets to our turn there are two pairs I like, and the shop assistant goes off to find my size, and while she's gone I see the price on the shelf. I'm not sure Linda's seen it so I point it out to her expecting her to say it's too much and we'll leave while the shop assistant's off looking. But she just says, 'I know, school shoes are a ridiculous price,' and waits for the shop assistant to come back. When she reappears, I look at Linda and she nods at me, so I sit down and take my trainers off. Actually I don't really have to take them off, I just undo the Velcro and they fall off my feet like they've got no energy to do anything and they just need to lie down for a bit. I can smell the trainers, and I can smell my feet smelling of the trainers. I feel myself going red and kick the

160

trainers away like they belong to someone else. The shop assistant bends over like she's going to help but I snap at her that I'll do it myself and she leaves me to it. I pull the shoes on, then stand up and look at them in the mirror, then I try on the other pair. The pair I like are the most expensive ones, but Linda just says to me, 'If you like them let's take them.'

Then she glances at the trainers that I've kicked into the middle of the floor. No one's daring to go near them.

'Why don't we get you some new trainers too?' she says, and sits waiting while we go through the whole thing again. I pick some trainers with purple on them, and the assistant goes off and finds my size. I try them on and of course the ones I like are really expensive, but Linda says okay again.

The shop assistant asks me whether I want to put my old trainers in the new box, but she says it with an expression on her face like she's smelled them, and no way is she going to pick them up, so I just shake my head. When I turn around, Linda's already picked them up and put them in a plastic bag so they're not left on the floor.

When we're back in the car park she holds up the plastic bag and says, 'Shall I bin them?' And I say yes, so she puts the bag in the bin, and it feels funny to leave them there after they've been on my feet for so long.

Then we're getting back in the car with me wearing my new trainers and Linda says, 'What's with the long face? Don't you like your shoes?'

'Yeah, I do,' I say, and we set off. But it's just going around and around in my head and I keep trying to bite it back but I can't stop myself.

'Do they pay you a lot, then, to look after me?'

She glances across at me. Then she says, 'It's not supposed to be a salary or anything like that, it's supposed to cover all your expenses – like new school shoes – and compensate us.'

'But you do make money out of it?' I'm not going to give up. 'I mean you make money out of me?'

'Some,' she says, and I can see her mouth getting tight.

I nod. It's what I thought. Now I know what's in it for her.

She sighs.

'I could've made you buy the Tesco shoes,' she says. 'They fitted and they were twenty pounds cheaper.'

'I know,' I say.

She's right, it would've been twenty pounds in her pocket.

'I could take the money and feed you gruel,' she says.

'What's that?'

'Porridge but worse.'

I don't say anything. She could still feed me porridge, and maybe she will. Maybe she's just being nice to me because it's the first day and because her daughter was rude to me. Just because she's bought me shoes doesn't mean I'm going to grovel around and say thank you.

'I'm not saying you shouldn't be angry,' she says as she drives us out of the car park. 'I expect you've got lots to be angry about. But don't be angry at all of us. There are people who are trying to help you. Your school counsellor is dead set on finding some funding for your school trip, you know.'

'I know,' I say. 'Mrs Franklin's alright. She's mad, but she's alright. But Bocock . . . She's evil.'

She doesn't say anything for a few moments. Then she says, 'I certainly didn't take to her.'

When we get back to the house Donald's watching the news. I sit on the couch and stretch my toes in my new shoes and watch TV with him. I'm hoping he'll remember about the phone charger so I take Jude's phone out of my pocket and play with it, sighing a bit. I can see Susan and her little brother in the garden throwing a frisbee to each other, both of them in shorts and T-shirts. The afternoon sun is fading, but it's still warm. I'm bored by the TV, and Donald's obviously not thinking about phone chargers, so I go outside, not expecting to play just to hang around and watch. There's a swing attached to a tree, and I sit on that and sway a bit. They glance at me and they carry on throwing the frisbee to and fro between them, but they're not very good at throwing it, so when it comes towards me and lands on the lawn by my feet I bend over and pick it up. Then I throw it to Susan. A couple of throws later it comes in my direction again, and this time I realise it's not just bad throwing, the little boy is throwing it in my direction on purpose. I stand up, grin at him and throw it back to him, and he grins at me too. Even Susan joins in, catching it from Sam and throwing it to me. Round and round it goes from him to her to me, round and round in a triangle, and I'm laughing as the frisbee gets stuck in the tree then falls on my head and we're all laughing.

And then she stops throwing it to me.

It's my turn, so I'm standing there ready to try and catch it, and she throws it to him instead. I think she's trying to break the pattern, try something new, so I turn towards him and get ready to catch it from him. But he throws it back to his sister. He doesn't even look at me. It's like I'm not there. I stand there waiting, but they just carry on throwing it to each other in a straight line, back and forward, back and forward.

I stand there feeling like an idiot.

After they throw a few more times between them I drop out, not wanting them to notice, and I sit back down on the swing. Then after a few minutes Linda comes out to call us in to eat, so we all walk back into the house together like nothing's happened.

Tea is sausages that we bought in Tesco's and baked potatoes, and salad that only Linda eats. Nobody says anything much. They're all trying to be polite, and I don't want to talk to anyone. When I've eaten my potato I'm suddenly exhausted. I can't keep my head upright. I think I'm going to fall asleep there at the table, there's nothing I can do about it. My eyes are going to close and my head will fall flat on the table, and if I'm unlucky it will land in the butter.

'Why don't you go to bed, Sarah?' Linda says, looking at me. 'This has been a big day for you.'

'I know,' I say, and get to my feet. I stand there for a moment. Linda's smiling at me and saying something about sleeping well, and Donald's watching his wife, and the two kids are looking at me like I'm an alien.

'Sorry,' I say.

'Sorry for what, love?' Linda says.

But even half asleep I know I can't say what I mean. I'm not even sure I know what I mean myself.

'Nothing,' I say, and head upstairs.

I manage to get my shoes off and then I fall down on the bed with my clothes still on. I sleep deeper than I've ever slept before.

Then suddenly I'm wide awake. My eyes are open and my heart is beating extra fast, a zillion beats a minute. There's black all around me and Jude is very close. I can feel her in the room. I call her name but she doesn't reply. She needs me, and here I am buying shoes and eating sausages and soaking in the bath. She needs me and I've stopped looking for her. I can feel a hand squeezing my heart like someone's wringing the blood out of it. It must be Jude, she's the only one here, but why would she do that? I try to speak to her but I'm running out of oxygen. I can't even whisper her name. I can't get air into my lungs. I'm really trying, I'm opening my mouth wide and trying to gulp it in but it can't get any further than my throat so all the air is building up but I can't get it down inside me where it needs to be and I'm going to explode. I reach out my hand. If Jude takes it, she can pull me up and then I'll be alright, but she doesn't. She leaves me gasping. Well, why not? I've abandoned her. I try to sit up but there's a lead weight on my chest. I can roll onto my side so I do that, and then I push myself up so I'm sitting, but I knock something off onto the floor with a crash. I don't know what it is. I just know I've got to breathe so I can speak to Jude. I need to explain to her.

Someone else comes into the room.

'What was that noise?'

She must be able to hear me panting. She switches the light on and I scream but it doesn't come out. I scream because the only person in the room is Linda.

'Oh dear lord,' Linda says when she sees me. She hurries over and sits down on the bed. She starts to rub my back. Her face is inches from mine and I'm looking at her and I want her to see in my face that I need oxygen.

'Sarah love, calm down,' she says, 'you're breathing too fast.'

I try to tell her I'm not breathing fast enough, but I can't speak. I've got pins and needles in my fingers. I'm freezing cold and sweat feels like ice on my forehead. I'm going to pass out.

'Calm down,' she says, 'calm down. You've got to breathe more slowly.'

She tries to make me cup my hands over my face and tells me to breathe in through my nose and out through my mouth. When I don't do it she says, 'It's this or a paper bag, love,' and I give in and do what she says. Then she starts counting elephants, like 'one elephant, two elephants …' and making me take a breath every four elephants.

After a while, I can breathe again. Linda picks up the bedside light I knocked onto the floor. She switches it on and off, and the bulb still works.

'There,' she says, 'no harm done.'

I start to sob.

'Sarah love.' Linda tries to hug me but I push her away. 'What is it, Sarah?'

But I don't tell her my secret. Jude was here and now she's gone.

TWELVE

I've been at Linda's a week when the first day of the trial arrives. During that week, I go to school but it feels like I'm on a different planet. I can't talk to anyone about what's happened, not even Sheena. When she tries to talk to me, I cut her off, and after a while she stops trying. I walk around the school on my own, and I eat on my own, and in class I don't listen to anything that's going on. In my head, I'm thinking about everything, over and over. About Mum getting killed, and the terrible things Millie said about her, about how she didn't care about us, and about Zoe getting killed, and Jude abandoning me, and Omar betraying me, and how I'm all alone now.

I keep seeing Omar in the distance at school, but we don't speak to each other, because I hate him for what he did.

Mrs Franklin tries to help. When she can't make me talk about Ben and Jude and Em, she tries to jolly me along, nattering about the Paris trip, getting me to sign papers she's got from social services to apply for a passport. I just do what she says and forget about it. I know there's no way I'm going to Paris, and even if there was, I wouldn't care.

Every day I read the news about the investigation of Zoe's death. Her parents have warned the parents of other

167

teenage girls to be more vigilant, to ask their daughters where they're going, and to check they're home at night. The week feels like a lifetime. Linda and Donald try to be kind, but Susan and Sam are wary of me, and I'm wary of them. I don't want to 'settle in', I don't want to feel 'at home'. I just want to be with Jude. And I want the trial to be over.

'I'm sure Miss Malik has described to you the arrangements for witnesses such as yourself,' the lawyer says on the morning of the trial when I go to court. 'The lawyers and the judge will remove their wigs – you'll see us in all our balding glory . . .'

'I don't care about the wigs,' I say quickly. 'You can wear wigs if you want, it doesn't bother me.'

'To tell you the truth, it doesn't much bother me either. I'd just as soon not wear one and I'm sure my colleagues feel the same way, so you can think of it as doing us a favour. You'll have to forgive us if we all scratch our heads, it will feel very strange to us, all that fresh air around our ears.'

I shrug. I don't like him patronising me.

He sits back in his chair, observing me like I'm a specimen. It doesn't seem to occur to him that I'm still standing up. His eyes glance over my school uniform.

'Could you lose the, er, hoody or whatever it is?' he asks. 'It slightly spoils the image and I can't believe you need it to keep warm.'

I shake my head and pull it closer around me.

'Why?' he asks. 'Is it a lucky mascot? It looks well worn.'

I shrug.

'Very well, if it makes you comfortable. But can I ask you not to shrug in the witness box,' he says. 'For one thing we can't hear it, can we? And we need to hear what you have to say, loud and clear, that's the only thing that counts. For another it doesn't give a good impression.'

'I know,' I say.

He looks at me for a minute, like he thinks I'm being sarcastic.

And I don't know if I am or not. Miss Malik brought me here to meet the lawyer prosecuting Borys for killing Mum, and I've never been in a room like it before, so old-fashioned and so filled with paper and books.

'Of course you'll be giving evidence via the video link, I think you'll find it far more conducive . . .'

'She doesn't want to,' Miss Malik says. 'She doesn't like the room.'

'You don't like the room? Has Miss Malik taken you there so you can see it for yourself?'

'It's nothing to do with the room. I don't want to be shut in.'

'Do you suffer from claustrophobia, perhaps?'

'I just don't like being shut in.'

'Did Miss Malik explain that on the video link you won't have to see the defendant. If you give evidence in court, you'll very likely see him. I suppose we could put up a screen, but . . .'

'I don't want a screen, I don't care if I see Borys. I should see him.'

'Should you?' The lawyer frowns. 'Are you sure that you wouldn't be intimidated by the defendant's presence?'

'Why would I be intimidated by Borys?' I say.

'Well . . .' he looks a bit surprised, 'the defendant is

charged with killing your mother. I think if it were me, I'd find that a little intimidating.'

'Well it's not you, is it?' I say. 'If he did it I want to look at him and I want him to look at me.'

He stares at me for ages. Then he says, 'Well, I'll have a word with the judge and see what we can do. It's not the only matter to be dealt with today before we get started so I'm afraid you may have to wait some time, and the waiting room is scarcely better than the video link room. I hope you've brought a good book with you.'

'I've got my music with me.'

'Ah,' he says cheerfully, 'very good. Bach, is it? I always find him very soothing.'

His face makes me smile in spite of everything that's happening. 'It's not Bach,' I break it to him. 'You wouldn't like it.'

'Not Bach?' He looks shocked, but I think it's fake shock, like a joke. 'What is it, rap? Lady Gaga?'

'Something like that,' I say, still smiling at his face, and the way he says rap and Lady Gaga, like he's got a bad taste in his mouth.

'Ah well,' he smiles. 'Then you're right, I probably wouldn't like it.'

He glances down at his papers, then back up at me, frowning now.

'I understand no one can find your sister,' he looks down again and then adds, 'Judith.'

'No one's looking for her except me,' I say. 'No one cares. I told the police, but I don't think they're looking.'

He looks back down at the file.

'I understand Judith is on a methadone treatment programme.' He looks up at me like he's expecting me to confirm what he's saying. I stare back at him. His eyes go back to the file. 'She's trying with limited success to kick a heroin habit,' he murmurs, 'she recently gave birth to a baby born with a methadone dependency . . . he's in a treatment centre where he's expected to stay for another two to three weeks until he's weaned off . . . There are concerns for the wellbeing of the older child, who remains in her care . . . Well . . .' He stops reading abruptly, straightens the stack of papers in his file and looks up at me. 'I doubt your sister would have coped well with the rigours of a trial.'

He looks as though he's expecting me to say something but my jaw is clenched so tight that I'm not sure I can ever speak again. His words are echoing around my head . . . *to kick a heroin habit . . . born with a methadone dependency . . . in a treatment centre . . .*

How has she hidden this from me? Or have I been blind? What have I seen and not wanted to see? I remember the blue marks on her arms when she was lying there in the hospital. I think about the syringes discarded in the stairwell . . .

I open my mouth.

'I know,' I say.

I don't know if there's anyone else in the waiting room except for me and Miss Malik, because I don't see them. I press my shoulders against the metal frame of the chair and I close my eyes. I listen to my music and I bite my nails until I taste blood.

When they come to take me into court I feel like I'm floating. My feet are doing that thing again where they don't touch the ground. I'm afraid my head's going to come off like it did the day Jude disappeared. People are looking at me all weird, and then I realise that I'm holding my head on. I mean I'm *actually* holding it on so it doesn't come off in public. My hands are over my ears pressing my head down onto my neck. I take my hands away from my head and I force my arms back down to my sides and I give myself a talking-to. I tell my head it's not going anywhere. I need it to stay where it is.

The first thing I see in the court is Borys. He's sitting behind a glass screen. I know he's going to be there of course, but it's still a shock to see him. He's wearing jeans and a long-sleeved shirt which is done up with a tie so you can't see his tattoos except at his collar where they go up his neck. He's leaning forward with his elbows on his thighs. He's got a sheaf of papers in his hand, and when he sees me he drops his head so he's staring at the floor like he doesn't want to look at me.

Seeing him there behind his screen, with a guard next to him, scares me.

The things I'm going to say are going to put him in jail.

Me. The things *I* say. *I'm* going to put him in jail.

My heart starts pounding.

I walk up the steps into the witness box. I'm really high up. Miss Malik follows me up the steps and sits down behind me. I can't believe there are so many people. At least if they had their wigs on I'd know which ones were lawyers. They've got their laptops out on benches in front of them, and big fat red books. Up

172

above them is the judge. There are piles of paper all around him. He's looking at me over the rim of his glasses. He tells me about things like the wigs, and asks me the same question the lawyer asked me about whether I really want to give evidence in court, and I say I do. So he tells the jury that that's what I'm going to do although I had the choice. And he tells the jury about the wigs, and that I can have a break any time. He says it all like he has to say it, like when they read you your rights when they arrest you. They don't really want to give you your rights but they've got to say it because if they don't then they're in trouble.

I keep glancing at Borys. I can't help it.

I can't smile at him because of what he's done. But I've never been in the same room as him and ignored him.

Then the lawyer I met stands up and starts to ask me questions. He's got no wig on, and no gown, just a suit and tie, and his hair's quite messy.

'Sarah, you lived at Number 87, Shepherd's Way Block A?'

'I did, I don't now.'

'Now you are living with a foster family,' he says. 'But I'm going to ask you some questions about your own family and about what happened nearly eight months ago. If you need a break just let us know.'

I nod. Then I catch his eye and I say, 'Yes,' quite loudly.

'I'd like you to describe to us your living arrangements. Who were you living with in November last year?'

'My mum, my sister Jude, and her baby, Emma.'

'Your mum, that's Dianne Carnaby?'

'Yes.'

'Did she have a job?'

'Not really . . . She sometimes did odd cleaning jobs. She helped out in the shop a bit. Not very often . . .'

'Did you get on well with your mum?'

'Most of the time.'

'Did you do special things with her?'

I shrug, and even when he asks me to speak out loud I can't think of anything to say.

'I've heard she used to call you her pot of gold as a term of affection.'

'Jude too, it wasn't like I was special.'

'She meant by that, I assume, that you were like treasure to her, that she valued you highly.'

'I suppose so.'

He looks disappointed, and the next question is different.

'And your sister, does she work?'

'She's got Em.'

'She's a full-time mum, then?'

'I suppose so . . .' It feels like I should say more, like I should explain. So I say, 'I don't know where she is at the moment.'

Something catches my eye and I glance up. There's a balcony with people in it hanging out over the court. At first I don't think I recognise any of them, then I see Carla and Mrs Franklin and Peasgood, and I feel a bit stronger than I did.

'How would you describe your home life, Sarah? Was it happy?'

I shrug. He looks at me, to remind me to speak up, so I grunt loudly.

174

'You and your mum and Jude, you all got on?'

'Most of the time.'

'Can you tell us about the defendant? What part did he play in your family life?'

I look at Borys. He's still leaning forward with his elbows on his knees and his grey eyes glued to me, but his face isn't telling me anything, I can't tell what he's thinking.

'Borys was Jude's boyfriend.'

'When did they start going out? Can you remember their first date?'

My head is spinning round and round. I've told my brain so often not to think about everything that happened that now it's like it just can't do it. Now when it hears the lawyer asking about Jude and Borys my brain just goes into overdrive in the opposite direction. If it spins fast enough it'll unscrew my head from my neck.

Everyone's watching me.

I shake my head. Which is quite hard when it's going round and round.

'Speak up,' the lawyer says in a jokey way, 'we need to hear what you have to say.'

I swallow.

'I can't remember,' I say.

'Alright, I'm going to suggest that they started seeing each other a year ago, and that Jude marked the beginning of their relationship by tattooing her upper arm.'

I remember the tattoo now. A rose on her shoulder, the first flower in a garden of flowers. Jude's really proud, so she makes me look at it as soon as she gets home, but it's all inflamed and red, and it makes me wince. I can't look at it.

'Yeah,' I say.

Now we've got through that question my head's slowing down a bit. It's still spinning, but I think it will stop in a little while. It's like I've crashed through a barrier. Now I'm inside the danger zone and I've got to take care.

'Where did the defendant live?'

'He was always around at ours.'

'Did you like Borys Kawolski?'

'He was alright,' I say. But it sounds insulting with him sitting there, so I add more. 'He was nice to me.'

'How was he nice to you?'

'He gave me sweets and cans of Coke, and stuff. He was funny.'

'So you knew him well. Well enough to know him when you saw him?'

'Of course. He practically lived with us.'

'Did your mum like Borys Kawolski?'

'Not much.'

'Why not?'

'Why not?' I repeat the question, because the question surprises me.

'Why didn't she like him?'

'She said he wasn't good enough for Jude. She didn't want him hanging around our flat.'

'Did your mum and Borys argue?'

I glance at Borys. His head is down, watching the floor.

'Sarah?' The lawyer's trying to get my attention.

'Yes?'

'Did they argue the night before your mum was killed?'

'Yes.'

'I'd like you to take your time, and to tell us about that argument.'

'It was just an argument.'

'How did it start?'

'My mum bought pizza for tea and Borys helped himself because he was there, and she got angry. She said there wasn't enough for him and he didn't live there so he should eat his tea somewhere else.'

'How did Borys respond?'

'He said Jude offered it to him and it was too late, but he could vomit it back up if she wanted.'

'Was that supposed to be funny?'

I think about that for a minute.

'Funny but not really funny.'

'Did he often speak to your mum like that?'

'Sometimes, if she had a go at him.'

'Had he been drinking?'

'I don't know. He didn't smell of it.'

'How did your mum respond?'

'She said, "Okay then, vomit it back up then get out of here."'

'But he didn't.'

'He didn't vomit, and he didn't get out. The two of them started to argue about everything, like why did he think he was good enough for Jude and that. My mum said he was trouble and she didn't want his trouble in her house and he said *she* was trouble too and she was the one should stay away from Jude.'

'Did he hit her?'

I glance at Borys but all I can see is the top of his shaved head. I shake my head.

'You shook your head, Sarah, does that mean no?'

'It means I don't want to talk about it.'

'Why not?'

I stare at the wall. I want to get out of here. I want to turn round and walk out.

'Do I have to answer the question?' I ask the judge.

'You do,' he says. 'It's a simple yes or no.'

'It's embarrassing!' I burst out.

'Sarah, did he hit her?'

I shake my head. Then I remember to say, 'No.'

He looks at me and waits. So in the end I say, 'The other way around. She hit him.'

'Your mum hit him? What did he think about that?'

'What would you think about that?'

'I'm afraid I ask the questions, Sarah, and you answer them.'

'It's embarrassing. He's a man and she's a woman.'

'So what did he do?'

'He said, "I've had enough of you." Then he left.'

'He said, "I've had enough of you?" Were those the exact words?'

'Well . . .' I hesitate, but the lawyer asked the question so he's only got himself to blame. 'He said, "I've had enough of you, you bitch." Then he left.'

'Do you know where he went?'

'No.'

'Where would he usually spend his time when he wasn't at yours?'

'There's a squat he stays at with some of his friends.'

'Did anything happen that evening or the next morning that was unusual or out of the ordinary?'

'I can't remember anything.'

'Well, Sarah, I'm afraid I'm going to have to ask you

now about the discovery of your mother's body. Are you up to that now?'

I don't answer right away because I'm worrying about my head again. It's stopped spinning but now it feels really light, like there's nothing inside it. I feel dizzy, like I might pass out, but I don't want to look like I'm making up reasons not to answer questions.

'Alright.'

'Do you remember the events of that day?'

'Yeah.'

'Can you tell the court how you spent that day?'

'I was at school.'

'If I'm not mistaken, that is Gelthorne School?'

'Yes.'

'What year are you in?'

'Year 9.'

'That is to say, you are thirteen years old, is that correct?'

'I was. I'm nearly fourteen now.'

'Was it a normal day at school?'

'It was boring.'

'Does that count as normal?'

'Yes.'

Someone laughs at that, and I glance up at the public gallery again. I don't understand why they're allowed in to watch this. It's not a show, you can't buy tickets.

'Did anything unusual occur?'

Borys definitely isn't laughing. He knows it's not a game. This time when I look at him I can see that he's really scared. I stare at him. I can't see him shaking or anything and he's so big that no one would think of him being scared, but he is.

179

'Sarah, I'll repeat the question. Did anything unusual occur?'

'No.'

'Were you in a good mood when you came home?'

'Not bad.'

How did you get home from school?'

'On my bike.'

'Ah,' the lawyer says. 'A very healthy mode of transport. And environmentally sound.'

I don't get it. Perhaps he's trying to be funny. He's giving me a little smile like he wants to cheer me up. I don't understand why anyone thinks I can be happy about any of this.

'What did you do with your bike once you got back to your estate?'

'I carried it up to the flat so no one would nick it.'

'Very sensible. Now, did you see anyone on your way up?'

'Before I got to Level 7 I saw Omar coming down,' I say.

'And Omar is?'

'He's a boy from my school.'

'Did you stop to speak to him?'

'He said he'd seen Borys at my flat.'

'How would he know that?'

'He must have seen him on his way down.'

'Did he say anything else about Borys or your flat?'

'No.'

'And after that encounter, you carried on up the stairs with your bike, you arrived at Level 8, and what did you see?'

'Borys,' I say.

'Where was he when you saw him?'

'Outside our door. Squatting down.'

'Was the door open or closed?'

'Closed.'

'What was he doing when you saw him?'

'He was putting something in his pack.'

'Did you see what it was?'

'No, he had his back to me. But I saw that he had the bag open, and was moving stuff around inside it.'

'Did you speak to him, call out to him?'

'No. I didn't want to talk to him.'

'Because of the row?'

'Yeah. I waited till he left, and then I went into the flat.'

'You got to Number 87, where you lived. Was the security grille padlocked?'

'No.' I shake my head. 'It was open.'

Out of the corner of my eye I can see Borys lift his head and stare at me.

'And what about the door?'

'That was locked.'

'And what did that arrangement tell you?'

'It told me someone was in.'

'By someone, you mean your mother?'

'Yeah,' I say, 'I mean my mother. Or Jude.'

'So you got your key out and you unlocked the door.'

I nod.

'When you got *in*side did you leave your bike *out*side?'

'No. I took it in. That's where I keep it so they can't steal it.'

'When you say "they", who do you mean? Who might steal it?'

'You know. Gangs . . .'

'Would you like a drink of water?' the judge asks.

I nod, and someone brings me a glass.

'Miss Carnaby, would you like a short rest? We can break here . . .'

I don't want to stop now. If I stop, I'll never start again.

'I didn't realise at first,' I say. 'I thought she was asleep. I got on with other things.'

'How did you discover she wasn't asleep?'

I don't answer.

'Did you go over to her?'

I sigh.

'Yeah, I went over to her.'

'Could you see her moving at all, or breathing?'

'No.'

'How did you find out she was dead?'

'I poked her shoulder, and when she wouldn't wake up, I tried to make her sit up, and her face kind of flipped over, and there was blood everywhere.'

I glance at Borys.

'What did you do?'

'She was dead. What could I do?'

'I mean, did you cry out, did you step away from her?'

I'm shaking.

I think my knees might give out.

I nod. I make a noise that sounds something like yes.

'She had her eyes open,' I say. 'I thought she was going to yell at me for waking her up.'

That shuts everyone up for a minute, even the lawyer, who looks at his papers before asking the next question.

'What did you do after you realised she was dead?'

'I can't remember.'

'You can't remember what you did after you found your mother dead?'

'I can't remember anything. I was in shock.'

'Can you describe that feeling?'

'It's like a blank. I don't remember anything.'

'And how long did the shock last? Was it just a few seconds, or a few minutes, or an hour?'

'I don't know. I wasn't looking at my watch. I was in shock. I think it must have been a long time. It's like time vanished.'

He nods and looks down at his papers, and I think he's ticking something off.

'There's a record of a call to the emergency services from that address. Was it you who called them?'

'Yes. Who else would it be?'

'What exactly did you tell the emergency services?'

'That . . . that she was dead.'

'What did they say to you?'

'They told me to wait, that someone would come and get me and Mum.'

'What did you do after calling the ambulance?'

'Nothing.'

'The emergency services came into the flat while you were there?'

'Yeah.'

'And the police?'

'Yeah.'

'Did they tell you she was dead?'

'I could see that already.'

'And they took her away?'

I'm staring at the wall. It's easier than looking at the piles of paper and all the lawyers in front of me.

'Sarah, I'm sorry, can you answer me, please? I asked you whether they took her body away.'

'Yeah,' I say softly.

'Well,' the judge says. 'We will end there for today. Miss Carnaby, be sure to have a good rest. Tomorrow will be a long day.'

Miss Malik says she's got a good way to get out of court without people seeing, so I follow her. I don't know where I am. All I know is that the Old Bailey feels like a prison, with guards all over the place and narrow corridors and dark staircases and bare waiting rooms. No one's supposed to feel at home here. So anyway, I just follow Miss Malik, and I'm walking down a corridor with her when I see Borys walking towards me. He's not on his own, obviously, he's got guards either side of him, and he's got handcuffs on. As soon as I see him I want to turn round and run the other way but it's too late, he's already seen me.

'Sarah,' Borys shouts, 'Sarah, tell me, is the baby born?'

Miss Malik grabs my wrist, but I stand there for a minute, because I don't know what to do.

'Sarah.' Borys is trying to get to me, but his guards are holding him back. 'Tell me, please, no one will tell me.'

But then his guards get the better of him, they manage to turn him around so now his back's to me.

'Yes, a week ago,' I shout out. Born and gone already I should say, but with Borys right in front of me, even Borys's back, I can't bring myself to say it. 'It's a boy.'

'He's a boy!' Borys shouts with joy as they drag him off. He calls to me, over his shoulder, 'Did you call him Ben?'

'Yes,' I shout back, but I'm crying now because he's so happy and because everything is so screwed up. I don't even know if his foster parents call him Ben.

'Tell Jude I love her.' Borys twists out of his handlers' grasp and turns back towards me for an instant. 'Tell her I did it for her.'

Miss Malik's pulling at my arm but I stand still staring after him.

'That shouldn't have happened,' she's moaning like it's my fault, 'you shouldn't have spoken to him.'

On the way out of court she's gabbling to me about how I mustn't listen to Borys, that he's trying to get my sympathy. But all I can hear in my head is, 'Tell her I did it for her.'

I'm coming out of the court into the fresh air when Omar comes up.

'They're using you,' he hisses at me.

I stare at him. I hardly know him, I'm thinking so hard about Borys.

'They're using you,' Omar hisses in my face.

'I'm just telling what happened,' I say.

'What you *think* happened,' he says, and then he looks round him like they do in spy movies, where there are microphones in people's hats, and pens and everywhere. He says, 'Borys was your friend.'

I'm not going to stand for that, not today. Not after he said he did it to my face. So I get angry really fast.

'What happened then, Omar? Tell me, was it aliens

killed my mum? What am I supposed to do? You saw him too, right outside our door with her dead inside.'

'How do you know I saw him?'

'Because you told me, you idiot,' I say.

Omar shakes his head.

'Sare, you know what I'm saying.' He looks miserable. 'You just don't want to think about it.'

'You know what?' I say to him. 'I've got loads of time to think now I'm locked up with a boring foster mother and her boring children. Thank you for that, Omar. Thank you very much.'

I see a flicker in Omar's eyes and I turn around. Linda is there, with the children. They look like people who've been standing in the same place for more than five seconds. Which means they heard every word I said.

'We came to take you home,' Linda says, really quiet.

In the car, no one says anything all the way back, except that the stupid kids whisper to each other and giggle. I close my eyes and try to ignore them.

When we get back to the house, I go to my room until it's time to eat. Donald knocks on my door and when I say come in, he opens the door part way and passes me a phone charger, which I thought he'd forgotten about. He waits for a minute while I check that it fits my phone, and it does, which is a relief because it's almost out of battery. Then, when he's gone, I take Jude's phone out my pocket and plug it in and a few minutes later it's come back to life, but then Linda calls me for tea.

I'm rude about the food because I'm embarrassed. I know that doesn't make sense. If I'm embarrassed, I should be trying to make up for what I said. But in my head, they shouldn't have snuck up on me like that when I was having a private conversation. In my head, it's their fault, they've got only themselves to blame; they shouldn't have been listening.

Also I'm in a hurry, because I want to get to Jude's phone, so I eat quickly and then Donald wants seconds and then Sam wants ice cream so it's all taking too long.

When we've all finished eating and I'm sitting there glowering at everyone, Linda tries to ask me how things went in court, but her heart's not in it. She's hurt by what I said, calling her boring. But she is, and her stupid children are, so I can't help it, and I just say nothing happened.

When I say I'm going to bed everyone's relieved, including me.

Actually, I'm not going to bed, I'm going to look at Jude's phone.

It's interesting, Jude's got no messages waiting for her. After my first call when she disappeared and then I realised she'd left her phone behind, there's nothing. No one trying to call her, no one trying to text her. I think about Jude's social life. After she met Borys, Jude slowed right down, she hardly ever went out. Since Mum was killed, she hasn't gone out at all. It's like us and Em have been hibernating. But then I think about her texting in between contractions and texting the night before she disappeared. So I go to Messages, then Sent Messages, but the settings on the phone are wrong, she doesn't save her sent messages, the folder's empty. I go to her Inbox and there's only one message, like she deleted all the rest.

I think about Keith Butcher going into our flat and searching for something. If he was looking for Jude's phone, did he know about this message? Was that why he wanted the phone? For one message? For two words?

I stare at the screen. I check the Sender but there's no name, it just says XXX like kisses or pornography.

There's a mobile number for XXX in Jude's contact list.

I take a deep breath and then I call it from Jude's phone.

It rings a long time and then someone picks up. It's a man, and I can hear a TV on in the background.

He doesn't say his name, he says, 'Who is this?'

He sounds wary and worried. Whoever he is, I don't think he's expecting anyone to call him from Jude's phone. That's why the first thing he wants to know is, who's got the phone. When I don't say anything, he says, 'Who is this?' again, more impatient this time.

I can't think of anything to say but the truth.

'I'm looking for my sister, Judith Carnaby.'

There's a long silence, except I can still hear the TV.

Then he says, 'I don't know who you're talking about. How did you get this number?'

And I say, 'It's on her phone.'

'You've got your sister's phone?' he asks quickly, like he's not thinking about what's coming out of his mouth.

'Yes,' I say.

Then there's another silence except for the TV.

And then he says, 'Well I don't know how my number got into the phone of someone I've never met. Has it got my name there too?'

And I say no, but I don't explain about the Xs.

And he says, 'Well it's obviously a mistake, so I don't see how I can help.'

And I say, 'You sent her a message saying you'd pick her up.'

And he says, 'You've got the wrong number. You're wasting my time. I don't know anyone by the name of Jude.'

And he hangs up.

I called her Judith and he called her Jude. He was worried that I've got her phone.

He knows her. And I kind of know him. I know his voice. I've heard it before, I just can't place it.

I get into my pyjamas and I lie down but I don't sleep for a long time.

Someone picked Jude up the night she disappeared. So does that mean she's safe, or she's in danger? Is he the man, the one I spoke to? Is he still with her? Why can't I remember where I've heard his voice before? Was she there with him when I called him? When he hung up, did he say to her, 'That was your sister,' and did she care even if he did? Why did she never tell me about him? And if he knows where she is, why won't he tell me? All these things go round and round and round in my head until I'm so dizzy and miserable that I can't tell one thought from another. And then I fall asleep.

THIRTEEN

Next morning, something's changed in court. I can feel it. It's in the way the lawyer looks at me. When he was questioning me, he was okay, he looked at me like I'm a human being. Now he's avoiding catching my eye. I tell myself not to worry, that he's nothing to me.

The lady lawyer isn't wearing a wig but her hair is like a helmet and she's big and fat.

'I'm going to take you back over the same period. Don't worry if it feels as though you're repeating yourself. We just need to be clear on one or two facts.'

She sounds friendly enough. I know it's her job to defend Borys, so she might try to say I'm wrong about seeing him. But I don't think she'll be able to do it. I'm just going to answer all her questions like I answered the other lawyer. Now I'm used to the court my head's not spinning any more. I feel more normal. It doesn't matter speaking about that day. I've said what I'm going to say. She just wants to hear it again.

'The court has heard about the unusual living arrangements at Number 87 Shepherd's Way.'

'What do you mean, unusual?' I say.

'I simply meant,' the lawyer says, 'the way you lived with your mother and your sister, and with the defendant, Borys.'

190

'Okay.'

'Can you remind us how many rooms there are in the flat at 87, Block A, Shepherd's Way?'

'There are two bedrooms, a lounge, and a little kitchen and bathroom.'

'Where did you all sleep?'

'My mum had one of the bedrooms. Jude and me and Em all slept in the other one.'

'And Borys?'

'He didn't live with us.'

'You said he did.'

I don't know what she's on about.

'What?' It comes out sounding stupid.

'My learned friend asked if you would recognise the defendant, and you answered yes of course, and I quote, "He practically lived with us."'

'I said he *practically* lived with us. I meant it was *like* he lived with us because he was round at our flat a lot.'

'Ah,' she says, like I've told a joke, 'so you said that the defendant *practically* lived with you, which might be taken as meaning that he lived with you for all practical purposes. But now you say you didn't mean that at all. In fact you meant it was *like* he lived with you?'

'Yes,' I say, but I know she's making fun of me.

'Please try to be more accurate when you're answering questions,' she says. 'Was there a room for the defendant and your sister, Judith?'

'No.'

'So where did he sleep when he "like" lived with you.' She makes quotation marks with her fingers around the word 'like', and the other lawyer – the one from yesterday

– rolls his eyes. I don't know if the jury see him roll his eyes, but it's almost like he does it on purpose so they'll see. I try to concentrate on what the lady lawyer said.

'Jude made me go away, or she told me to sleep in with my mum, or on the couch.'

'How did you feel about that?'

'I was alright with it.'

'Your sister's boyfriend tips you out of your own bed, and you expect us to believe that you're alright with it?'

'I'm not saying I liked it,' I say. 'But I liked it when Jude was happy, and she was always happy when Borys was around.'

'Ah,' the smarmy lady lawyer says. 'Borys made your sister happy, you say. How did he do that?'

I shrug. 'I suppose he liked to look after her, make sure she was alright. He used to mess around to cheer her up . . . he'd sing and dance, not that he was any good, he was terrible, but he made her laugh. And he was good with Em.'

'What did being good with Em entail? Can you describe their relationship?'

'He just played with her, so she was happy and she didn't go bothering Jude all the time.'

'So in fact Borys helped to care for Em. Perhaps he babysat sometimes?'

'Yeah.'

'Did he ever get angry with Em?'

'No.'

'You've told us your mum and Borys didn't get on. You've described one row. At the time of that row, had your mum been drinking?'

192

I don't feel like answering that.

'Well? You were happy enough to answer a question about whether my client, the defendant, had been drinking. Had your mother been drinking?'

'I don't know.'

'You said you couldn't smell drink on Borys, is that right?'

'Yeah, that's right.'

'Could you smell drink on your mother?'

'I can't remember.'

'You can remember that you couldn't smell drink on Borys, but you can't remember whether your mother smelt of drink?'

'Yeah, that's right.'

'Can I put it to you that you have a very selective memory?'

I stare at her.

'What does it matter what my memory's like?'

She sighs like she's frustrated.

'I'm afraid that the convention of the court is that I ask questions and you answer. The fact is that you don't like Borys, do you?'

'I just said I liked him.'

'You may have liked the sweets he gave you, but you didn't like being evicted from your own room, did you?'

'He never evicted me.'

The lawyer doesn't say anything for a minute. She just stands there drumming her fingers on the bench, like I'm so stupid she can't even think of another question to ask me.

'You say on the night of the row your mum hit Borys, is that correct?'

It's like she thinks I'm telling her lies.

It feels very hot in the court. I can feel myself sweating.

'Yeah. She hit him in the face, under his eye.'

'Did he hit her back?'

'No, I already said.'

'Had she hit him before?'

'She pushed him around a bit when she got fed up with him.'

'Did he ever push her back?'

'Not in front of me.'

'Did he ever hit Jude or push her?'

'Never. No.'

'Did he ever harm Em in any way?'

'He would never.'

'Did he ever hit you or push you?'

'No.'

When I've said that, she doesn't ask anything for a long time, like she's giving everyone time to think.

Then she asks, 'Did you ever see Borys hurt anyone?'

'I never saw him hurt anyone.'

'Did you ever see him hit out at anyone who challenged or confronted him?'

'No.'

'Or anyone who offended him?'

'No.'

I glance at Borys. He's watching his lawyer. I think she's really good. She's making it sound like butter wouldn't melt in his mouth. For the first time I think she might get him off. But he can't get off.

'. . . But then he killed her,' I burst out, 'so it doesn't matter that he was nice to me and nice to Em, he's still a murderer.'

'My lord!' the lawyer appeals to the judge, and the man lawyer jumps to his feet too, but the judge is already leaning down from his perch and reading me the riot act. I mustn't volunteer information. I must only answer the questions put to me. I must abide by the discipline of the court.

'But what I'm saying is a fact,' I interrupt him. 'She's the one who's talking about things that don't matter. The fact he gave me sweets and I never saw him hit anyone doesn't make him innocent. He's hurt someone before and gone to court for it . . .'

They all pile on top of me like a ton of bricks then, all jumping up and down and getting overexcited.

In the middle of all of it, I glance up at the public gallery, and I see Carla there. She's looking a bit worried, but she gives me a big smile and a little wave that nobody else sees.

The judge sends the jury out, and then he tells me off. He's saying – almost shouting – that any previous arrests Borys may or may not have are not, as yet, permitted to be discussed during this case. He may or may not consider at a later date submissions to place any further information as might be available before the jury, but as yet that has not happened.

'Well they know now,' I say.

Which makes the judge shout again, and when he's stopped shouting he sends everyone home for the day.

That night, two things happen. The first is I get in trouble at Linda's. It's teatime, and her kids are talking about school, and football and school trips.

'You can't go on your school trip,' Susan turns to me and says.

'Why can't she?' asks her little brother.

'Because she's on trial,' the girl says. 'You can't go on a school trip if you're on trial.'

'She's not on trial.' Linda starts speaking quickly. 'She's a witness, that's all . . .'

But something's happening to me. I'm half out of my chair, and I'm reaching out and swiping everything I can reach off the table. Plates, cups, pickle jars, they all fall onto the floor, with food everywhere, and some of them smash.

'I don't want to go on the stupid trip anyway,' I'm yelling, and Susan's bursting into tears, and Linda is shouting for everyone to calm down.

I stomp out the room, but Linda comes and gets me and tells me I'm cleaning up the floor and then I'm going to my room.

She looks tired and disappointed.

I hate myself for disappointing her.

That's the first thing that happens.

The second is, when I'm in my room as punishment after I've cleaned up the floor, I get a text.

It's nothing, just an address.

Number 35A Hibernia Place, Edinburgh EH3.

I stare at my phone. I don't recognise the number, but it has to be from Jude. It can't be from anyone else. Who's going to send me a random address?

My heart starts beating really fast. I'm so excited.

196

I text her back.

Jude is that u?

I wait. And I wait. But there's no reply.

Jude???

Nothing. I'm desperate.

I call the number. If she answers, I'll whisper. I don't want anyone in the house to hear me on the phone to Jude.

The phone . . . *Her* phone is switched off.

There's a knock at the door, then Linda's voice.

'Sarah love, can I come in for a chat?'

'No,' I call out, 'I want to go to sleep.'

I can hear her standing at the door, waiting, and then after a while she goes away.

All night I'm texting Jude and I'm calling her number. She has to switch it back on sometime, and when she does, I'll be there.

But by four in the morning her phone's still dead and my phone falls out of my hand onto the pillow and I fall asleep.

FOURTEEN

Next morning I'm back in court but I don't care any more. I know where Jude is – or I think I do – and that's all that matters. As soon as the trial's over I can go and find her and we'll be together. I don't need to spend any more time at Linda's. Bocock and Peasgood will never be able to find me . . .

'You have said that you carry your bike up the stairs to the flat each day to make sure it's not stolen by gangs.'

'Yeah.'

'There is substantial criminal activity at Shepherd's Way.'

I don't say anything. It sounds like she's stating a fact. I glance up at the public gallery. Carla's there again. I feel surprised and pleased.

'Well, is there substantial criminal activity at Shepherd's Way? It's a simple question.'

She's doing it to make me look stupid, asking a question that's not a question.

'There wasn't crime when Shepherd's Way was full of people, but once they started moving people out the gangs took it over and started treating it like their property.'

'Thank you,' she says, 'I'll take that as a yes. And do these gangs go around armed with knives?'

'Go around where?'

'Generally speaking, do they arm themselves with knives? That is the question.'

'I don't know, I don't ask them. Why would I ask someone if he's got a knife?'

'From the time that you entered your building to the point when you reached your front door with your bike, who did you see?'

'I saw Omar on the stairs between Level 6 and 7. He was coming down, I was going up.'

'Did you speak to each other?'

'Yeah. He told me he'd just seen Borys at my house.'

'Did he actually say that?'

'He said he could see the future – he's always reading minds and predicting the future – and he said Borys was in my flat.'

'So it was a joke.'

I shrug. 'It was a joke, but he'd definitely seen Borys because then I saw him.'

'You're assuming that Omar saw Borys, but he may not have. It may have been a joke, pure and simple.'

'It's obvious,' I say. 'Otherwise it wouldn't be a joke. If he hadn't seen him, he wouldn't say it, would he?'

The lady lawyer pretends like she's really tired and fed up with me. She sighs.

'That's your assumption, you have no proof that he saw Borys, have you?'

And I say, 'No.'

'And Omar goes on down the stairs?'

'Yeah.'

'And you go on up.'

'Yeah.'

'Was there anything unusual about Omar's appearance?'

'Why should there be?'

'Was there anything unusual?'

'No.'

'And was it normal to see him around that time on the stairs?'

'Yeah.'

'You don't know where he was coming from, do you?'

'His flat's on Level 9.'

'But you don't know that's where he was coming from, do you?'

'I don't know, no, because I don't have eyes that can see where someone's been . . . What are you saying?'

'I'm not saying anything,' the lawyer says. 'The court will decide for itself whether the police have explored every avenue open to them. To get back to that day. You proceeded to Level 8. You claim that at Level 8, as you reached the walkway, you saw Borys.'

'Outside my door.'

'Can you describe for me the lighting situation in the stairwell?'

'There isn't any lighting situation.'

'So it's dark.'

'Not all the time.'

'Please try to be more helpful. When you say it's not dark all the time, exactly how much light is there in the stairwell?'

'It depends. On a sunny day daylight gets in there, on a dark day it doesn't really.'

'And that day?'

'Dark.'

'Well,' she sighs, 'and after all that, it's dark. I put it to you that coming out of a dark stairwell into the open-air walkway, you would not be able to identify Borys from the back with any level of certainty.'

'That's wrong,' I say. 'I could see him. I know Borys.'

'From the back? In bad light, and at a distance of almost twenty-five metres? I think you made it up.'

'What?'

'You may have seen someone, you may not. I think you're accusing him because you don't like him.'

Everything explodes inside me.

'I'm not a liar!' I'm shouting. 'I saw him.'

'Oh I think you are lying,' she says, raising her voice. 'I think you don't like Borys, and you don't know who did this to your mother, and you are blaming him because you can.'

'My lord,' the man lawyer has got to his feet. 'My lord, the girl is thirteen years old. This questioning is quite inappropriate for a child.'

'My lord,' the woman interrupts whatever the judge was about to say. 'My lord, I am questioning a child who is apparently quite prepared to convict an innocent young man of murder! Is my learned friend suggesting I should let her get away with it?'

Then all of a sudden there's another voice protesting from the public gallery. I look up. Everyone looks up. And there's Carla standing up and jabbing her finger towards the woman lawyer.

'She's twisting everything Sarah says! My lord, why don't you stop her?'

The judge stares at her in disbelief, and the lawyers smile, and one of them laughs.

I'm gazing up at her, and I'm embarrassed but I'm also pleased. No one's ever stood up for me before, like literally stood up like Carla's doing.

The judge is calling for the clerks to throw Carla out, but they're already on the job, coming towards her, closing in on her, but she carries on with her speech: 'I thought her job was to get the truth, but all she's doing is confusing Sarah . . .'

You can see them thinking twice before they lay a hand on her because she's such a size. But she knows when her time's up. She gives me a little wave, shouts, 'You stand up for yourself, Sare!' and then she waves her arms to clear the clerks out of her way, and leaves the gallery.

When she goes, there's a bit of laughing, but the judge shuts everyone up. He's really annoyed.

'Miss Blunt,' the judge says when everything's calmed down. 'I know where you are going, and I will permit the line of questioning, but no more of this innuendo and speculation.'

The lady lawyer mutters, 'Of course, my lord, of course.' Then she turns back to me.

'I want to turn now to the period after you found your mother dead on the couch. Can you tell us why you were trying to wake your mother?'

I don't mind this question, I've answered it so many times.

'I wanted to talk to her.'

'What did you want to talk to her about?'

'I was hungry.'

'And was your mother going to cook for you? Was that why you were trying to wake her?'

I stare at her. Then I think I want to speak to the judge.

'Why's she asking me that? She knows my mum wasn't going to cook.'

'Does she?' he answers. 'She doesn't know until you tell her.'

'Yes she does.' I can't let it go. 'She's asking to make fun of my mum.'

Nobody says anything for a minute. Then the judge says, 'Miss Blunt, let's move on.'

'Very well,' she says. 'I'll rephrase that. Were you going to tell your mother you were hungry?'

'I was going to ask her for money to buy chips.'

'You were going to ask her for money to buy chips,' the lawyer repeats it, like it's significant. Then she asks, 'You didn't have any money of your own?'

'No.'

'No pocket money?'

'No.'

'No money saved in a money box?'

I turn to the judge. 'She's making fun of me again.'

I wish Carla was still here. She'd stand up for me. Literally. She'd stand up and shout for me.

'Miss Blunt,' he says. 'The girl is both sensitive and sharp. I suggest that you step carefully. This is not the time or place for teasing.'

'I can assure you, my lord,' she says, 'that you'll see from what I am about to say that I certainly do not intend to make fun of anyone or anything concerned in this quite terrible situation. This has nothing to do with fun.'

'Quite,' he says, like he doesn't believe it. 'Well, get on with it.'

Then she looks hard at the jury, and then at the man lawyer, as if they should really listen to what she's about to say.

'The call to the emergency services came at 6.17 p.m.,' she says. Which doesn't sound like a question to me. But then she adds, 'What time do you get out of school?'

'Three-thirty.'

'And how long does it take you cycle home?'

'Depends.'

'Roughly speaking?'

'Thirty minutes, forty-five minutes?'

'So you reached Shepherd's Way, let us say, at four-fifteen at the latest.'

'I don't know. I didn't look at the time.'

'But unless anything unusual happened, it can't have been much later.'

'Alright.'

'Let's allow a few minutes for you to wheel your bike up the stairs . . .'

'It's a hundred and sixty-eight steps,' I say, interrupting her, because this is a question I know how to answer, 'and it's more like carrying my bike, not wheeling it, it takes a long time.'

'I see. Well, even if it took you fifteen minutes, which seems a generous estimate, you would be home by four-thirty. Your mother is dead inside. But you don't call the emergency services until almost two hours later. I find that hard to understand.'

'I told you already. I tidied up.'

'Ah yes. You tidied up. Can you tell us exactly what your tidying consisted of?'

'I threw out the rubbish. I did the washing up. I washed my uniform . . .'

'We've all had experience of teenagers tidying up. It's not an hour's worth of work, is it? It never is. Let alone two . . . So . . . you got hungry.'

I shrug. Everyone gets hungry. She can't tell me off for that.

'Sarah, I'm asking you, did you get hungry?'

'Yeah. It's not a crime.'

'You tried to wake your mother up.'

'I told you that already.'

'You discovered she was dead.'

'Like I told you.'

'And when you discovered she was dead, you went through her pockets for cash.'

'No!' I'm staring at her. What's she saying? 'I told him.' I'm pointing at the man lawyer now, and I'm shouting at her. 'I was in shock. I didn't do anything like you're saying. I was in shock. That's why it took so long. Wouldn't you be in shock if your mother was murdered?'

'You picked up her bag, you rummaged through it. You stole anything of value.'

'No! It wasn't like that.'

'You put your hands into your dead mother's pockets, and you pulled out her money and you stuffed it in your own pockets . . . you took her jewellery off her dead body.'

'No!' I shout. 'No, no no!'

I'm clutching my ears.

205

The man lawyer's jumping up and down now, and the judge is talking to the lawyers.

'Enough,' he's saying angrily to her. 'Enough. I need to talk to you both.'

He tells me to sit down.

Someone touches my arm and guides me to a chair. Someone puts a cup of water in my hand and tells me to drink.

My hands are shaking too much. I spill the water, and it soaks through my school skirt and onto my legs.

The judge sends the jury out.

He tells me to go back to the waiting room until he calls me back in. He needs to talk to the lawyers.

They take me to the waiting room, but I can't sit down.

I can't believe she can do this to me.

I can't listen to my music.

I can't close my eyes because of the things I see.

They call me back in. I turn to Miss Malik.

'I want to go home,' I tell her.

'I'm sorry,' she says, 'I expect they still need to ask you some questions.'

'But I've said everything.' I'm nearly crying.

'I know it doesn't feel very nice,' Miss Malik says. But she says it like she thinks perhaps I deserve it.

'She said I'm a liar and she said I robbed my mum, and I told her that's a lie. There's nothing more to say. Can she keep saying I did those things?'

'I don't know what they're going to ask you,' Miss Malik says.

'Is she even allowed to keep asking me questions like that? Isn't that just bullying?'

She tries to pat my arm, but I push her hand away a bit roughly, and her face goes hard.

'Come on,' she says. 'They're waiting for us.'

When I climb the steps back into the witness box my heart feels like lead. The lady lawyer's waiting for me.

The judge tells me that I can ask for a break any time. I can ask him any time if I think the question is inappropriate.

I speak to the judge, trying to sound sensible.

'I've already told her everything,' I say. 'Is she allowed to keep accusing me of things I didn't do?'

For a moment he stares at me over the top of his glasses.

'She may continue to question you, so long as I feel the questions are appropriate,' he says. 'Just tell the truth clearly and simply. Now, the defence and I have agreed to allow the prosecution to introduce new evidence. Unfortunately we haven't had time to examine this material as fully as we would wish, but I don't want you to have to come back here again, Miss Carnaby, so let's get it dealt with now. Go ahead, Miss Blunt.'

The lady lawyer stands up and says she hopes I'm feeling calmer now, which I ignore.

'I'd like you to watch something on the screen in front of you,' she says.

Which isn't what I was expecting.

There's a screen set up just in front of me. It wasn't there before, but it's there now.

'Okay,' I say. I'm relieved that it's not a question. I just have to watch something.

When the picture comes on the screen I don't recognise it at first. It's indoors, the lighting situation is gloomy, and it's like I'm looking down. People are moving around slowly, up and down a corridor, up and down the staircase. I can just see some shop fronts at the edge of the corridor, which is when I realise I'm looking at CCTV footage of the Egleton Shopping Centre.

There's a date and time stamp in the bottom right-hand corner of the film. 20th November, 17:32.

Which is when my heart basically stops beating.

The picture is focused on the base of the staircase, where there's a stall. I know already what's written on it.

Pounds for Gold.

A figure approaches the stall. She's not very big compared to the women around her, and she's wearing jeans with a hoody, the same hoody I'm wearing over my school uniform in the witness box. I know the girl's head has flown off. She's about to do something she would only do with no head, because if she had a head then her head wouldn't let her do it. I know her feet aren't touching the ground. She's pedalling thin air.

I can see her face.

If you wanted to see, like, a single freckle, then the picture's not clear enough.

But if you want to see if it's Sarah then it looks like her.

She stops in front of the stall and she talks to the man who's sitting there looking bored like he doesn't get many customers. There's no soundtrack, so nobody but me can hear what they're saying and I can only hear because it's in my head.

Nobody needs to hear a single word.

The girl unzips a pocket in her hoody and reaches inside it, then she raises her hand – it's clasped tight like a fist – and she opens up her fist and lets something fall on the table.

The man peers at it and he picks it up, dangling it from his fingers. Whatever it is, it's small. Too small for the CCTV camera to pick up anything except a little glint.

But I know what it is.

He puts it on a scale and he says something to the girl and she says something back.

Something's going wrong. She's angry and he's shaking his head. He takes the thing off the scale and throws it back onto the table in front of her. She snatches the thing back off the table, stuffs it in her pocket, and turns around.

She walks towards the camera, and as she gets closer her face gets clearer. The girl who looks like Sarah is definitely Sarah.

The moment she's out of the frame the screen goes blank.

I look down at my hands. I'm clutching the wooden barrier in front of me. My fingers are white because I'm clutching it so hard. My head's still on my neck. I think it's still there because you can't watch yourself on film with no head at the same time as your head's flying off. It's just too many heads flying around. Somewhere a head has to stay in the right place.

'As a word of explanation,' says the lady lawyer, 'this particular CCTV camera, which is placed inside Egleton Shopping Centre, is situated above the entrance to the Sunshine Café. Therefore, the girl we saw in that footage, who has apparently just offered an item for sale to a gold dealer, is walking toward the door of the café as this piece of footage ends. We cannot be sure, of course, that she did not turn away just before she reached the door. Now, Sarah, can you tell me who that girl was in those pictures?'

I shake my head.

'Sarah?'

I shake my head again.

'Very well, let me put it to you that it is you. The film, as you'll have seen, was shot at around 5.30 p.m. on the day of your mother's murder. According to your own account, you had already found your mother dead at this point. This girl goes to the shopping mall, tries to sell a piece of jewellery, and then walks towards the café at a time when you have said you were in your flat in shock, staring at your mother's dead body for nearly two hours.'

I can't think of anything to say at first. I'm paralysed. Then I manage to fight back a bit.

'Perhaps the date is wrong on the film. I think I remember doing that on a different day.'

'That is always possible,' she says. ' Later in the trial, we will be talking to witnesses from the security firm hired by Egleton Shopping Centre who can clarify for us whether the date and time were set accurately on the film. Meanwhile, I wonder if you can enlighten the court as to the nature of the item the girl offered to the gold dealer in the Egleton Shopping Centre just minutes after your mother was murdered.'

I stare at her.

'Your mother has just been stabbed to death,' she says. 'She's all alone in the flat, isn't she? You've gone out to the mall with pockets full of cash and jewellery stolen from your mother.'

'No! It's not true!'

'Later, we will interview the man buying gold that day. He will identify the girl who approached him. He will describe to us the item she wanted to sell, and he will tell the court that he would have bought it if the girl had been able to produce ID that showed she was over eighteen. He remembers the girl protesting. She didn't know about the age requirement. When he refused to take the item she was disappointed and angry, as we observed on the footage.'

I'm staring at her. I don't understand how she even started looking for this film. I don't understand how she knows all this. I look at the man lawyer, but he's got his head down. He's avoiding my eyes, he doesn't want to help me. He's cutting me off. I'm no use to him any more. Then I remember Millie on all fours in her flat, after I broke her ornament, looking up at me and saying, 'I saw you.' Millie who spends half her life eating chicken wings in the Sunshine Café. It's like she's smiling at me. Like she's saying I told you so, I told you I'd get you back.

'Sarah,' the lawyer says, 'would you like me to tell you what the item was? According to the best recollection of the Pounds for Gold representative, it was a gold heart-shaped pendant.'

I'm shaking my head really fast. My whole body's shaking, not just my knees, everything from my toes to my eyeballs. Not this. She can't know this too.

'It's your mother's pendant, isn't it?'

My head snaps up. This is why my head didn't spin off. My brain's got work to do.

'You're right, it's my mum's,' I croak.

The whole room is shocked. No one moves. The lady lawyer loves it. She loves the silence. She lets it go on for ages. Then she says, 'Thank you for your honesty, Sarah. Now, can you tell me how you came by the pendant that afternoon?'

I don't want to say it. I feel like I'm going to be sick.

'I took it off her neck,' I say loudly. 'When she was dead. She didn't need it, so I took it. I thought I could get cash for it.'

There is a gasp that slices my head away from my body. It goes spinning off across the courtroom.

Someone's tipping a vat of shame into the open veins where my head was.

I'm choking with humiliation.

That's all I remember.

FIFTEEN

It's a week since the lady lawyer humiliated me in front of everyone in court. I'll never forgive her for what she did. It's also my fourteenth birthday. Jude and Sheena are the only ones who ever remember my birthday, so it's not as though I've got high expectations. This year, I don't want anyone to remember. There's nothing to celebrate. Getting born was a big mistake.

Linda and Donald keep on pretending that everything's alright. Linda keeps saying, 'Don't worry, love, it'll all be over soon, it'll be alright.' But after what happened in court, nothing can ever be alright again. So when Linda gets them all to sing 'Happy Birthday to You' at breakfast, I just want the kitchen floor to open up and swallow me. She hands out chocolate muffins for breakfast with candles on top, and I only eat a bit of mine because I've got no appetite since the trial. Then Linda gives me an envelope, and I have to open it, because what else can I do, and inside there's a passport.

'Thank you,' I say, but what I'm thinking is, 'What good is this to me?'

Then Linda says, 'Look in the card,' and I look in the card, and it says, 'Congratulations, you're going to Paris! Happy Birthday!' and it's like a knife in my heart.

'Mrs Franklin got funding,' I whisper, and Linda shakes her head and says no, it's a birthday present. She and Donald have gone halves with Mrs Franklin to pay for it. I look at them and I don't know what to say, because I'm not going to Paris. It's my birthday, and I'm running away to Scotland.

I stuff my clothes into the bag Linda bought me for the Paris trip. I roll up my second best pair of jeans and shove until they go in the bag and then I zip it up. Linda didn't let me choose the bag, she got it one of the days I was in court, so it's pink and shiny, and now it's full of clothes it looks like a shiny pink slug. I sit back on my heels. I came here with nothing and now I've got so much stuff it won't fit in the bag.

My school books are in a mess on the floor. I'm not taking them with me. A school can't help me. Nothing in those books can help me.

'Sarah love,' Linda calls up the stairs, pretending everything's alright, 'do you want to come down for a cup of tea?'

'I'm going to bed,' I shout down the stairs.

But I don't go to bed, I just sit there.

The room feels empty with all my stuff cleared up. There's the books between the bookends still on the windowsill – I haven't read one of them. There's the *High School Musical* poster on the wall and the poster with the poem on it.

Whether or not it is clear to you,
No doubt the universe is unfolding as it should.

I go up to the poster and I rip it off the wall and then I rip it into tiny bits and put it in the bin. I don't want to make a mess.

I check I haven't left anything out of my bag except my scissors, which I need.

I've made my bed, so it looks really nice with its matching duvet and pillowcases. I know Linda will strip them all off to clear the room for someone else. So I don't know why I made the bed.

I think about Linda walking into the room and seeing it empty, and knowing I've gone.

She'll be pleased.

No one could want me in their house.

There's so much poison in me. I look like a fourteen-year-old girl but I can poison your whole house. I can poison your family. Your lovely children throwing frisbee to each other in the garden, they'll be infected too. They'll start to lie and steal. They'll wish their parents were dead so they could have their stuff. It's good that I'm sitting here in the room on my own. I can't infect anyone that way.

I feel cold.

I pull on my hoody. I pat the pocket. I've got everything I need, even my passport.

I sit down and wait.

When I've gone, Linda will look to see if I've nicked anything.

I feel so cold.

I look at my watch.

It's not time yet. Not for hours. But I've said I'm going to bed, so I turn the light out or Linda will come in and see me all packed and ready to go.

In the dark I hunch my shoulders against the cold and huddle on the bed, and I wait.

I can tell them all by their footsteps.

Susan and Sam go to their rooms first, bickering all the way. They clatter around the bathroom, running water and flushing the toilet. They always leave the towels on the floor.

An hour later, Donald heaves himself upstairs, the floorboards creaking under his weight. He breathes heavily.

A few minutes later, Linda walks upstairs, and after she closes the door to their room I don't hear anything else.

I wait a really long time until the house is so quiet you can almost hear them snoring. Then I pad across the landing to the bathroom. I pee because I've been waiting so long. Then I open the bathroom cabinet. Linda's blonde hair dye is there.

But first I cut. I just want it different, so people don't recognise me. I try cutting about three inches off, but my hands are shaking so much that I cut a really jagged line, and when I try to cut it straight it gets shorter and more jagged. My hands shake even more. And I try again, and it's even worse this time.

I start to cry. I throw the scissors on the floor. I look ridiculous.

I tear open the hair dye box, and I'm too worked up to read the instructions, I just mix it all together, and spread it all over my hair until I've got a mound of guck on my head that looks like it came from the sewers.

I start to cry again when I see myself like that in the mirror.

I know I have to wait, but I didn't look at the time when I started, and I've got no way of telling how long it's been on my head. So I wait, and then I wait some more, and more.

Then I stick my head under the water, and I rinse and rinse, until the water runs clear. Then I rub my hair in a towel, and I lift my head and rub my eyes and look in the mirror.

I stare.

My hair's white with sick-looking yellow streaks.

I want to scream, but I've got to stay quiet or they'll wake up. Sobbing, I sink to the floor. I'm surrounded by chunks of hair. My old hair, dark and shiny. What have I done? I'm poison, and I'm a thief, and I'm stupid.

Eventually, I stand up and look in the mirror again. It's as bad as it was the first time, even though my hair's almost dry. For someone who's trying to be inconspicuous, I've just done the opposite. I brush it back from my face and gather it in a ponytail, which I never do in real life.

Then I open the bathroom door, pad back across the landing, pick up my bag and put it over my shoulder.

I open the door to my bedroom, and creep downstairs. There's a light on on the landing, but downstairs it's dark. That's where Linda always leaves her bag. I fumble around for it. I'm not sure it's going to be there. I thought maybe she'd be more careful now she knows about me. Someone like me, I'll steal from my own mother's dead body . . . My hands are shaky, but I can feel the leather.

The bag is where it always is, on the hall table.

I unzip it and stick my hand in, feeling for her wallet. I get hold of it and pull it out, and feel for what's inside it,

217

running my fingers over the shape of things. There are endless cards, but without the pin numbers they're no good to me and besides, it's a lot of trouble for Linda to cancel them and get new ones. Then I feel the long sharp edge of a banknote, and there's a few of them. I can't see the numbers on them in the dark, so I pull them all out and stuff them in the pocket in my hoody. Then I put the wallet back on the table. There's no point in trying to cover up, or wipe off my fingerprints or anything, she'll know it's me.

I reach out to the front door, and as quietly as I can I pull back the bolt and unlock it.

But there's a noise behind me.

I spin around. Linda's at the top of the stairs.

She's peering down, ugly and old-looking, blinking in the light with her hair all roughed up and a baggy nightdress. I have an urge to run to her and throw myself into her arms, which isn't what I expected. I'm running away from her.

'Sarah?' She says my name like an idiot, like she can't believe it's me, when it's obvious.

Really slowly, she looks down at her bag on the hall table, and really slowly she looks back at me, and she's frowning like she still doesn't understand.

I don't want her to look at me.

I pull open the door and I run.

I can hear her behind me shouting, 'Sarah! Sarah! Come back!'

But I keep on running.

I've got a long way to go.

SIXTEEN

Just in case anyone's looking for me, I try to throw them off my track. I catch a night bus, then another night bus in the opposite direction. When I'm the only one on board except for a drunk who's fast asleep, I pull Linda's money from my pocket and I count it. I've got twenty-five pounds, which will get me where I want to go. But when I get to Victoria coach station it's still too early for the first coach. I buy my ticket, feeding Linda's notes into a machine. It costs me nineteen pounds. But then I don't dare sit down and wait in case someone spots me. So I walk around the streets instead. The shops are really posh. There's one that's all hats and they all look like a joke, like out of *Alice in Wonderland*, and I'm guessing the price tag's a joke too.

I catch sight of myself in the window and I want to die because I look like I feel, which is like a stray animal.

So then I don't look in the windows any more.

I feel for my ticket in my zip-up pocket and I can't find it, and I stand in the street pulling everything out of my pockets. Then I crouch down and pull everything out of my bag in the street like a crazy beggar or something, because I can't afford another ticket if I've lost it.

I find it in my pocket after all, where it always was.

219

I'm standing there with all my stuff around my feet when a really posh lady walks past me and goes up to the door of the hat shop and turns a key in the lock. She turns around and looks at me down her nose.

'Can you move on?' she says. 'I'll call the police if you stay here.' Then she turns away from me, and opens the door to the shop and goes inside.

I want to throw something through the window of her shop, but I haven't got anything heavy enough or hard enough. My pink-slug bag would just bash into the window and slide down to the ground. So I just move on, like she told me.

Near the coach station there's a newsstand. There's a picture of Zoe on the front pages again. I stand and read. Police have taken a man in for questioning. He's suspected of killing her. He's a drug dealer who lives in Shepherd's Way, a supplier to local kids. I think of the lawyer telling me Jude used to inject heroin. I think of the blue marks on her arms that I saw in hospital, and I wonder if this is the link between them.

When the driver calls for passengers for Edinburgh I get onto the coach and find a seat at the back. I keep my head down. I put my bag down next to me, because I don't want anyone to sit there, but I needn't have worried because there's almost no one on the bus.

It's when the coach pulls out the station that I see there's loads of messages on my phone.

Where are you, love?

Come home, Sarah, there's nothing to worry about

Are you alright?

Just let us know you're safe

Call us

We're worrying about you

I scroll down.

Endless Linda.

For a minute I want to stop the coach and get off.

Then I think that probably the police told Linda to pretend she wants me to come back, and then how could she say no, I don't want to do that in case Sarah really does come back? She couldn't. So she had to send the texts.

Then I turn my phone off, because maybe they can track me. I'll get a new simcard when I get where I'm going. When I think of the word *new*, like *new simcard*, I feel strange. It's a shivery strange, like being scared, but not bad like being scared. Like there's a tiny bit of me inside that thinks a new simcard will be like a new life. Which of course it won't, it will just be a new simcard.

I stare out of the window and count the newsstands until I fall asleep.

When I wake up there's an old man standing in the aisle. He's looking a bit pissed off and he's gesturing at me to move my bag, like he can't just open his mouth and talk to me. I give him a look, but he doesn't move away, so I move my bag off the seat and put it in front of my feet.

I don't want to talk to strangers. They'll ask me questions and then I'll have to lie. You'd have thought he'd have got the idea from my bag on the seat that I don't want to talk but no, he's hardly belted himself in when he asks me where I'm going.

'Edinburgh,' I say, hoping one word's enough to shut him up.

'All on your own?' he says. 'Forgive me, but you seem very young to travel so far without your parents.'

'I always travel on my own,' I say.

'Is that so? Are you going to visit friends?'

'I'm going to live with my sister,' I say, because actually I don't have to lie about that. 'She's got a flat there, and a job, and a little girl, and I'm going to live with her and go to school there.'

'I see,' he says. 'I'm going to visit my sister too, but I'm not going as far as you are.'

Then he doesn't say anything else and I put in my earphones to show I don't want to talk. I listen to my music and I can feel all the bits of me relaxing. I've been so worried for weeks now, worried about Jude, and about baby Ben, and worried about the trial, worried about running away from Linda's. There's been nothing but worry. Being on the coach I like the way the engine purrs, it's really soothing. I like the way the world moves past me through the window. I don't have to do anything, I don't have to fight anyone or argue about anything, it all just flows past me. It's raining, and I like that too, because I've been feeling like things are too hot, like I'm burning up, and now the rain is cooling everything down so I can rest. I don't have to answer stupid questions from the stupid lady lawyer and I don't have to remember the thing that happened to Mum and I don't have to think about the things I did.

'What does your sister do in Edinburgh?' The old man's talking to me again, which is really irritating because I have to start talking, so I can't rest. I pull out my earphones.

'She's got a job,' I say again, and then I know what his next question will be. 'She's a hairdresser.'

I'm making it up. Jude's never mentioned a job. She's never said a word except for an address. But she's got to have a job or how's she coping? And she had a Saturday job for a while sweeping the floor in a hairdresser's, so she's got the experience. So when I say she's got a job in a hairdresser's, I'm guessing but I'm not lying. Not at first, anyway. Then he keeps asking questions, so I've got no choice but to lie.

'It's in a lovely salon in the city centre, all the rich people go there to get their hair cut,' I end up saying. 'And she gets loads of really amazing tips, so she's got a flat like a penthouse, all modern. She sent me a photo of the kitchen, it's all marble and glass.'

'Well,' he says, 'that sounds delightful.'

'Her little girl Em goes to a nursery while she's at work, with good facilities and that. And there's a really good school with nice girls, and that's where I'm going.'

'Well,' he says again, like he's impressed, 'the two of you really do have everything worked out, don't you?'

'Yeah,' I say, and I realise I'm smiling, because for the first time I think it could be like that. It could really be like that. We could live together in a really nice flat and work things out and Jude can get a job and I'll go to school, and when it's all working we can show Bocock, and maybe they'll let Jude have Ben back. And for a millisecond I start to feel light, like all my troubles have flown off my shoulders up into the air and vanished.

He's got a newspaper folded on his lap, and I can see a headline that says, 'Teenager Takes Stand Accused of Stabbing Death'. I don't want to see it, but I have to. I try to read what it says on his lap, but his arm's across it, so I can't see it clearly.

'Can I borrow your paper?' I ask him, and he hands it to me.

Nineteen-year-old defendant, Borys Kawolski, gave evidence yesterday at the Old Bailey to answer charges that he stabbed Dianne Carnaby to death in November last year.

Kawolski, who has pleaded not guilty to murder, told Anji Blunt QC, appearing for the defence, that he had been with friends in a squat when the murder took place. Cross-examined by Michael Zakari QC, appearing for the prosecution, Kawolski denied that he had gone that afternoon to the flat where Carnaby's body was discovered by her thirteen-year-old daughter.

Kawolski denies being at Number 87, Shepherd's Way, where the murder took place. He also denies all knowledge of a knife, found in an alley just yards from the squat where he resides with friends. This knife, the prosecution alleges, is the murder weapon. Fingerprints and DNA evidence have been found on the knife.

During cross-examination, Michael Zakari QC asked Mr Kawolski about a letter he sent from prison to his former girlfriend, Judith Carnaby, the daughter of Dianne Carnaby. For the prosecution, Zakari quoted the letter, in which Kawolski wrote: 'Now you are free I do not care what happens to me, only care about you and our baby. I do not regret.'

Questioned by the prosecution about the letter, Kawolski said, 'I didn't mean anything by it.'

'Are you following the case?' the old man says.

I give him a sharp look but he's just making conversation.

'A bit,' I say. 'Do you think he did it?'

'Perhaps he did,' he says, 'but whatever else he does, I rather think the judge should put the teenage daughter behind bars. She's a cold-blooded little thief, she's said as much herself. If she can steal from her own dead mother's body, who's to say it wasn't her who stuck the knife into her? She had plenty of time, she can't account for her own movements. There are hours unaccounted for, hours!'

I don't know what to say. This man suspects I might have killed my own mother, and it's my own fault because of what I said in court. I can't say anything to him. I can't even sit next to him.

I grab my bag from in front of my feet and I stand up, pushing past him.

'What's the matter?' he's asking. He's all flustered. But I ignore him. I go further back down the coach and find a double seat that's got no one on it and I sit down and I put my slug bag on the seat next to me. I pull my hoody around me so I don't feel so cold. I turn my head against the window and close my eyes.

I don't want to talk to anyone again for my whole life.

The coach journey lasts forever.

SEVENTEEN

It must be summer in Edinburgh too but it's really cold. I haven't eaten anything for hours and I don't know where I'm going. So when I get off the coach I go to McDonald's and spend 99p on a burger and 99p on a Coke. Then while I'm eating it I go and ask the bus drivers where to find where Jude lives, and then I find out it's really close and I can walk there.

I don't know what the equivalent of Shepherd's Way looks like in Scotland. Maybe it's got tattered tartan curtains at the broken windows and drunks clutching bottles of Scotch. But the roads I'm walking down don't look anything like that. On both sides of me are tall grand houses. I can just see into some of the rooms, and they're as big as waiting rooms or classrooms, but you can tell people live there because there are paintings on the walls and thick curtains that swoop in curves or hang in great big bunches.

Even when I get to Hibernia Place it's still so grand, and I'm beginning to worry.

What if someone sent me that address by mistake?

What if it wasn't Jude?

What if it was a posh Scottish person who sent it to the wrong number?

When I reach No 35A, I stop and stare. I think I've come all this way for nothing. Jude can't be here. It doesn't make any sense.

Number 35A is down some metal steps. It's a basement flat, but it's still got windows. But I can't see in the windows, because there are blinds down over them.

I can't go back all the way I've come, and I've got nowhere else to go.

So I go down the steps.

I press the buzzer and then I stand right back so I can run if I have to.

Then I hear Jude's voice from inside the flat like she's talking to Em, and I know it's alright.

That's when I feel really excited because I'm going to see Jude and we're going to start a new life.

Jude opens the door. She looks terrible. Her skin is stretched over her cheekbones and the red blotches I noticed on her face in hospital are angrier than ever. She's been itching them, some of them are scabbed. Bits of her face look like they've collapsed. Her left cheek, for instance, it looks like whatever was keeping it up has disintegrated. For a moment she doesn't see me or doesn't realise it's me, and I can see her getting ready to snap at me to go away.

Then she wails, 'What have you done to your beautiful hair?' For a minute I think she's going to cry, but then she opens her arms wide, saying my name over and over.

I give her a huge hug, closing my eyes tight to enjoy the feel of it more. I can smell her smell. She's breathing and laughing in my ear. Through her T-shirt I can feel her ribs pushed up hard against my chest. I can feel the bones in

227

her back too under my hand. I open my eyes to get a better look at her and her eyes are level with mine and I realise I'm as tall as her now. Then I realise I've grown even in that little bit of time we haven't seen each other. It's just a couple of weeks, and maybe I've grown just a millimetre, but I was shorter than her before and now I'm not.

Then I see Em standing behind her in the hall. She's in a nappy, nothing else, and her face is furious and a bit scared at all this commotion. I push past Jude and kneel on the floor to grab Em up in a bear hug.

She screams and hits me hard on my ear. I'm not expecting her to do that. I put her down.

'It's me,' I say to her, 'me, Aunty Sarah. You remember me. And now I'm deaf because of you.'

She frowns at me for a bit, still howling her head off but thinking at the same time. Then she stops abruptly and gives me a great big beaming smile. I hold my arms out to her, and she waddles into them for a cuddle. I hold her tight. Her little body is solid and warm.

I twist my head to speak to Jude.

'She's walking all on her own,' I say, grinning. 'How did that happen?'

Jude says, 'You should see how much she eats.'

'You look like you should be eating more yourself,' I say to her. Her wrists are sticking out of her sleeves and they look like you could snap them with your hands.

Still kneeling down, with Em pinching my face and giggling, I look around. There's a stale smell like the windows have never been opened. And through the door to one of the rooms I can see it's messy with clothes lying all over a couch and I can see at least one used nappy sitting on the floor. Still, if Jude wasn't living here, you'd say this was a nice place. There's no damp or cracks. The floor is polished wood and the blinds at the windows all match and they haven't got bits hanging off them.

'How are you living here, Jude?' I ask, looking up at my sister. 'Who's paying for it?'

'Mind your own bloody business!' she snaps, really vicious. She turns away.

I just kneel there with Em and don't say anything. It hurts my feelings that she talks to me like that after I've come all this way to find her, but talking to Jude is always like walking across a minefield. You never know when you're going to step on something that blows up.

'Have a look around,' Jude says, trying to cover up.

I stand up and lead Em into a lounge. There are bookshelves on the walls with books in them and a couch and two armchairs that match. Apart from the mess, it's the kind of room you dream about living in.

I try a grin at Jude. 'Looks like you've been waiting for me to do the cleaning, you messy cow.'

Jude smiles and shrugs. 'I knew you'd come,' she says.

'You going to show me around, Em?' I say. I point to a door. 'Shall we go and have a look in there?'

I open the door and it's a cupboard, big enough to walk into, and Jude laughs.

I open another door.

I peer inside, and I don't know what to say. It's a nightmare. There's a big bed, and all Jude's clothes are mashed together in a big ball and there are empty drinks bottles knocking around. She's only been here two weeks, and she's made this much mess . . .

Not Em's bottles. Jude's.

There's a can of Coke that's lying on its side and dripping into a puddle on the carpet.

'I'll give it a clean,' I say.

She puts her arms around me, and because I've got Em in my arms it turns into a group hug, with Jude's nose in her daughter's hair and Em shrieking in delight.

'I've missed you and your rubber gloves,' she says.

'You haven't got any though, have you?'

'Rubber gloves?' She just grins and shakes her head. 'I've got better things to spend my money on.'

And what money would that be, I'm thinking, but now I don't dare ask.

'Kitchen?' I ask Em.

When I see the piles of dirty crockery, I nearly drop Em.

Jude must see it on my face.

'I'm doing my best,' she says, and then she goes and bursts into tears.

I put Em down and give Jude a cuddle. I can feel her crying into my shoulder. Her tears are making my shoulder wet. I can feel her jutting ribcage shaking and shuddering against me. I don't like the feeling. She's never cried on me before. I don't know what it's about.

'Nice you're so pleased to see me,' I say in her ear, and I can hear her catch her breath at that and chuckle a bit.

I pat her awkwardly on the back. I don't pat her too hard in case I break a bone.

'Come on, it's alright,' I say. 'You're just tired because you've been poorly, and you've been on your own looking after Em. And all that business with . . .' But I can't bring myself to say the name Ben. It's best for both of us if he doesn't exist any more. 'Come on, stop crying, you're scaring Em. See, she's crying too.'

Jude raises her face and wipes her eyes, holding out her hand to Em, who's bawling her head off because she doesn't like to be outdone. But for all the tears Jude wipes up there are more rolling down her face. It's like her plumbing's gone wrong, she just can't stop it.

'We're going to be alright,' I tell her. 'I'll clean it all up, it'll be a great place to live. We'll be fine. You go and have a lie-down.'

Jude sniffs and nods.

I don't want her in the bedroom while I'm cleaning up so I push her towards the couch and she lies down and closes her eyes.

I tell Em she's going to help me. And I turn away from Jude and take her daughter back out to the kitchen.

'We'll start in here,' I say to Em, 'you've always got to start a clean-up in the kitchen.'

You have to do the washing up before you do anything else. Otherwise your sink isn't clear to wash anything else.

I run the tap. Cold water. My heart sinks. Then I think I can feel the water getting a bit warmer. After it's been running for a bit it's not hot, but it will have to do. I dig around for detergent, but I can't find any. No washing powder, even. I look for a bathroom, dreading what I'll find, but it's not too bad, just mouldy-smelling and a bit messy with a hairball in the plughole in the basin, and soap gunge around the taps. It's actually a nice bathroom, with blue and white tiles on the walls, and towel rails, and everything. There's a nearly empty bottle of shampoo, so I take that back to the kitchen and squeeze the last of it into the sink. It's probably the same stuff anyway. Or perhaps not. The sink whiffs of shampoo. I pick up the bottle and have a look at the label.

'Like the smell?' I ask Em.

She looks at me with her head on one side, but she's not interested in chatting.

'It's guar hydroxy . . . hydroxypropyl . . . trimonium chloride.' Still Em doesn't look impressed. 'With a hint of grease. Very nice.'

I have to chisel some of the old food off the plates, it's been dried on so long. I feel a bit queasy doing it, like I would for a stranger. In my opinion, doing gross things for your own family isn't the same thing as doing gross things for a stranger. Take changing a nappy. You do it for your baby – or for your sister's baby – but you wouldn't do it for any old baby. It would make you throw up. If you're a nurse or a doctor, throwing up must just be part of the job, you must feel like puking all the time. Just like leftovers. You don't expect to feel queasy when you're hacking dried-up leftovers off a plate if it's family leftovers.

There are no bin bags so I take my school shoes out of the Safeway bag where I've packed them in my pink-slug bag, and the Safeway bag becomes the bin.

My eczema starts to throb at the sight of the sink full of soapy water. I feel like I'm plunging my hands into a bucket of paint stripper. I think about going to find a shop that sells rubber gloves, but I don't know my way round here and I don't want to leave Jude. She's obviously in a state. And even if I did leave Jude I couldn't leave Em here with her mum passed out.

First I wash a few things for Em to mess around with, some spoons and saucepans. There's nothing to dry them with, so I get a clean T-shirt out my bag and use that instead. She bashes on a saucepan with a spoon for a bit, then staggers to her feet and starts running up and down the corridor like a mad thing, howling with laughter, her little legs pumping up and down. I stand and watch for a bit, smiling at her antics. Then she trips and sprawls on the floor and howls, so I have to go and pick her up and give her a hug.

Soon the clean plates are stacking up. My T-shirt's soaking wet and I'm not going to use all my clothes as tea towels. I've got a feeling that as long as I'm living with Jude, clean clothes will be like gold. So I just stack the dishes clean and wet. There aren't that many of them, not as many as it looked. Four big matching plates, four small plates, four bowls, a few coffee cups and saucepans, and bits and bobs of cutlery. I take a look inside the cupboard, but there's no more crockery. Every last plate and bowl has been used. I wipe down the counter with the sodden T-shirt and then I decide it's time for the final sacrifice and I use it to wash the floor. Then the soles of my shoes don't stick to it like they did.

I take a look at Jude, who's lying curled up on the couch, either asleep or pretending to be. Then I take Em by the hand and we venture into Jude's room. The telly's still on in there. It's got no coin meter attached to it, so I suppose Jude doesn't need to worry about it running out. I fiddle around until I find a kid's show, and clear a space on the carpet and stick Em on her bottom in front of it. Now she's remembered who I am, she's acting like I never left.

I can't help giving her a once-over. My sister adores Em. She'd never let anything bad happen to her. Still, you can't help checking. She's not got as much baby fat as she did. But that's why it's called baby fat. She's a toddler now, and slimming down. Soon she'll be skinny enough for the Miss World toddler contest. She'll do well in the nappy competition. I can't see anything wrong with her. No bruises.

What would we do with another one? I can't help thinking it.

'Where's your bed?' I say to Em. She must have grown out of the pushchair now. Perhaps she sleeps with her mum in the big bed, or on the couch? She ignores me. 'Em, where do you sleep then?' I ask her again.

She's glued to the telly. So I look around.

There's a dog basket in the corner of the room. One of those wicker things with a padded base and sides. But there's no dog.

I go and have a look. It's dirty, with trails of snot and worse over the dark blue material. One of Em's toys has rolled into the gap between the padding and wicker. There's a towel screwed up.

'Is *this* your bed, Em?' I say softly.

She doesn't hear me. It doesn't matter. I know the answer.

My niece, the dog.

I'm rooted to the spot staring at the dog basket.

I think of Jude saying, 'I'm doing my best.'

I think of Jude lying on the couch in the other room, curled up like a baby herself.

I feel like I'm crumbling inside.

I try to pull myself together. It's a dog basket. So what? She can't roll off it, she can't get her head stuck between

234

bars. It's a bit dirty, but she'll never get sick. *What to Expect When You're Expecting* says it's good for a baby to have contact with germs.

Besides, the bed's a bit padded.

Probably it's never been used by a dog.

Probably Jude got it new.

I can scrub the padded base of the dog basket.

So that's what I do.

I feel a bit better after that and I go back to cleaning up. But once in a while I find myself just standing there, not really doing anything, just looking at the dog basket. Like the dog basket can tell me something. Which obviously isn't going to happen.

After a while, Jude gets up and comes out of the bedroom, rubbing her eyes.

'Sorry,' she says.

'What for?'

'For the mess.' She waves her arm. 'I get used to it when it's just me.'

'That's alright,' I say. 'I knew what it would be like.'

Jude answers with a question.

'You did, did you? You knew what it would be like?'

I leave that question well alone. There's a tone in Jude's voice. The tone when you don't cross her because she's unhappy and when she's unhappy you don't know what she's going to do.

She sighs.

'It's not much of a welcome. I wasn't expecting you.'

'I know,' I say. I don't say, but you asked me to come. I'm not sure she can remember what she did five minutes ago, let alone five days or five weeks.

'Don't get me wrong, I'm really pleased you're here, I missed you.'

'I know,' I say again.

'Come on then,' she says, opening her arms, 'give me a hug.'

I give her another hug. I don't remember her wanting hugs before, and I don't want to be doing it all the time. Her ribs creep me out.

'Let's have a rest, watch some telly,' she says.

She goes and gets a bottle of Coke and some biscuits. We settle on the bed, leaning against the wall. When I take a swig of it the Coke's flat, but it gives me a bit of a lift. I pick up Em so she's on my lap and we flick through the channels until all three of us agree on *The X Factor*.

After a while, Jude says to me, 'Got your hairbrush, Sare?'

I get up and find it in my pink-slug bag and hand it to Jude. She kneels behind me and starts to brush, pressing the palm of her hand against my scalp so she doesn't pull.

'It's a real mess,' she says. 'Did you put conditioner on it after you washed the dye out?'

'I can't remember,' I say, because I don't want to remember last night and stealing from Linda's wallet.

'It'll probably all fall out,' she says.

But she keeps brushing. When she gets to knots she brushes gently until the strands separate again. Soon the brush is sweeping through my hair from root to tip, and the bristles of the brush prickle the skin on my scalp. She can't see my face so I close my eyes. I drift off. It's been a long day and I'm dozing but awake if you know what I mean. I can hear the telly on but I can't make sense of it. All I know is that the TV is laughing and singing and applauding. It sounds so happy. I feel so happy. I feel like I'm wrapped in happiness. I've got my sister's warm body pressing against me and little Em asleep on my lap and it feels like all of us are part of the same big breathing thing, not separate, just one set of lungs, one heart, one mind, and a lot of arms and legs. Even Jude brushing my hair feels like some cosmic thing where me and her and Em are all being rocked back and forth by this head massage, this brushing and pulling and letting go, and brushing and pulling and letting go. I'm floating in and out of sleep. My head's all over the place, it's here in the flat, it's back in the old flat, it's even further back, in the flat before that. I'm remembering this brushing and pulling and letting go, the brushing, pulling . . .

I don't even think about it, I just open my gob.

'You brush like Mum,' I say.

Jude doesn't say anything but her body goes all tense. She doesn't stop brushing, but she pulls away from me so the weight of her on me is gone. On my lap Em moves and whimpers like she knows we're not the one-lung, one-heart thing any more.

'What's the matter?' I ask.

'Nothing,' Jude says. For a while she doesn't say anything, just keeps on brushing. But she's not brushing like before. Now it's like she might as well keep brushing because she's busy thinking, and you can't just think so you might as well keep on brushing. Then she says, 'Why are you talking about her?'

'Why shouldn't I?' I say.

She brushes another six times, and then she says, 'I don't want to talk about her.'

She stops brushing.

I sit there thinking what exactly it is I want to ask her.

'Why did you run away?' I say in the end.

She looks at me for a long time.

'I couldn't deal with it,' she says in the end.

'I know,' I say. 'But that doesn't mean you have to run away.'

'It was you who said I should go so they couldn't find me and Em.'

'Not without telling me,' I say. 'I didn't know where you were or if you were alright or anything. I can't believe you did that.'

'Sare, I'm sorry,' she says, and she really looks cut up, and I haven't got the heart to lay into her about it. I know she's not going to tell me what I want to know: how did you get here? Who's helping you?

I glance at the TV screen. It's the news, and there's a journalist speaking outside the court.

'Today the court heard from sixteen-year-old Omar Jones,' the journalist is saying. 'Questioned by Anji Blunt QC for the defence, Mr Jones said that he had not seen the defendant, Borys Kolowski, outside Number 87 Shepherd's Way where Dianne Carnaby was found stabbed to death shortly afterwards.'

'You liar,' I burst out, shouting at the telly. 'You saw him, Omar, you know you did, you liar!'

Jude steps over to the TV and switches it off just like that. I stare at Jude. Just for a minute, I forget Omar and his lies. Because I'm thinking, does Jude even know what happened with me in court? Does she read the newspapers? No one could've missed the newsstands, but I'm not even sure she leaves the flat much. What if she didn't go out the day after the lady lawyer humiliated me in court? What if she didn't watch the TV news, or listen to the radio news, or buy a newspaper? Until now I've been thinking that we both know what's going on, we're just not talking about it. Now I'm thinking perhaps she doesn't know.

'Don't you even want to know what's happening with Borys?' I ask.

She gives me a look like she despises me.

'You should want to know,' I say.

'And you should shut up,' she snaps at me.

'You should want to know because Borys did it for you,' I say, because she doesn't seem to get it, and because I can still see his face in court, all fear and longing.

'He did it because he wanted to live with you and Em and the baby, and he thought Mum wouldn't let you, so he killed her.'

'Shut up if you know what's good for you, Sare.'

'He killed Mum because of you,' I taunt her.

Jude is gazing at me and she's running her tongue over her lips which are all dry.

'What you're saying is crap,' she says slowly.

'I saw him in the court, he was asking all about you and about the baby, like he really loves you.'

'What are you on about?' she bursts out. 'What do you know about love, you nosy cow?'

She turns and heads for the door.

'What are you doing?' I'm panicked too now, and I follow her, but she turns around and shoves me away from her. I say shoves, but there's no muscle in it. It's like being shoved by an angry feather. 'Where are you going?' I want to know. She pushes past me, and it's like a ghost is drifting past me, all I can feel is a breath of air. She pulls open the door and heads out into the dark. I'm going to run after her, but then I hear Em wail behind me, and I know I can't leave her behind. So I leave Jude to go wherever it is that she wants to go, and I turn back inside. I go and pick Em up and cuddle her so tight she cries. So I apologise and I tell her that I was cuddling her to make me feel better, not her.

I don't sleep well. Jude's bound to come back, so I leave the bed for her and sleep on the couch. After I've given Em a bottle I put her in her mum's bed, but she won't settle there. She frets and fidgets, and tries to climb out although the bed's so high she can't get her feet on the floor without falling. In the end I worry she'll fall, so I help her off the bed and watch what she does. Half asleep, with her two little hands still holding her bottle of milk in her mouth, she totters across to the dog basket and curls up in it, with her back pressing against the padded sides. Her eyelids close, and she goes straight to sleep. I look at her asleep, still sucking now and then on her bottle. Except for the bottle of milk, she looks like those diagrams in *What to Expect When You're Expecting* of a baby in a womb, its back pressing against the round line of the tummy, its head tucked into its chest.

I take the couch. There's no bedding, so I pull on an extra sweater from my bag so I keep warm. I lie down, and I fall asleep.

I don't know what time it is when Jude comes in but I hear her opening the front door and stumbling noisily in the dark. I hear her going to the bathroom and not washing her hands. She staggers past the lounge, and through the connecting door I can see her fall into the bedroom and land full length on her bed. She's either drunk or off her head from something I don't want to think about. I drift off to sleep again but in the night I wake up. She's moaning. She sounds scared. She flails her arms as though she's fighting someone off. I get up, ready to go and comfort her. I can see her in a shaft of light shining in between the curtains. She's lying there on her back with her eyes shut. She cries out again.

'Jude?' I say. And then she falls back into a deeper sleep. I lie there awake for ages. I don't understand what's going on. All I know is that I've found Jude, and I've found Em. I've found my missing bits. But the bits don't fit like they used to. It's like while we've been apart she and I have grown jagged edges, and we can't get close to each other without cutting each other open.

EIGHTEEN

When I wake up the sun's already shining through the window. The sky is blue and clear, and all at once it's like everything's going to be alright. I've got Jude and Em, and I'm in a whole new world. There's no school, no nothing, we're free as birds, we can do what we want. It's amazing that a blue sky can do that.

I get off the couch and go into Jude's room. Jude is still flat out. She's face down and she's not moving. I approach the bed. Em must have crawled into her bed in the night, because she's sleeping peacefully snuggled against her mum. It freaks me out seeing Jude there like Mum, so still.

'Jude,' I say loudly.

Em's eyes open and she lies there gazing at me. But Jude still doesn't move, and my legs go weak. My heart's pounding.

'Jude,' I say again. I can hear the panic in my voice.

Her back rises and falls with a deep breath, and then she hauls herself over and blinks blearily at me.

'What?' she says.

'I thought you were dead,' I say, forcing a laugh now I know she's not.

'What are you on about?' she frowns.

'You weren't moving,' I say . . .

242

'I was asleep, of course I wasn't moving,' Jude says.

'I know,' I say. And then because I don't want her to think I'm a total idiot I say. 'It's just that Mum, you know, I thought she was asleep, and . . .'

'Just shut up about Mum,' she says, and the way she says it makes me decide to shut up.

I turn away.

'Thanks for leaving me the bed,' she says.

'You're just trying to change the subject.' I round on her. 'What's so bad about thinking about Mum? She did her best.'

It's what I said to Millie, that Mum did her best. I don't believe it any more, not after what Millie said, and what I can remember now about 'Uncle Keith'. What mother pushes her fifteen-year-old daughter out the door to go clubbing with a grown-up man and takes money for it? I think I'm saying it because I want to hear what Jude says to it.

Jude's half propped up on the bed. She looks like a real mess with her blotchy skin and last night's make-up smeared on her collapsing face and her hair all knotted and greasy.

She's watching me, not so bleary now. After a while she starts to speak.

'Course she did her best, Sare,' she says. 'That's why I don't like to think about her. It really upsets me. It'll upset you, too, if you think about her too much. Best to put it behind you and move on. We've got to try and make things better, we can't dwell on the past.'

So she wants to lie to me. She doesn't want to tell me what really happened. She doesn't want me thinking too much, and that makes me angry.

'That's what this is, is it?' I say, wanting to hurt her. 'Having Em sleep in a dog basket? This is you making things better, is it?

Em starts hitting Jude's arm, asking for food and attention, but Jude just ignores her and sits there. She looks at me for a long time and then she says, 'Yeah, that's what this is. This is me making things better.'

But she says it so hard and cold that I wish I'd never brought it up.

We don't talk to each other for a while, but then Jude makes me a cup of tea, and she washes the cups up right away, like she realises she let me do everything and clear up all her mess the day before. While she's at the sink she turns to me and says, 'I know what you think, but Em chose the dog basket, I didn't make her sleep there. It was here when we got here, and when she got tired she'd go and curl up in it and have a nap. And then she wouldn't sleep in the bed at night, she'd just cry for the dog basket, so I let her. She can't come to any harm, can she?'

I shrug. I don't know whether she can come to any harm. She can't hurt herself. But what does it do to a kid's head if it grows up knowing its mum let it sleep in a dog basket? I think about Linda, and what she'd say, and Carla. She'd have a fit. Mrs Franklin would love it. She'd be scribbling notes like fury.

'He's going to get me a proper cot,' she says.

'Who is?' I say. 'Who's going to get you a proper cot?'

She takes a deep breath and shakes her head, like she knows she's screwed up.

'Leave it, Sare,' she says, turning towards me. 'Just leave it, okay?'

She goes to the bathroom and when she comes out she looks almost normal.

'Is there anywhere to go?' I say. 'I don't want to stay in.'

Jude looks doubtful.

'I've got some bus fare,' I volunteer.

She shakes her head.

'I don't need your money,' she says. 'I should be the one looking after you, and I've got enough to be going on with.'

'You've got money?' I can hear myself sounding surprised.

'Yeah,' she says, but she doesn't explain, and I bite back the question.

Then she says, 'There's a bus round the corner, we can catch it to Portobello.'

Once we're on the Number 26 bus, I'm still worrying about how Jude lives here. I'm thinking that the only way she could get hold of money would be by signing on, but if the welfare know she's here, how long will it take for the Bocock to come and take Em away? Then I'm thinking perhaps she hasn't thought about that. Or perhaps she thinks she can get away with it. The alternative, which is that she's making money some other way, is worse. I remember what happened in hospital and the lawyer saying Jude was on drugs.

'How did you find the flat?' I ask her.

'Through a friend,' she answers.

'You know people here then?'

'Someone I've known for a while.'

'How can you know someone in Edinburgh?'

'I mean,' she says, turning to look me in the eye, 'I mean someone I've known for a while, from before, not from here.'

245

'Okay,' I say. And she gives me a look, like, 'stop being nosy'.

'Will I meet the person?' I ask. 'I mean if I'm going to live here too . . .'

'No,' and this is the one thing she's clear and firm about. 'No, you won't meet them,' she says. 'They wouldn't be able to help you.'

'Okay,' I say again.

'Okay,' she says, and the way she says it, it's the last word.

I concentrate on what's going on outside the bus windows. We're driving along more grand roads with old posh buildings, tall and sandy-coloured. Then we go out of town a bit and past a stadium, and eventually the bus drops us on a street with shops on.

'Come on,' Jude says.

We walk around the corner and there's the beach.

There's the sea.

I've never seen anything like it.

It's like the whole universe is in front of you. No buildings, no people, just sand that disappears into the sea, which dissolves into the sky, which dissolves into the sea, which dissolves into the sky. It's so big. How come no one told me it was so big?

I turn to Jude and find her standing smiling at me, watching my expression. I grin at her and then I start laughing.

'You're mad,' she says, 'it's just the sea.'

'I know,' I say. 'But I've never seen the sea before.'

She shakes her head and tells me I'm mad again.

We walk along the promenade pushing the empty pushchair while Em toddles along holding on to it.

I'm so happy I'm actually skipping. Which I would never do around Shepherd's Way. This is the new life I was thinking about. Not the flat and all the mess. The blue sky and the blue sea that stretches for miles and miles.

'Let's go on the sand,' I say. I pull off my shoes and climb over the little wall and step onto the sand, and the minute I'm on there I start running. I can't stop. I just run and run, and my feet are in heaven beating down on the wet smooth sand. I didn't know feet could feel like this. It's like they've been dead till now. Like I didn't know I even had feet. First I run down to the edge of the sea, and I shriek as the freezing water washes over my feet. Then I run along the edge of the water, so every step my feet send water splashing. I'm laughing again, and running. It's ages before I stop and look around for Jude, and see her miles off, struggling with the pushchair that's stuck in the sand.

I run back to her.

'I'm glad someone's having a nice time,' she says.

'Stop whingeing,' I tell her. 'I'll take the pushchair, you can go and have a paddle. It's amazing. It feels like your feet are literally freezing and then they stop freezing and they feel really warm, and the sand feels all prickly. You've got to try it, Jude.'

I take the pushchair off her and wave her away.

'I'm not bothered,' she says. But then I pretend I'm going to chase her and she actually laughs and then she shrieks and breaks into a bit of a run to escape me, but she doesn't run more than a couple of steps, and then she stops and holds her tummy, and I think it must still hurt from Ben's birth.

I sit down on the sand with Em and watch Jude walk down to the water's edge. So much has happened since

Ben was born, but actually it's not long since she had him and gave him away. She hasn't even mentioned him. She looks so tiny down there, like a scratch or a speck of dust, like something that's so light it could be rubbed away. She looks out to sea for a long, long time, and then she seems to get cold, because she wraps her arms around herself and walks back up towards me.

Em is excited by the sand. I take off her shoes and socks, and she stamps up and down screeching like she doesn't know whether to be happy or scared. Then she starts running, hurtling around, and because it's sand she doesn't cry when she falls down.

I lie back on the sand. It's still a warm day, but clouds are blowing in across the blue sky. I watch how they move even when you think they're not moving, so the shapes that are there one minute are all changed the next minute even when you think the sky is standing still. And I watch how the clouds move in layers, so some of them are hidden and it's only when the ones at the front blow away that you see the clouds behind.

When Jude comes back I tell her to lie down, and when she's lying next to me I point out the polar bear who's carrying an umbrella across the sky, and the ballet dancer doing the splits in a tutu. She grins and she says I'm mad. When I ask her what she can see, she says she can see a vampire, which makes me laugh a lot because I can't see it although she points it out to me a million times. And then she says she can see a baby's face blowing a bubble, and I can see it too, and it actually looks like Ben, which is amazing but I don't say it. I think she sees it though, because she goes very quiet. We lie there a bit longer but the breeze from the sea is cool and I start to get cold so I scramble to my feet.

'I want to go to the Bahamas,' I say.

'What's the point of that?' Jude says.

'What's the point? What's the point? We could just sit on a beach like this all day long and never get cold.'

She doesn't say anything right away, and then she says, 'It doesn't matter where it is, though, does it? I mean even if I went to the Bahamas, it would still be me sitting on a beach, I can't change that, so it doesn't really change anything.'

'Well . . .' I try to sort out in my head what she's trying to say. 'It would still be you, but you'd be warm and happy.'

'Would I?' she says. 'I don't think I could be happy now, it doesn't matter where I am.'

'Well I hope I'm the one who wins the lottery,' I say, 'because I'm going to the Bahamas whether you come or not.'

I think about Sheena. She'd want to go to the Bahamas.

For lunch we have fish and chips and a Coke each and it costs us £11.90 and Jude pays. We sit inside the shop, looking out through the window at the sea. I notice Jude is always playing with her mobile, glancing at it to see if she's got texts, but I don't know who she's expecting to text her. I've still got her old mobile, so this must be a new one. I wonder who bought it for her. I try not to wonder too much. I try not to think about anything like that. The fish and chips are fresh and crisp and salty. I could eat them every day until I die. We talk a lot, or I do, and I even tell her a bit about Linda's, and about school, and Sheena and the school trip to Paris I'm missing even though Linda got me a passport. I've never had a better day in my life.

249

'What're we going to do, Jude?' I ask as we head home on the bus.

It's like when I ask her something there's a whole conversation going on in her head before she replies.

'We can do this every day,' she says. 'We had a good time, didn't we? Em liked it.'

Em's fast asleep on Jude's lap, her fat little face squidged against Jude's chest. Jude's resting her face on her daughter's head.

'You liked it too, didn't you?' I ask her. 'You look better after a day in the sun. You've gone a bit pink on your cheeks. You look really pretty.'

Jude smiles.

'Don't sound so surprised,' she says.

Because of that smile for the rest of the bus journey I think everything's going to be alright.

Then, after we get off the bus at Prince's Street and cross the road, her mobile rings, and when she pulls it out her pocket and looks at the screen her face sets hard. She answers it, though.

'Yeah?' She's speaking to someone she knows but not someone she wants to think about, someone she's embarrassed to be talking to in front of me. I can tell it's a man because I can hear his voice, not what he's saying, just that he's a man.

'No,' she's saying. 'Not tonight. I'm not in tonight.'

As far as I'm concerned this is a lie. I don't know of any plans we have to be out, and Em's got to go to bed. Em's not big on clubbing. Then I think perhaps Jude's going to go out like she did last night and she's going to leave me with Em and she's going to come back stoned out of her head again. My heart sinks. I don't want tonight to be like last night.

'No,' she repeats. 'I can't, not tonight.'

But whoever it is won't give up. She glances at me, still with the phone to her ear. And although she's still got her hard face on I think for just a millisecond that she's going to cry. Then she turns away and she doesn't cry so I must have got it wrong.

When she hangs up she doesn't say anything for a while. Then she turns on me, her lips pressed together, and she's frowning.

'I've got my own life.'

'I know,' I say. I'm thinking that what's coming is that she's going to go out and I'm to look after Em.

'So you'll have to look after yourself tonight,' she says. 'You can't come back with me.'

'What? Where am I going to go?'

She blows up at me then.

'I should never have told you where I was. There's nothing here for you, I didn't ask for you to come. I've got my own life.'

I step back like she's hit me and there's a man behind me walking his dog, so I bash into him, and instead of telling me off he gives me a look like he's scared of me and I get a flash in my head of what he sees, two teenage girls having a fight. He doesn't want to get involved. It's like I'm standing outside myself looking at us. I can see me, shocked.

'Yeah,' I say, trying to sound normal. 'I know you've got your own life. I don't have to stay, I just wanted to make sure you're alright.'

'I'm completely bloody fine,' Jude shouts. 'Can't you see that?'

'Good.' I'm struggling to hold it together. I put my hand out towards Jude but she won't take it. 'Are you sure I can't come back with you? I don't know where to go . . .'

But she's already got her back turned on me and she's hurrying away from me, bent over Em's pushchair.

'When can I come back?' I shout after her. But it's a weedy shout and she doesn't hear it. Or she does and she ignores it. But Jude's not like that.

I stand there by the side of the road and after a minute another Number 26 bus comes along and some people get off, and after a minute the bus still hasn't gone and the driver shouts to ask me if I'm getting on or not. I wasn't going to get on and I don't know where the bus is going but I'm cold standing by the side of the road so I get on and give him 70p, and he prints me off a ticket. I move down inside the bus and find a seat on the back row next to the window. Once I sit down I feel a bit better. The bus is nearly full so there's a woman squeezed in next to me and her body heat warms me up and then I don't feel so shaky.

There's a couple of women sat opposite with shopping bags and stuff on their laps and they're chatting in Scottish accents about some dress they both tried on and it made one of them look fat and not the other one. I could've told them that's because one of them's fat and the other one isn't. But I don't. Still, they make me feel better, like I'm part of the real world, the normal world, where your sister doesn't throw you out onto the street after you came all the way up the country to see her. When I think about that I can feel tears welling up in my eyes, and the woman sitting opposite me is looking at me so I turn my face so I'm looking out into the darkness. The women sitting opposite me get off the bus and I stay on. The warm woman sitting next to me heaves herself onto her feet and gets off the bus, and I stay on. After a couple more stops the bus driver calls out to me, 'End of the line, love.'

I look out the window. I haven't a clue where I am.

It looks like a residential street, and I don't want to keep going too far in case I can't get back. So I get off the bus.

'Alright, lass?' the driver calls after me.

I can't trust myself to speak so I just nod.

I can feel his eyes on me so I start to walk like I know where I'm going. I've got my hands in my pockets, counting what I've got left in coins. There's five coins that Jude gave me for playing the slot machines on the promenade at Portobello which I didn't end up doing.

If there's a café that's open this evening I can buy a cup of tea and sit in there and stay warm. Or if there's a church where something's going on, maybe I can beg a cup of tea. There are dark alleys in between some of the shops, and I hurry past them. I can't see a café, but there's a pub, with a banner outside advertising Sky Sports. A pub means people, at least. I stop outside the pub and try to see inside, but the windows are covered. If I go in, what's the worst that can happen? They can refuse to serve me. Usually I wouldn't want to walk into a strange pub on my own, but tonight I feel like it's not me pushing the door open, like the insides of me have been drained out and there's someone else wearing my skin.

Inside, it's a bright lights and empty bar stools kind of a pub, with a barman with a sour face and eyes that sit on top of folds of oily skin. He eyes me up as I enter the bar, and I make my way to a table as far from him as possible. I sit down with my back to him.

'What are you doing?' he asks. I look around, hoping that he's addressing this to someone else. But the only other customer is an ancient man who looks as though he's been pickled, and his dog.

'What does it look like?' I challenge him. 'I'm waiting for someone.'

'We're all waiting for someone, darling,' he says, and I can tell he's not from round here, because he doesn't talk like them. 'Anyone wants to sit down has to buy a drink.'

I know he's challenging me. I get up and walk to the bar.

'I'll have a Coke, then,' I say.

He looks at me. 'Cash or card?'

I pull a hand from my pocket and drop a couple of coins onto the bar.

'Well,' he says, 'the last of the big spenders. Can I interest you in a packet of crisps too?'

I really want a packet of crisps, but I'm worried my cash is running low.

'Cheese and onion,' I say.

He nods slowly, staring at the coins, then reaches into a cardboard box and pulls out a packet of crisps, throwing them onto the counter in front of me.

'That's another pound, then,' he says.

I push the crisps back towards him.

'I'll just take the Coke,' I say.

'You shouldn't be in here at all, a young girl like you,' he says with his back to me. When he bends down to get a glass for my Coke, most of his bum escapes from his

254

jeans. The band of his spotty boxers is halfway down his butt, which makes me feel sick. It still feels like none of this is happening to me. It's all happening to someone else. It's like I'm looking down at myself sitting at the bar in a city I don't know and looking at the yellow dimply buttocks of a man I don't know.

'Like I said, I'm waiting for someone,' I say. I don't want to tell him I've got nowhere to go. I know enough to know I'm safest if this man thinks there's someone who knows where I am, someone who'll be here soon.

'And who would that be?'

He puts the glass of Coke on the counter in front of me, and watches as I take a sip. Even that one sip perks me up.

'That would be my brother,' I say. 'He lives round here. I'm visiting him.'

But I know as soon as I've opened my mouth that I should've shut up.

'Where round here?' the bartender asks, propping himself against the bar with hairy fat arms.

'I don't know,' I say back, 'that's why I'm meeting him here. He'll show me where he lives.'

'Why don't you call him, tell him you're here then?'

'I already texted him,' I say.

'If you've got no home to go to I'll help you find somewhere to stay,' he says.

He's fat and oily and gross, but his face isn't mean. If he can find me somewhere to stay, tomorrow I can find my way back to Jude's. She'll be alright by tomorrow. She was just throwing a wobbly. Even if she's not alright I can collect my stuff and get back on the train. But first there's tonight.

'I'm alright,' I say. 'I'm going to look for my brother.'

255

He watches me sip at my Coke. He's frowning.

'Do you want me to walk with you, help you find him?' he asks.

He pushes my two pound coins back across the bar, and I snatch them up.

'I don't need your help,' I say. I get up and hurry out the pub. Outside, on the street, I take stock. I look at my watch. It's still only nine o'clock.

I start to walk back the way I came, thinking about trying another pub. But I know if I try too many I'll be bound to find trouble if I haven't already. Behind me someone's leaving the pub. I can hear the door closing. Then coming towards me there's a bus and I start to wave it down. The driver doesn't see me or he ignores me and drives past me, and then the bus pulls into a bus stop and two men get off. I run towards it and jump onto it just as the doors are closing. As we pull out into the road I look behind me. The barman is on the pavement watching me with a frown on his face. I don't know whether to wave or to ignore him. If only I knew what was going on in his head. If only I could be sure he didn't mean any harm, then I might have taken his offer of help. In the end we just look at each other until the bus turns a corner and I can't see him any more.

I'm the only one on the bus. I go upstairs so the driver doesn't get too curious about me. I look at my watch. There's still hours and hours and hours of night-time till I can go back to Jude's. And what then? I huddle next to the window and stare out. I haven't got the foggiest where I am.

I'm really hungry.

I'd eat anything I could get my hands on. If a live chicken came and sat next to me on the bus, I'd eat it and spit out the feathers.

What's wrong with Jude? What's come over her? It's like the man who called her on the phone has some power over her, like a magician. I don't know who he is but I hate him. One minute she's my Jude. Next minute she's something else. Because I'm weak from being hungry, thinking like this makes me cry. I've got tears running down my face and snot hanging out my nose and I've got no hankie so I wipe it on my sleeve.

The bus stops and three boys come upstairs. I say boys, because they're not grown-up like men. They're wearing jeans that sit so low on their hips their underwear is ballooning out. They've got chains and keys hanging off their belt loops like they own anything that might need a key. They've got piercings anywhere there's a bit of skin big enough to get hold of – lips, noses, ears. I don't want to think about the other bits of them. They see me and one whispers something in the other one's ear and the second one laughs. I try to ignore them but I've still got tears running down my face so they're bound to notice. They come and sit behind me and their voices are loud, and their accents are so strong it's like they're speaking a foreign language. I can smell them because they've been sweating and they haven't washed.

They're eating something and the smell of it wafts over me, hot and fat and salty.

'I thought ye were allergic,' one of them says to another, 'you kenna eat tha'.'

There's the sound of swallowing and then a loud belch.

'Ah'm jest a wee bit allergic.'

It's burgers or kebabs or something. Something hot and meaty and rich. The saliva's running in my mouth. I want to turn round and rip the food out their hands and stuff it straight in my mouth. My belly's really hurting so it might even be worth it to get punched in the face if my belly would stop hurting.

'Lass, d'ye want summa this?' I shake my head.

'Ah've git chips,' one wheedles.

If I don't eat, I'm going to pass out. I can hear them churning the food in their mouths. I can taste it. The oil, and the salt, and the soft potato.

Then one of them stretches over the back of my seat and waves the box of in front of me. There's burger and chips, soft and golden and oily, all in a white cardboard box with a picture of a fish on it. I don't think about it, I lunge for the cardboard box. I snatch it and half the food falls out, but what's left ends up in my hands and I stuff it in my mouth as fast as I can.

Behind me he's shouting.

'She took it oot ma bloody hand! Oot ma bloody hand!'

I brace myself to get hit. But I keep on stuffing the food in my face. One of them swings around from behind me and sticks his face in front of mine.

'We've git a hungry lassie here!' he says.

Now the tears are running down my face again.

'Ach dry yer eyes,' says the one with his face in front of mine. 'Dinna cry!'

'Shut yer gob, ye bumshite!' one of the others says to him. 'Tha wes our breakfast!'

I'm looking from one to the other of them but I don't

know where I am or what's going on and I'm still crying but at least my belly feels warm and full.

The bus is slowing down and I stand up and rush down the stairs so fast I almost fall down them. But even while I'm hurtling down they're howling with excitement and getting up and following me. So when I jump off the bus they're right behind me. My feet keep going, one foot in front of the other, in front of the other, in front of the other. This is where it starts, where they start to taunt me, then someone thinks verbal's not enough, they should get physical. If I break into a run they'll chase me and outrun me. They're bigger than me.

It takes me a minute to realise I'm back in Portobello by the promenade.

But now the blue sky is black and the big sea is black and frightening.

Behind me, they're regretting following me off, because they got off at the wrong stop. Their footsteps keep a steady pace behind mine like they're following me but they're losing interest in me. They're trying to work out how to get home.

'Hey, chip thief!'

I don't respond. I keep on walking . . . Then their voices are moving away from me and soon they're gone completely like they were never there.

There's a bench, and suddenly my knees give out, and I sit down hard. I sit there shivering, looking out to sea. So, after all that, the lads meant me no harm, they were just messing about. I'm scared someone else is going to come along who does mean me harm. There's nowhere for me to run, no one to run to.

After a little while, I get up and I walk down onto the beach. I can't see where the sand turns into sea, but I know that it does because I can hear the movement of the water. It's like a secret sea, right in front of me but I can't see it. All I know is if I stood up and walked straight ahead of me I'd walk into the dark sea and that the dark sea reaches to eternity.

But it's the sky that makes me catch my breath. It's like the sky has come alive. Like it was a secret in the day, fooling me with clouds and stuff, and now at night it's showing me what it's really got up there, pinpricks of light scattered in great patterns across the sky, patterns like I've never seen, like it would take forever to look at them all. As soon as you think you've got the pattern in your head more stars appear out of nowhere. Everywhere you turn the sky is covered in them. I fall back so I'm lying on the sand for I don't know how long. My body's getting rigid with cold. I can't feel my fingers in the sand. But my eyes are wide open. If this is the first time I've seen the sky in fourteen years then it might be another fourteen years till I see it again.

When I can't feel my legs any more I make myself stand up and I jump up and down on the sand until I can feel all the bits of me again. I make my way to the road and I wait for the night bus to go into town.

I'm the only one on the night bus. When we reach Princes Street I get off and walk down the street past the shuttered shops. I'm not the only one with nowhere to go. There are people sleeping in doorways. Men mostly, and dogs. I pass a woman and I think about stopping and asking her for advice but when she raises her head to me her eyes frighten me and I run off down the road.

My legs get to feel like they can't keep going any longer.

I'm passing a doorway so I sit down, pulling my knees up to my chest and hugging them to me. I tuck my head in so my forehead's on my knees. It's a bit sheltered from the wind but the cold from the pavement works its way up through my bum until all of me's frozen. I feel something digging into me where my hip is flat on the ground. I reach into my pocket. It's my mobile phone. I haven't even thought about it since I turned it off on the coach to stop people trying to find me. I think I might as well turn it on. They're never going to find me in a shop doorway in Edinburgh. And I'm beginning not to care if they do. When the phone beeps back to life, it says I've got fifty-seven new messages. Thirty-one of them are from Linda, just a few words each time.

Pls ring us

Let us know you're alright

I'm so sorry

Everything's going to be alright if you come back

We let you down

How can you do this to us?

And so on, more of the same. Fifteen from Mrs Franklin.

Running away won't solve anything

I can help you if you'll let me

Let's face this together

Exactly one from Bocock:

Unxceptbl bhvr rtrn imdtly

I delete her.

There's three messages from Omar. I cry when I read them because they make me think of his arm around me, and how safe it made me feel.

i need 2 talk to u

where r u girl?

im sorry

I can't believe I was ever angry with him. He was only trying to help me. It's me who's got myself into this mess, not him.

There's loads from Sheena, and she makes me smile although I'm still crying.

paris wont b fun w/out u

cheese sare u and me got to eat french cheese!

iffel twr sare u and me got to clm 2 the top!

me in paris u?

sare r u alright?

seriously call me!!

There's one from Carla. It's only short, but I like it best of the adults' messages because she doesn't sound panicky like Linda or touchy-feely like Mrs Franklin.

just let us know where u r love and we'll come and get you

u can share Sheena's room

I close my eyes tight. I can't think of Sheena's room now. I can't think of Omar or Sheena, I miss them too much. I even miss Linda and Mrs Franklin.

I still hate Bocock.

I'm freezing cold.

I'm thinking of Zoe Brown lying outside, like me, strangled. She must have been so cold.

And I'm furious with Jude.

I unzip my pockets and I shove my hands deep into them, and my fingers touch the gold chain.

How can she do this to me? She asked me to come, and now she's thrown me out onto the street, and I'm so angry that I can't even sit still. I stand up and start jumping up and down, but that makes me even more angry, like I'm getting ready for a fight.

I don't know why I'm even listening to Jude. Why am I doing what she says? Where does she get the right to order me out onto the street? She's older than me, she's got a duty to look after me.

I start walking towards where I think Hibernia Place is.

If she doesn't like it, she can bugger on off out the flat herself and sleep in a shop doorway.

When I reach Number 35A Hibernia Place, the door to the flat is locked so I press the bell but no one comes.

I put my ear to the door. I can hear someone moving around and that makes me even madder. She's in there and she's ignoring me.

I start bashing on the door, and it's the middle of the night, so one way or another I'm going to wake someone up.

Then I start yelling, 'Jude, I know you're in there.'

When she comes to the door, she only opens it part-way. The look of her shocks me all over again. She's a wreck. Her eyes won't meet mine.

'Go away,' she says.

'Jude,' I beg, 'I've got nowhere to go.'

'Go away,' she says again.

It's when she tries to close the door in my face that I explode. I block it with my shoulder and shout at her.

'Don't you dare shut me out, you ungrateful cow!' I shout.

I shove as hard as I can, and because she's got the strength of a flea she shrinks back and I burst into the flat.

She flinches, and I get angrier.

I slam the door behind me.

'You run off and leave me and I travel hundreds of miles to find you and I spend hours cleaning up after you and you throw me out, then you shut the door in my face. I don't know what's going on with you. I just want to help you and you don't tell me anything!'

She's literally cowering, all bent over and hugging herself. She's staring up at me. Her lips are pressed together and her skin is grey and clammy.

'Not now,' she's whispering. 'I've got someone here, you can't . . .'

'Do you know what I did for you?' I'm screaming at her now, not even listening to what she's saying. 'Do you even know?'

I unzip the pocket in my hoody and I pull out the pendant and I shove it in front of her nose. She stares down at it.

'Recognise it?' I'm screaming. 'Do you recognise it? Because you should recognise it. It's yours.'

She raises her hand and touches it.

'How . . .?' she's muttering. 'How . . . you . . .'

'How did I *get* it? How did I *get* it?' I'm almost beside myself but I'm not shouting now, I'm hissing. 'I took it out of Mum's dead hand, that's how I got it.'

Jude covers her face with her hands.

'Her fingers were all stiff and I had to pull it out. I wanted to sell it so they would melt it down and no one would ever see it, but they wouldn't let me. So the question is, how did she get it? Isn't it? That's the question. And the answer is obvious, isn't it? You were there. You were there when Borys killed her.'

She's taken her hands away from her face and she's looking at me now, eye to eye. She's freaking me out because we haven't ever looked at each other like this before. I swear it's like she's trying to tell me something, but her eyes are huge and glassy, and I think she's not really seeing me.

'What have you taken?' I want to know. 'Look at the state of you. And you with Em to look after. No wonder they took the other one off you.'

She wails at that and runs to the kitchen and before I know it she's got a knife. Her back's to me but I can see what she's doing. She's got the blade of the knife up against her skin and she's pressing and after a moment the blood starts to appear in little beads and then in drops that drip onto the floor.

'What are you doing?' I'm crying. I get closer, but she waves the knife at me to make me back off.

'Stop it,' I'm shouting at her. 'Jude, stop it!'

She opens her mouth and sounds come out, but I can't make out what she's saying for the rattly breathing and the snot muffling what she's saying.

I'm staring at her face and I see something change in her eyes, and that's when I look behind me and realise there's a man there.

I can't believe what I'm seeing.

It's the man from the council, the man from the hospital café, the man I was going to meet about a new flat.

Michael Finch, with the blond curls.

He's standing there, very still. Something about the way he's watching us starts to ring an alarm in my head, but I need him to help me.

'Stop her,' I beg him, 'or she's going to kill herself.'

He doesn't move, but she stands there frozen with the knife in her hand, watching him as though she's mesmerised by him.

266

'She hates herself,' he says quietly. 'She hates herself for what she's done.'

'What's she done?' I mutter.

He shakes his head.

'You'll despise her for it,' he murmurs. 'You won't be able to forgive her.'

I'm frowning and shaking my head. I don't understand what's going on.

'She killed your mother,' he says with a vague smile. 'Don't you understand?'

'You?' I say to Jude. 'It was you?'

But as soon as he said it, I know it's true.

She wails again and slashes at her wrist, but I lunge towards her and grab at the knife and because she's got no strength I get it off her.

We stand there staring at each other.

Now I know, she looks like a stranger to me.

'I could kill you like you killed her,' I'm hissing at Jude, but I'm crying at the same time. 'I could stab you till you bleed to death.'

I wave the knife at her.

'You should,' she mutters at me. 'You should kill me.'

Hearing her say that makes me drop the knife.

It clatters onto the kitchen tiles.

Now I know, it's like I'm in a dream.

I watch Finch come over and put his arm around Jude's shoulder. He walks her towards the couch and makes her sit down, then sits down next to her. He's stroking her as if she's a dog. I feel like I'm going to be sick.

In my dream I think, where's Em? I leave them there and hurry into the bedroom, but Em's asleep in the dog basket, sucking on an empty bottle. Something about the way she's curled so tight makes me think she's made herself go to sleep. This is her way of hiding.

I go back through to the lounge. Jude is still sitting there huddled round herself on the couch, crying. Her face is grey and streaked with tears and blood and her clothes are so messed up she's half naked.

I know what she is now.

I don't mean just guessing, or thinking perhaps, or just trying not to think it.

Now I know, I've got to watch her.

Now I know, I can't let Em out of my sight.

Jude's not to be trusted.

I notice a passport lying on the coffee table in front of her and a wrap of white powder that's lying open.

Jude looks up at me. Her eyes are hopeless.

One thing I notice. She's clasping her mobile tight in her fist, and she's trying to keep it out of sight of Finch.

'Get out of here, Sare,' she says. She's saying it like she's angry, but I don't think she's angry. I think she wants me to go so I'll be safe. I think that's why she wanted me out of the flat. She knew I'd be safer on the street than with Finch.

I glance at the door that leads into the hallway outside.

When Jude sees that I'm not going anywhere, she starts to cry.

'Sarah, you can be useful to us here. I'm trying to explain something to your sister,' Finch says to me. 'But she's being a bit dense. Perhaps you can help me.'

I don't think Jude's even listening. She's still crying, rocking to and fro.

Someone's at the front door. I hear it open and close, and footsteps, and I'm shrinking into the wall expecting a stranger, wishing I'd made a break for it when Jude told me to go.

It's not a stranger.

It's something much worse.

It's Keith Butcher. 'Uncle Keith', the man who passed Mum a wad of cash when he took Jude out. The man on the bus, the man who broke into our flat and tried to find Jude's phone, the man I followed back to his place, and who tried to catch me.

Well, he's got me now.

I'm the only one surprised to see him.

'What's she doing here?' Butcher says to Finch, jerking his head towards me.

'I'm hoping Sarah here is going to help us explain to Jude,' Finch says to Butcher.

'What are you trying to explain?' I ask. I can hear my voice a long way off like this is happening in another world.

'Jude's not herself, she's been under the weather. She needs to take a holiday somewhere warm,' Finch says. 'I've got tickets for a flight tomorrow morning but she doesn't want to go.'

'Why would she want to go anywhere?' I say.

'It's for her own good, the press will come after her,' Finch says, 'she's got twenty-four hours at most.'

'The press?' I echo, still not understanding.

'Borys Kawolski was released yesterday,' Finch says, irritated. Then, when he sees the surprise on my face, he says, 'Don't you watch the news? The case collapsed for lack of evidence. The DNA on the knife was unreliable, Omar says he never saw Borys there, and you—'

Butcher interrupts him, '—No one believed you because you're such a dirty little liar.'

'So if Kawolski's been released, they'll come after you, Jude.' Finch's voice is soft and quick. 'If it wasn't Kalowski, then who was it and why did he take the blame? That's what they're thinking. It's like a *CSI* – don't you get it, Jude? Eliminate one suspect and it must be another one. She didn't kill herself.'

'What do you care?' I burst out. 'What is it to you if they come after Jude? I don't know why you're here. Why don't you just go away and leave us alone? Me and Jude can decide what to do, we don't need you.'

No one answers me. Finch is shaking his head at me.

'What is it?' I'm looking from one to the other. 'Why are you even here? Why did you take Jude away? What does it matter to you if the police get her?'

'Leave it, Sare,' Jude begs me, but she's below my contempt now.

Then I say what comes into my head. 'Is this about Zoe, is that what it is?'

Finch and Butcher go quiet. I see them glance at each other.

Jude says, 'What about Zoe? What do you mean?'

Which is when I realise that I never told her. She still doesn't know.

Then Butcher's got one hand over my mouth, and he's got his other arm around me so I'm struggling, but I can't speak and I can't move. He drags me over to right in front of Jude.

'You're getting on that flight tomorrow morning, do you get it now?' he says to her, and then he raises his fist and it moves fast towards my side.

Jude shouts, 'No!'

She lunges for Butcher's arm, but he kicks out at her and she seems to break against his foot, and she collapses onto the ground.

He hits me hard just under my ribs.

In the middle of everything I catch sight of Finch. He's standing very still and he's watching Butcher hurt us. His eyes are glittering, and he's got his hand in his mouth and he's nibbling his fingernails.

Butcher's fist moves again and this time I hear my rib crunch under his fist.

'Get it?' Butcher shouts. 'Do you get it now?'

I'm crumpled on the floor. Beside me, Jude has hauled herself onto her knees.

'I'll go,' she's wailing. 'I'll go. Just let her go. Don't hurt her.'

I try to stand up, but I can only get as far as my knees.

'Zoe got strangled,' I shout. 'It must have been them . . .'

Then Butcher grabs me again and lifts me clean off the floor and out of the room. He opens the cupboard door and throws me inside.

I curl up like a ball on the floor where I land.

I hurt too much to move.

The cupboard door's slammed shut and a key turns in the lock.

I am in darkness.

NINETEEN

I wake up. Or I think I do. There's a voice in the dark whispering my name. Above me, a shape darker than the darkness moves. Something glints, catching on a scrap of light. I think of Finch's watery eyes.

The light is coming from a sliver at the door.

'You've got to come with me now, Sare.'

The voice is so quiet it's hardly there.

My heart's pounding because I'm afraid the voice is in my head. I'm afraid I've gone mad like at Linda's house. I reach out towards the shadow.

A hand clasps mine tightly. The fingers are cold and bony. Another hand finds its way across my shoulders, up my neck and to my face, it pushes my hair from my ear. She leans in close and I can feel her chilly lips against my ear.

'Get up, Sare, you've got to come with me.'

I reach out and my hands find Em, bundled up against Jude's chest. She feels solid there, like she's been put in some kind of baby carrier, or like Jude's tied her there with a strip of cloth. I can hear Em's breathing now, quick shallow breaths.

'You mustn't go with them,' I hiss.

'Trust me,' she murmurs back.

Trust her.

I pull her close again.

'Tell me what's going on.'

'Don't ask any more bloody stupid questions, Sare. Just come with me now. Have you got your passport?'

I don't think about why she's asking. My passport hasn't moved from the pocket of my hoody, and my hoody hasn't moved off my back in days. Still, I find my pocket and run my fingers over the outline of the passport.

'What about them?'

I'm clutching her wrist, and when I move my hand to hers I realise she's holding something in her right hand. I move my hand down, and I can feel a blade against my fingers.

'What're you doing?' My voice comes out loud, and she clamps her hand over my mouth and I can feel the knife against my cheek.

'Swear you'll be quiet,' she's begging me.

I twist my head under her hand.

'Swear on Em's life,' she says, and lifts her hand from my mouth.

'I swear,' I say, and she grabs my arm and pulls me up and towards the door.

The pain in my side is nothing compared with my fear.

The door swings opens silently, and I follow her into the corridor. My heart's pounding and my ears are listening out for tiny sounds, like a footstep or someone lifting a glass to their mouth, or turning a page. The hallway's dark, but there's light coming from the lounge and we have to pass it to get to the front door. My legs feel weak. What happens if my legs collapse under me? I can feel Butcher's fist like it's still stuck in my side.

Jude pushes me back against the wall and we take turns peering in. Finch is asleep in an armchair with his head thrown back.

'Where's Butcher?' I mouth at Jude, and she shakes her head to tell me she doesn't know. We're pressed against the wall, with Em like she's never been born, like she's still inside her mother's tummy, head buried in Jude's chest, her back all round like a huge pregnant belly.

Finch's throat is exposed, tight over his Adam's apple, then fleshy under the chin, unshaven. Under his chin, I can see right up to his ears. His shirt collar is open, and there's flesh and hair there too.

Anyone could kill him now. If they did it quickly, if they just stuck the knife in, he wouldn't wake up. He could be sitting there asleep one minute, and dead the next.

Jude's hand is in mine, and I can feel her straining to do it, and her wanting spreads to me, so I want to do it too.

We're one heart, one lung all over again, and this time we're one knife, too.

I want to do it, but I'm waiting for her. I'm letting her decide.

I stare at Finch.

I can see the white of his eyes.

My heart bangs against my chest wall.

Either he sleeps like this with his eyes not shut or he's watching us.

Jude grabs my hand and drags me to the door. She fumbles with the lock, pulling the door wide open, creaking, and our feet are on the stairs, pounding up to street level, and then we're bursting out onto the street, and

274

we're racing along the wide pavement and the cold night air is in our lungs and it feels like the craziest drug must feel, like I could fly.

Jude seems to know where she's going. We don't stop moving. I just float with Jude through the streets. I don't notice which way we're going. But after a while the good feeling I had from escaping is gone. My side is hurting too much to think. I can't keep up with her.

'Where are we going?' I ask, when I get my breath.

But she just shakes her head and keeps on walking. She walks faster than me, so I can see her up ahead, a shadow in the dark, walking fast, like a ghost flitting through the streets looking for something.

I don't understand what's got into her.

Then she waits for me, and I catch up with her under a streetlight, and when I catch sight of her face it's got fear in it and hope.

We reach the train station and she starts looking around like she's waiting for someone. Then a man walks out of the shadows towards us. And when he gets close to us I can see by the streetlight that it's Borys.

He walks up to Jude and takes her in his arms and Em is in between them almost smothered in their hug.

And then I understand.

TWENTY

Borys says they'll look for us at the train station, and the train doesn't leave for hours, we can't just sit there and wait for Finch to find us. We need to keep moving, he says. So we get on a night bus, and we buy tickets that let us sit there on the buses all night. Sometimes we move from one to another one. Mostly I sleep. My side is aching really deep down, but I don't want to make a fuss. I can hear Jude and Borys whispering, and Jude telling him about Butcher hitting me. She wants to take me to hospital, but Borys says they'll look there too. She's telling him about Zoe, too, because I can hear her say the name, and when she talks about Zoe she cries.

When the sun comes up, we go back to Waverley station, and we catch a train. I'm not thinking about where it's going, I'm just following Borys.

On the train, even though I'm hurting, I start to think about happy endings. It's because of seeing Borys and Jude together, and Borys holding Em safe while she stands on the chair and looks through the seatbacks at me behind and plays peek-a-boo with me. If you just saw them on a train, you wouldn't know, you'd think there's a happy family. You might get a bit sniffy about the tattoos, and if you were good at looking you'd worry about Jude, too.

You'd think she's as skinny as a skeleton and you might see the bruises on the inside of her arm. And if you knew how old she really is, which is eighteen, you'd think she looked double that. But when you saw them with Em, your heart would melt. And when you saw Borys holding Jude's hand tight when it shakes, and tracing the outline of the flowers on her arm, and holding her to his chest when she gets weepy, and kissing her straw hair, and whispering hopeful things into her ear, you'd think he loves her enough to cure anything.

But Jude's a murderer and a murderer can't be anything except a murderer for the rest of their life.

I close my eyes and lean my head against the coach window and memories pour out of the box in my head.

Uncle Keith has introduced her to a boy – actually he's a man, he's called Michael and he's got money. They go to pubs and clubs, cool places she's never had the money to go to before. He's going to take her out at the weekend shopping for clothes. For clothes! Ten-year-old Sarah is so jealous.

At the weekend Jude practically skips out of the house, she's so excited. She comes back with bags from Primark and tips everything out onto the bed, flirty little skirts and canvas ballet pumps and skinny T-shirts. Even underwear.

'Didn't you feel embarrassed buying this with him?' ten-year-old Sarah asks fifteen-year-old Jude, picking up a pair of knickers that looks like a piece of string. She tells me to shut up, not to be nosy.

Mum's stopped shouting at Jude, except one time when Jude won't lend her a top. At night, on the nights she's not out, Jude whispers to me about her man. Jude's dopey about him. He loves her. He loves her like no one's ever loved her. He never shouts at her, he's never rude to her. When they go shopping he looks into her eyes and tells her how beautiful she is and how he wants to be her boyfriend forever. When they've finished shopping they go to a club called Denny's under the arches and he buys her drinks like she's a grown-up.

Then, bit by bit, things change. One night Jude comes back drunk and it's the first time ever. She throws up on the carpet, and Mum yells at her when she has to clean up after her but she doesn't stop her going out. Another night she doesn't come back at all but Mum doesn't seem to notice, it's only me worrying when I wake up and she's not there.

Jude's not back by the time I go to school. She misses school. The next time I see her, she's changed. She won't tell jokes, she won't laugh at my jokes. She lies on her bed and listens to the radio. She leaves the radio on all night. When I try to ask her about her boyfriend, she won't talk about him.

I guess that they've broken up. So I'm surprised she's not crying about it and pouring out her troubles to me. Instead she turns in on herself like whatever is going on she doesn't want to talk about it. So I assume, if it's all over, that there's no more pubbing, no more clubbing or shopping. But then, the very next night, the doorbell rings again, and Mum goes to answer it, and calls Jude like she always does.

This time I sneak up close to catch sight of the boyfriend but it's Butcher again. When Jude comes to the door she looks at Mum, like, please don't make me go. But Mum just takes hold of Jude's shoulders and pushes her out the door.

Outside, Jude's dragging her feet. I lean out the door and call out to her, 'Jude, where you going?'

Butcher looks back and sees me.

'Hello,' he says, smiling, 'next time you come along with me and see.'

Jude's face is terrible. She waves me back inside like she's frantic.

'Is he your boyfriend, then?' I call out, and Butcher laughs.

'I'm just the delivery boy,' he calls back.

My mother's hand lands on my shoulder, and she hauls me back inside, slamming the door.

'Where's she going?' I ask Mum.

'She's going to have some fun. She gets little enough around here. Look, if you nip down to the shop you can buy yourself an ice cream. She's getting a treat, you shouldn't be left out.'

And she pulls a pound coin out of her pocket and presses it into my hand. Ten-year-old Sarah notices her mum's not short of money since Jude found her first boyfriend.

Then Jude has Em, and then she meets Borys, and everything changes all over again. Every night Jude is screaming at my mum that she only wants Borys, she doesn't want to go out with anyone else. She doesn't care about the clothes, she doesn't care about the money, she doesn't even care about the drink and the other stuff. I'm twelve years old when Em's born. I don't understand what's going on. All I know is, we don't have money any more. It's not like we were rich, but while Jude was going out with Butcher there was enough to put food in the fridge and now there's not enough money to turn the fridge on.

Mum keeps threatening Borys to keep him away.

Butcher keeps arriving at the house.

When Jude goes out with him to shut Mum up, she comes back looking like a zombie.

Here and now, on the train, Borys has fallen asleep with his head banging against the window and Em asleep on his lap. Jude slips into the seat next to me. We sit there for a long time not talking. She puts her hand on mine, forcing her fingers in between mine, lacing us together, but I yank my hand away from hers, so we're not touching at all.

'What's the matter, Sare?' she asks quietly. Like she needs to ask.

'What's the matter?' I hiss. 'After what you've done, you don't have the right . . . you don't have the right to hold my hand.'

'Sare.' She's pawing at me now, clutching at my arm with her hands, and I'm shoving her away. 'Sare . . . Sare . . . I'm sorry, you've got to say you forgive me. You've got to.'

'I haven't got to do anything,' I'm hissing.

'I can't go on if you don't forgive me,' she whines. I push her hand off my arm again, and I look out of the window, although the only thing to look at is the darkness. In my head, all I can see is Jude with a knife in her hand, slashing and stabbing . . .

Jude starts to whimper, and I ignore her. Even when she stops crying, her voice is so soft and wobbly that I have to strain to hear it.

'Sare, that afternoon I told her I'd made my mind up. I was going to take Em and live with Borys in his squat. I wasn't going with Butcher and his friends any more. Me and Borys, we were going to start our own family, get our own place . . .'

I don't want to hear this. I don't want to think about Jude planning to abandon me on my own. She's a double traitor now. But the double traitor is gabbling on.

'When I told her, Mum laughed at me . . . She said the only reason Borys was interested in me was because I could get cash from Butcher and Finch. She said if he couldn't be my pimp, he'd dump me. I told her Borys loves me, he loves Em even though she's not his, he's going to love our baby, and she said . . . She said love doesn't exist, it's a story people tell themselves. The only thing that matters is money . . . and you've got to believe me, Sare . . .' Jude's sobbing now, heaving for air, and her hands are shaking, 'You've got to believe me, I tried to ignore her, I didn't want to let her get to me. I said she can't do anything, she's got no hold over me. And then she said . . .'

When Jude stops, at first I don't know how the sentence ends, because anything Jude says is just an excuse. I hate her for killing our mother. But I have to know, so I ask it through gritted teeth.

'What does she say?'

Jude sniffs. She wipes her eyes on her sleeve.

'She laughed. She said fine then, go, she's already talked to Butcher, and Sarah can go in my place . . .'

She breaks off, snivelling again. I don't want to hear this, because now I've got to hate both of them. I've got to hate my mother for what she was going to do to me, and I've got to hate Jude for killing her, and that much hate would fill me up like a balloon. My veins would be running with liquid hate; every time I opened my mouth, it would pour out like a river . . .

'. . . When she said it, she could see the expression on my face, and she got scared. She said I should go and lie down. She knew I couldn't control myself. She knew I couldn't bear it, what she said . . . When I got the knife she laughed at me again, she said I'd never have the guts, she said I wasn't worth anything, she said I was dirty, no one loved me, not her, not you, not Borys. She said I deserved everything I got . . .'

She starts to cry silently, but even though she's done it to protect me I can't think of anything to say to comfort her. I can't agree with what she did. I can't tell her she did the right thing. I can't say thank you for sticking a knife in my mother, even though I should disown her as my mother.

'So . . . afterwards . . . when I saw what I'd done, I got out of there . . . I went straight to Borys. He asked about the knife, and when I said I'd left it there, he said he'd go and get it.'

I think that's when I saw Borys, and when Omar saw him, even if he says he didn't.

'When Borys came out of the flat, he said it was like he was going mad. He couldn't remember if he'd left the knife inside, so he told me he was squatting there looking for the knife, and then he found it.'

I think about what happened in court, about all the things the lawyers asked.

'Borys borrowed your keys when he came back, didn't he?' I say to Jude. 'The security grille was locked behind him, but Borys didn't have a key to that, only you and Mum had a key to that.'

'I was in such a state when I left the flat, I couldn't remember what I'd locked and what I hadn't. I thought I might have locked the security grille behind me, so I gave Boris my keys to open it when he went back in for the knife. In the end, when he got there, he discovered I'd left everything open, so he could walk straight in. Then, on his way out, he wasn't thinking straight, he locked everything, including the security grille . . . Borys told me in court you said the security grille was open . . .'

'I knew only you had a key apart from me and Mum,' I say. 'If the grille was locked, your keys must have locked it.'

She turns and stares at me.

'You knew, then . . .' she says. 'You knew it was me?'

For a moment I don't answer.

'I don't know what I knew and what I didn't,' I say.

Which is the truth.

I think everybody has some questions they don't want to think about, because deep down they think they might know the answer, and they don't want to know it. That's how it was for me.

'Why did you run away and leave me on my own?' I ask. When I say it I can hear the hurt in my voice.

Jude sniffs and mewls a bit more because she can hear by my tone of voice that I'm still angry. But then she starts talking.

'After Mum, they stayed away from me. They didn't know exactly what happened between me and Mum, but they knew she got killed. Then when I was in hospital Finch sent me a message saying I had to leave the hospital and go away with him. That really scared me, because I don't know how he found me in hospital. I thought the nurses must be talking about me. Then we saw Butcher on the bus and I completely freaked out. I didn't know what was happening.'

283

'It was because of Zoe, wasn't it?' I say.

'I didn't know about Zoe, but it must have been,' she says. 'Butcher took me and Zoe to Denny's all the time, and Finch was always waiting there. It's like a private club. They don't care there. Even when the girls are crying because they don't understand what's happening, nobody helps. I've seen them lock girls in so they didn't have a choice . . . So I didn't know about Zoe getting killed, but that was the same day Finch started wanting me to go away and Butcher was stalking me, and I was afraid if I didn't go with them they'd go for you. It wasn't safe to take the baby . . . so I gave him up . . . I didn't know anything about Zoe getting killed, or I wouldn't have gone with them. One of them must have killed her, and the other one's got to help cover up because when the police know what they did to young girls, they'll get both of them not just one of them.'

'You're lucky they didn't just kill you,' I tell her.

'Finch thinks Em's his because she looks like him. It's like he thinks she's a bit of him, and he loves himself. She's my protection.'

But I remember how Finch didn't take the knife off Jude, and then how he didn't take the knife off me when I was threatening to kill her, and I think Jude's fooling herself. I think if she'd stayed with him, he'd make sure she was dead one way or another, even if he kept Em alive.

TWENTY-ONE

When we get to Hull, we get off the train and find a McDonald's. We sit at a table, and Jude goes to the toilets to change Em's nappy. Someone's left their newspaper there, so while I'm eating I'm flicking through it and reading to take my mind off how much my side is hurting. At first I think that because the trial's over, there can't be any news about it. Then I see a little article headlined 'Witness Flees'.

A fourteen-year-old girl, Sarah Carnaby, has fled her home in South London a week after giving evidence at the trial of Borys Kawolski who was accused of murdering her mother and who was later found not guilty. The girl, who was repeatedly accused by the defence of lying about what happened when she found her mother's dead body in November last year, has not been seen since Tuesday. Police say she is being sought for her own safety. The body of Zoe Brown, who lived on the same estate and went to the same school, was found outside a nightclub in the area two weeks ago.

'What's the matter, Sarah?' Borys asks, and I say, 'Nothing.'

But there's lots the matter. If I run away, it'll look like I'm guilty.

If they're looking for me, and if they find me, then they'll find Jude.

Something's been worrying me.

'Jude was going to let you go to prison,' I say to Borys. 'Why do you even want to be with her?'

'When Jude . . . When Jude does it . . . I think she will be arrested, and then I think how can Jude have baby in prison?' he says. His face is very dark. It's so hard to think now about how we were all waiting for Ben. 'Of course when they arrest me I hope they will find me not guilty. I think if I make false confession, the police will see it is false, and then they will ask themselves why I make a false confession, and then they see that it was Jude. If I don't confess, it doesn't look like I'm protecting her.

'Every day I sit in prison waiting for the trial, I hope that Jude will take the chance that I have made for her to escape, but she does not. She stays with you. She doesn't want to leave you on your own. She is not thinking straight. She thinks all the time about what she has done and she thinks about me in prison for her. She is breaking inside. She cannot tell anyone what she has done.

'Finch is clever. He stays away because he knows she is trouble but he sends Jude drugs to comfort her. When she takes the drugs she doesn't think about what she has done. She doesn't think about killing. She doesn't think about me. Then they kill Zoe – I don't know which one killed her, but must be one of them – Jude doesn't know about it, but that's when Finch and Butcher start to panic, because they know Jude can tell the police everything. So they send her a message saying she must go with them. She is so scared. When social services take the baby away she is desperate, she knows she will lose Em. At least if she goes with them, she can keep Em. She thinks if she goes, it is safer for you . . .'

'Safer for me?'

'She knows if you get into their hands, the same things will happen to you . . .'

I squeeze my eyes shut and try to think through the things he's saying. Jude has told him they took Ben, she hasn't told him what she told me, that she wanted them to take the baby because she knew she couldn't protect him. I overheard her saying, 'Take him then.' But I have to believe one last good thing, that she only wanted to save him.

'She did do the killing,' I say. 'We're all pretending she didn't, like we should be sorry for her, but she did do it.'

Borys presses his fingers together.

'She cannot stay here,' Borys says. 'The press will come to find her and photograph her. Then the police will come . . . You know how that will be. She is too weak. She cannot survive.'

'They'll take Em,' I say.

'How can she keep Em? She cannot if they come for her,' Borys says.

'She could tell them about Mum selling her to Butcher, and what they did to her,' I say. 'They're not supposed to treat people like that.'

'Is it an excuse really?' Borys asks. 'If you hear someone else tell this story, someone who is not your sister, do you say well then, let's not call this murder, let's call this something like an accident? Or do you say well yes, we are very sorry to hear these terrible things that have happened to you, but there is still a crime.'

*   *   *

We get on a coach to the ferry terminal. It doesn't come as a surprise to me, because although they won't tell me exactly what's happening, I've been overhearing Borys and Jude talk about crossings and passports, and I'm not stupid.

We get off the coach and there are benches at the edge of the car park. I go and sit on one on my own because my side doesn't hurt so much if I'm sitting down. I'm beginning to feel like a spare part, and I don't like it when they keep kissing. It's embarrassing.

At first I can't see anything that looks like a boat, and then I realise that the thing as big as a building that's in the water next to the terminal is actually a ferry.

After a few minutes, Borys comes to sit next to me.

'This is it, Sarah,' he says. 'We go from here to Zeebrugge, twelve and a half hours, and from there to anywhere in Europe. It's a new life for all of us. You can be anything you want to be. I suggest Polish, like me, or you can be Frenchwoman, very elegant, or German . . . You have passport, we have passports. We will all start again.'

He's sitting on the seat next to me, with his elbows on his knees like I saw him sit in court so many times. He turns and looks at my face.

'You're not happy, even with new life,' he says.

I don't know what to say.

He stands up. 'We must buy tickets.'

I don't move.

'What's the matter?' he asks me.

When I still don't move, he says, 'You are not coming with us, are you?'

'I don't know,' I say.

288

He stares down at me, and I look up at him. I want him to understand, but my throat's too tight to speak about that.

After a minute, I say something else.

'Will Finch come after me if he finds out I'm still here?' I ask.

Borys sits down next to me again. His face is very serious.

'Jude is the only one who can send him to jail,' he says. 'You have heard what he did, but you have no proof. I don't think he will come after you, but you should be on your guard. You should be careful.'

I nod, but I'm trembling.

'And what if the police think I killed Mum?' I say. I can hardly get my mouth to make the words, they are so awful.

Borys passes a hand over his cropped hair. He doesn't like the question, and he thinks about the answer.

'Jude is on the run now,' he says slowly, 'the police know this is not a holiday. They will think why is Jude running and you are not. They will find out I am with her and they will think about if I am protecting her all along. I think they suspect about Jude. But if the police do ask you questions I know you will try to protect Jude.'

He puts his hand on my shoulder and gives it a squeeze, and then he goes and talks to Jude. When he has started speaking, she looks across at me, alarmed, and she stumbles over to me, pulling Em by the hand.

'You are coming with us, aren't you, Sare? You've got to come with us.'

I can't speak, so I shake my head again.

She clutches at me.

'You've got to come, I can't go without you . . .' Her voice is rising.

'You can,' Borys says holding her. But I'm not sure she can. I'm not sure Borys can hold her together, and I can't bear to see her fall apart.

Jude thrusts Em towards me, and I know she thinks that will make me change my mind. I hug Em tight, like I can keep her with me even when she's not there if I've hugged her tight enough. I start to cry although I'm trying to hold it in. I hug Em so much that she'll be safe without me but she starts to cry because I'm crying and because she doesn't understand. I pass Em to Borys and with my eyes I say to Borys that whatever happens to Jude, whatever happens, that Em is his now and he cannot let harm come to her.

Then I hug poor frail Jude whose bones feel like twigs in my arms and we sob and sob.

'You will come and see us when things are better,' Borys says. 'We will come back and show everyone what happened, and they will give our baby back.'

But that seems so impossible that I start sobbing all over again.

When he realises that I can't stop crying, he takes Jude by the shoulders and turns her away from me, and he takes Em by the hand, and leads her away, and I am alone.

I can't get up from the bench. People come up to me because they can see me crying. But when they speak to me, I tell them to get lost. Minutes pass like hours. Time doesn't mean anything.

I watch Jude and Borys and Em as long as I can see them, even just bits of them, their arms, the top of their heads, in the queue for the boat. Borys raises his arm and waves to me. Jude turns to look back at me, and when I see her face it's all I can do to sit glued to my bench. I know if I stand up and go nearer then I'll run after them and push my way through the crowds and go with them. Soon they've gone, disappearing into the ship. Gates clang shut, there is a great blast of noise, and the ferry pulls away from shore.

My head spins off, and it flies out to sea, and it hovers over the ship where Jude and Borys and Em are without me.

I'm afraid that some great storm will come, and that they'll be pulled under the waves.

If I try hard enough then I can hold them safe above the water.

I watch until the ferry's out of sight. There's a smattering of rain, and a black cloud overhead, but it looks brighter on the horizon, and I hope that's the direction of where they're going.

I'm freezing cold and my side is really hurting.

I'm not sure if my head is back on my shoulders or if it's still out at sea. I can't make sense of things.

I take my phone out of my pocket and hold it up in front of me.

I take a photo, and then I take a look at myself.

My skin is dead white, and my eyes are red and swollen from crying. My yellow hair is blowing crazily in the wind. In the background is a noticeboard. It says Hull Ferry Terminal.

I open my contact list. I select Sheena, attach the photo and send.

TWENTY-TWO

We're not supposed to be here.

At first Carla said no, it's too dangerous, don't even think about it. Then I told her I have to see, because one day I have to tell Jude. Then she said alright, if we stay at the back.

So we're sitting in the back of the café, me and Sheena and Omar and Mr Jones. Usually Mr Jones doesn't stop talking all about his battles with the council, and I hang on every word. But tonight there's nothing to hang on, because he's completely silent. Carla's given us a plate of nachos and cheese and mugs of tea, but none of us can touch any of it. I'm sitting bolt upright, and my hands are braced on the table. Sheena's covering my right hand with both of hers, and Omar keeps brushing my left hand with his long fingers like he doesn't mean to, but I know he does. We've all got our eyes glued to the window at the front of the café. We can see the neon light that says Denny's.

What we can't see is the police.

We know they're out there, watching Denny's. The question is, will Finch and Butcher walk into their trap?

When Carla found Zoe dead she was scared to say much to the police, because she thought Finch could find a way to get back at her. But after I told her about Jude, and what Finch and Butcher did to her, she went back to the police and told them everything, about seeing Zoe at Denny's, and about how she always arrived with Butcher and sometimes left with Finch, and how she could identify both of them. She told the police she'd heard about what went on in the club, about young girls and men who buy them drink and drugs, and what they did. She didn't tell the police she'd heard it from me.

That's when the police started watching Denny's. But for ages Finch and Butcher didn't go to Denny's, or if they did, the police didn't see them. Carla says they must have been staying away because of what they did to Zoe, they must have known the police might be watching Denny's. Then they started coming back again, like they couldn't stay away even though they knew they should. Sometimes some of the plainclothes police come into Carla's place, and today she overheard them saying if Butcher goes in with a girl tonight, they're going to raid Denny's.

So the police are waiting and we're waiting, and I can't bear it.

Then, at 10.30 p.m. I see him and I know they've seen him too. I can't see him very clearly through Carla's window because she's painted Carla's Café, Coffee and Carbs all over it in red and blue and purple. But I can recognise his shape and the way he walks.

He's got a girl with him. She's all dressed up, tottering on high heels, with a skirt up to her knickers. He's pulling her on behind him like she's not keen.

The door to Denny's opens, and a bouncer says something to Butcher, and they go inside.

Then it all happens quickly. The archway which was empty moments before fills with police. They've got body armour on and they're carrying weapons. There are flashing lights from the patrol cars.

'They'll scare him off,' I mutter, 'they're going to scare him off.'

Sheena clutches my hand.

It's completely silent, and all I can hear is my heart beating, and Sheena humming softly next to me.

Then they throw open the door and they pour into the club.

Everything's shouting then. Shouting from inside the club and shouting from outside.

When they start coming out, I can't help myself. I push past Carla and run to the front of the café to get a better look. My heart's pounding. I press my fingers up against the glass, and then I realise Carla's right there beside me. She's got a hand on my arm, to stop me just in case I try to run outside, but she's letting me see.

They've got Butcher with his arms handcuffed in front of him. He's looking round him like a lion in a cage. When I see him my body starts shaking. Even when they've led him off towards the police cars and I can't see him, I still keep shaking.

Then women police officers bring three girls out wrapped in blankets over their bare legs.

'What about Finch?' I'm saying, and I'm still shivering like I've got the flu. 'What about Finch? They've got to get Finch.'

Then there he is.

He's talking, talking, trying to talk himself out of it, trying to pull away from the police but he can't because he's handcuffed and they're not even listening to him. He looks so handsome and smart, like it's a mistake, like he should be at a business meeting, but his eyes are wild and scared.

He knows I'm there.

He glances towards the café and my heart stops beating.

But only for one beat, because I'm not scared of him any more.

He should be afraid of me.

Later that night, I'm lying in bed and I'm staring at the ceiling because I can't sleep because I'm still shivery from the day. Sheena's in the other bed, and I can hear music whispering from her earphones.

Like last thing every night I reach for my mobile phone.

Like every night, there's a message from Omar.

sleep well sare

im thinkin about u

Like every night, I press reply.

c u tomorrow

Sometimes I think Omar and me might be like Borys and Jude one day. I think they try to be better for each other. They try to make each other stronger. Omar and me, we do that too. Carla and Mr Jones keep their eyes on us, they worry that we spend too much time together, but we know that we're okay. We're never going to hurt each other.

Then, like every night, I look at my photos. They send me a photo of Em nearly every day, and I keep all of them. The photos are always of Em, never of Borys or Jude. Just one time I could see the hand holding Em was Jude's and I zoomed in and I examined it really carefully to see if it could tell me whether she was better, but it couldn't.

I glance over at Sheena to make sure she's asleep, and then I whisper to Em about what happened that day, about waiting in Carla's café, and the police going in and getting Butcher and Finch. In my head, Em can hear me, even though she's just a photo, and she can pass on all my news to Jude. Today I've got a lot to tell her. So I tell her the bad news is that Bocock's been promoted, but the good news is, she's been promoted to Nottingham. And I tell her tomorrow I've got something hard to do. I've got to go and say sorry to Linda. I keep thinking about what I did, stealing and running away. I don't know if Linda will forgive me, but I think she might. Then I tell her that Peasgood and Mr Jones have made it so next week I can go and see Ben with his foster parents. I'm scared, but I'm excited too, because visiting him could be the start of something new. Like Carla says, I've got a lot of possibilities in front of me. Maybe Ben and me can live together with a foster family, maybe even Linda if she forgives me. Or maybe I'll stay at Carla's. She says I can stay forever if I want.

When I've finished whispering my news, I kiss each one of the photographs even though I know Em can't really feel it. I'm crying, because they should be here. Jude should be here to see what I saw, Butcher and Finch in handcuffs. She should be here with Ben. Thinking about these things means I can't stop crying, so I cry until I'm drifting off to sleep.

Then when I'm far away, I can feel my head spinning. It starts slowly going round and round, and then it speeds up and flies off, but in a good way. I'm flying over all the sea, and it's blue underneath me, and the sun is glinting off the surf, and birds are swooping around me. And then there's land underneath me, and it's green, and there are hills and rivers and animals and birds. Then there's sea again, and land again, and then an island, green and round in the middle of a blue sea, and my head starts to fall, but in a good way, like I'm coming in to land. Then my head levels out and hovers close above the island just for like a millisecond, just long enough to see. And there is Em, and there is Borys, and there is Jude. They're sitting on a blanket on the beach, and they have food spread out in front of them, long crusty bread and all different sorts of cheese and fruit, a pile of grapes, and apples rolling off onto the sand, and Em is digging in the sand, and Borys has his arms round Jude, and her skin is healed, and her hair is soft and her face has put itself back together, and she's smiling at her daughter.

Then my head is spinning off again whisking me back across the land and sea and land and sea, through the blue sky, to Sheena's bedroom. My head settles smoothly on my neck where it belongs and I sink deep into a peaceful sleep.